DA CHEN

MY LAST EMPRESS

A NOVEL

Crown Publishers • NEW YORK

Published in the United States by Crown Publishers, an imprint of the Crown Publishing Group, a division of Random House, Inc., New York.

www.crownpublishing.com

CROWN and the Crown colophon are registered trademarks of Random House, Inc.

Library of Congress Cataloging-in-Publication Data
Chen, Da.
    My last empress: a novel/Da Chen—1st ed.
        p. cm.
    1. Americans—China—Fiction.   2. First loves—Fiction.   3. Empresses—China—Fiction.   4. Courts and courtiers—Fiction.   5. Intrigue—Fiction.   6. Beijing (China)—Fiction.   7. Paranormal romance stories.   I. Title.
PS3603.H4474M9 2012
813'.6—dc22   2011049964

ISBN 978-0-307-38130-9
eISBN 978-0-307-95270-7

Printed in the United States of America

Book design by Elina D. Nudelman
Jacket design by Melissa Chang

10 9 8 7 6 5 4 3 2 1

To Robert S Pirie, a generous mentor

MY LAST EMPRESS

PROLOGUE

I am old, decayed, and fermented. I am a dead tree with a rotten cavity within which grows a stem of flower—my last empress.

Sitting on the veranda, I feel my bones aching and my heart ready to dip down the horizon like the aging sun. I am alone now with In-In, the palace servant from my days tutoring the last emperor. He is as faithful as the thoughts of my Annabelle.

Age makes simple all urges. Only the essence of life remains; the rest matters not at all. Daily I rise to do one small task: write down what transpired from that initial spark to the final flame, patching pebbles of my past into the riverbed of the present.

For what reason?, you may ask. The answer is simple. So you will know that I have not lived a fruitless life but an immortal one.

I relive on paper the bygone days, savoring their glory the same way a shadow vies for the sun. This is a story of love and inevitability. I was nothing until Annabelle came along one fateful summer day.

"Your ink is ready, master," In·In calls in his soft voice, placing the inkwell before me. Ink gleams like the encroaching night. Carefully I dip the tip of my brush at the edge of the well, then let the brush glide over the porous scroll.

From my trembling hand bleeds forth the passion that I thought had died all those years ago. Yet still, I am forever burning, forever wanting.

I

There was no evidence or early trace of my penchant for the young, the tender, or the ghostly. Every branch of my family tree has been upright and shadowless, even in the afternoon slanting sun. Father worked at the family law firm of Pickens, Pickens & Davis, and he summered on his white yacht off the Connecticut coast with his white-shoed friends who doted over me, my father's only heir, a navy-suited blinking boy with blond eyelashes. Early memories are of standing in a ring of cigar smoke puffed from the admiring mouths of my father's friends, and the manly breath of whiskey amidst slurred New England syllables. Mother, a buxom matriarch, was the fruit of an even taller tree, the linear descendant of Elihu Yale, the founder of the famed college that bore his name.

It was never debated what the path of my own life would be: Phillips Andover followed by Yale, then days at the family law firm and evenings at the club. I too would drink whiskey and puff cigars and ogle the help while my bride, a thin blond wisp from a similarly upstanding family, would look the other way. It was the path that my father had followed and his father before him, and who was I to veer from it?

It started so innocently while I was still at prep school, culminating in my maiden encounter with one ripened maiden.

Mrs. D was the barren wife of the stiff-necked librarian. She idled her days away in the New England sun, devouring forbidden romance novels while her poodle, a big-snouted pooch, licked between her stockinged thighs. She had the dazed look of disillusion, her hazel eyes full of anguish and unknowable pain, which the entire campus unanimously blamed on her childless state.

Mr. D had the look of a seedless man, pale and thin, without a boisterous moustache or prickly chest hair, as seen on occasion during his reluctant and awkward participation in the faculty cricket games. Just as surely, gossip posited that she could be the culprit, for she had the docility of a guilty mute. They both could be conspirators in the childless game, each as barren as the other, or they both could be endowed with potential to bear, but the fire of lust had never been lit or lit rightly in their cold, separate bedrooms. It was a longstanding uncurriculumed subject that every Phillipian dabbled in during the last drowsy minutes before sleep stole our souls after the lights were shut. I felt a certain stir whenever the word *barren* was mentioned in the same breath with the sullen Mrs. D.

Her hair, not always neat, had an occasional strand falling over the bridge of her nose, fringing her often parted lips. Her hips were wide with the sacrificial openness of a fertile woman. How could anyone blame her for anything?

My heart still thumps at the memory of the first touch of her trembling hand.

It was my first Thanksgiving spent at school, away from the snowfall of Connecticut. The silence of the campus was deafening. Mr. D had gone to the mountain to hunt deer, leaving Mrs. D all alone in the company of an empty house. My duty that afternoon was to dust the small collection of toy yachts, canvas sails, and bamboo masts encased in the draped library of Mr. D's home. I arrived to find Mrs. D just awoken from a nap, lying starfished on a couch, book at her bosom, legs apart. The pooch wasn't around, though its stench hung thin in the air.

Mrs. D greeted me, cupping my face with her soft hands. I melted like a snowman in the sun, burying my face in the valley of her bosom. Her breasts were firm, her buttocks soft. She swayed to the crazed crawling of my fingers, her breath whiskied like the summered memory of my father's white yacht. In a blur of scenes—birds flying, windowpanes reflecting, pooch sniffing somewhere in the corner of the house, my mast tenting—she whispered her dearing words, and I felt the warmth of her hand hungering over my sword. Silky stockings ripped and I plowed blindly in the mud of her.

Oh, that long ago Thanksgiving Day, that woe of my youth.

We mated a few more times under the veil of Mr. D's suspicion till we could bear the suspense no more—I faced expulsion, and she the foreseeable loss of Mr. D's vocation, but the memory of her came to form the basis of my youthful arousal. Parted lips, loose strands of hair hanging over the face, an empty house, a cold sky laden with the angst of oncoming snow, and my heart would ache as it ached that dreary day, and my groins would burn with the flame of that afternoon.

I often plotted trespassing the ivied residence of Mrs. D again, impinging upon her shaded vulnerability and unearthing her muffled screams that she stifled under bookish breath. We came close only one last time at a pompous school event whereby all wives of the academic faculty were demanded at the angular dining table for the benefactors of the school, the elder Pickens included. I sat three heads and a table corner from Mrs. D and watched her chew her London broil. I smiled at her with code of our love, but she avoided my gaze.

A ball ensued. Old chaps of the school borrowed the young wives of others to hold in their arms, and I got to whirl her around the room in the guise of a waltz. She stayed silent with sullen face and begged me to stop halfway around the ballroom. Leaning on my shoulder with the world swaying on tiptoes, she uttered the three most horrifying words: "I am pregnant!"

I nearly let her fall out of my hand. I held my breath for the next three long and dying seconds until I felt a tap on my shoulder and heard the congenial Mr. D whisper, "Let me take over."

Was it relief or burden that I felt? I could not tell—the ring of her words still echoed in my ear. I swiped two tall glasses of some liquor from the dark corner of the ballroom, downed them, and rushed back to my dormitory.

This must be my punishment from God: fathering a bundle of sin. What would she do with him or her, the little me?

After a long week of fearing, the campus was suddenly abuzz with news of Mr. D's departure. Mrs. D's pregnancy had fulfilled a longstanding clause in his late uncle's will, a liquor dealer from Boston, bequeathing him, the only living heir of the Ds, a minority stake in a brewery on the condition that D produce an heir of his own blood and flesh. The Ds rushed off rather unceremoniously, and I have lived in cloudy ambiguity ever since.

For weeks after their departure, I was haunted by nightmares; each time, I woke up sweating and panting. Headmaster Herbert had called Father twice with mild compliments of my sporting verve but expressed concern over my general well-being. My eyes were circled with dark rims, and I was dispirited in religious assembly. A school nurse, after checking my pulse, scraped the moss from my tongue, tapped my echoing ribs with her knowing but misguided knuckles, and declared me a slight case of depression that a home visit and some sun should dispel. But it was the uninduced confession from another virile classmate of mine, one Samuel Polk III, the son of a mean-spirited financier, that cleared my guilt in toto.

One insipid Sunday afternoon after I had scorched my throat with much hymnal singing, Sam Polk strolled with me along a patch of lawn near the school chapel that afforded a slice of Mrs. D's former garden. The dreary day produced a dreary chat, and soon the New York boy was regaling me with his ventures with Lower East Side foreign whores whom he described as not only good with their craft but with their tongues.

"Got it, Pickens?" He chuckled at his own wit. "But you know, Pickens. I had more fun and less trouble right there behind those hedges." He pointed his toe at Mrs. D's garden.

"You what?" I sputtered.

"I had my way three times with that barren Mrs. D. Only made two trips to her house; the other time, I had her behind the hedge before it was trimmed and the leaves cleared."

I nearly choked the boy with my own hands.

I was let out of the jail of burden and breathed the fresh air of a sonless youth, but in that freedom I yearned for her—the hedge, the garden, the white house, the possibility that she would forever gaze at her child's face and think of me.

2

After the Ds' departure, Andover was as empty for me as the Forbidden City, under whose roof I now am penning this improbable diary. The colors were erased from autumn trees, and a certain buoyancy was amiss in the eyes of the young boys around me, mourning the fable that was Mrs. D. The vibrant PE teacher, Mr. Waldran, no longer sat on the short wall fencing off the Ds' former house in between his classes—another suspect. Cricket balls, footballs, any balls seldom found their way to that haunted garden anymore.

That shrine of our hearts soon was spiderwebbed as snow whited its shingles and ice icicled its roof, but soon came spring, and all dread vaporized upon the lilting sound of an exotic mellow flute. It came from the window of that white house, the Ds' former abode, hovering over the same garden.

Here and now I must pause. The hurried rustling of my brush must have awoken the demons of the night within the Forbidden City where I reside now: the footfalls of the night guards are nearing. You see, I am being watched constantly by the eyes in and beyond the walls. The flutist, creating the music that hung in the air over Andover that day, is the woman who links me to this fate within this red wall of the Forbidden City. She is the ebb and flow of my tide, the doing and undoing of it all.

She was conceived, as she would tell me in our initial shy encounter, on the Nile one rippleless night sailing through Egypt. She was born at dawn when the Qing Dynasty was dusking in the Manchurian port city of Dalien, where her father, and before that her grandfather, served as missionaries in the church of Jesus Christ, the northern division of their worldwide conference. The Hawthorns were a clan of proud missionaries with pious convictions and big-boned conventionality. Her father, Hawthorn IV, a blue-blooded Philipian himself, had lost a leg to a striped tiger in the Changbai Mountain. A reassignment by the North American Conference, his employer, landed the man back on the campus of his alma mater and his only daughter on my cold lap.

The blond and blue-eyed whimsical Annabelle, after growing up in the Orient, liked to dress up as a Chinese empress in an ornate embroidered coat, a gift from a local warlord. The cross-Pacific voyage had left her melancholy and stricken with longing for the only land she had ever known. The bamboo flute was a gift from a Changbai Mountain monk, and this flute, upon which she blew her scented breath to stir the melodies of that yellow dirt land, was her only solace in her uprooted existence. That is, until I came along.

We chatted behind our hymnbooks about eloping—she nineteen, an unbridled bride, and I eighteen, a doomed groom—to the foggy kingdom of her Shangri-la. She was full of myth and mythology. Our temple floated in the clouds and spring tasted sweet; she dreamed of being a ghost, dead from the inferno of a love affair, living thinly between the wall and its wallpaper. I boasted of becoming a fearless explorer with the sunlight my only guide, the moonlight my bed.

Quickly and clumsily we fell in love. Ache of that nascent love and the pain of our monstrous desire to possess each other nearly destroyed us during the honeyed month of our affair. She would ricochet between the imaginary summit of elation and the abyss of low and dark moods, while I languished in a permanent state of tented agony, hungry for every glimpse of her: strolling down the wooded path, a white lily in her hair; in a tree, skirt afluff, a blond butterfly in greens; laughing on the swing, my heart in flight.

Compared to Mrs. D, Annabelle was a tadpole in a puddle, an apprentice in the witchcraft of womanhood, a girl in waiting—waiting for the hands of her fate to unpeel her petals. During sleepless nights, the ghost of Mrs. D, the married martyr, would still creep to the edge of my canvas, elbowing aside Annabelle to make it a portrait for three. Mrs. D's sudden vulgarity shamed me—the rolling stomach, corrugated thighs, and copious breasts. Those signposts of age all burst into flames, and in its place rose the phoenix of Annabelle.

I still tremble at the thought of touching Annabelle's budding chest for the first time under the May maple tree. The hedges formed our barricade beyond which her mother was having tea with summer friends. Tree leaves played peek-a-boo with tea leaves upon their white-clothed tea table. Her young breasts were taut under her plain dress. Her face twisted in agony, she pressed my palm into her chest, her hands over mine, then slowly pushed it down to bury between her legs. We both drew in a long breath, suspending the moment into an eternity. My fingers were about to wriggle for its prey when suddenly, a bark was yelped at her puppy. Her mother called to her errant daughter from her shaded alcove.

When we emerged, I was poured a cup of tea, which I shame-lessly accepted.

The cravings germinated from that unfulfilled under-the-hedge hanky panky left our hearts sobbing with even more potent desire. Rubbing shoulders in the chapel's narrow cor-ridor induced dizzy spells; holding hands secretly generated electrifying lightning; drawing her name on the sandy ground rendered my knees weak and sword amast. We were stupe-fied by the storm of love ravaging our young bodies.

My hand is shaking now as I prepare myself to compose that fateful night when we met again. Even my palace ink boy, In-In, frowns with concern. Grind on, my boy, make it dark, make it silky, make it last longer than the etchings on my tombstone. I desire the world to know that truth—yes, the truth that begets no explanations.

It was love. It was the moon. It was fragrant June. All was quiet, a New England summer night, when I followed Anna-belle's instructions left in a coded note slipped into my Bible. A trail of yellowed leaves waited for me from the shadow of my window. A blithe jump landed me out the dorm, and I tiptoed along her Silk Road, my heart in my throat. Our tryst was a narrow isle between two looming haystacks reeking of stale autumn.

Annabelle sat on the hay, her hair tossed over her shoul-der, smoking a slender bamboo pipe tipped with a bubbling holder. The air was tinctured with the heady scent. "Smoke it." She puffed. "It's opium."

I took a long draw, swallowed it with a gag, then kissed her parted lips. Pain creased her forehead and pleasure quivered her lower lip. Weakened by desire, I lifted the hem of her skirt. She drew another puff, blowing it into me, and we fed on each other's hungry mouths. I thrust my hand up her skirt, sailing for my dark destiny, her scented Shangri-la, and she slackened her legs with a small cry. Heaven was near. Oh, that sweet, sweet spring. In an outburst of tenderest love, I let loose my painful sword. She took me in her slender hand, making it quiver, and opened her castle gate. I marched forward with stars blinking over my shoulders and was on the verge of possessing her, my darling, darling Annabelle, when the sparks from her damned opium pipe leaped into life. The flames, like a gale on a stormy sea, swallowed the haystacks.

All my feeble mind can recall is that she pushed me away as a bale of hay, aflame, fell hard on us. My foot caught on fire and a certain stench overwhelmed me. I remember pulling her slender arm, her bare feet; then another haystack toppled against my shoulder and I lost her hand. I was found unconscious, slightly burned and bruised, fifteen feet from her incinerated remains with my right hand reaching for her. From that cursed moment on, I have been living only to regret every second of life without her, my Annabelle.

When the authorities questioned me about the fire and my burned clothing, I was told not to mention our tryst. There were numerous clues linking me to that fateful night, but the tentacles of the elder Pickens made them all vanish. I was repulsed by the cover-up, and I wrote a moving confession of all the ins and outs of our affair leading to the climax of the fire. Upon reading the report, Annabelle's father and the principal not only burned it in my presence but also threatened prosecution with the possible charge of involuntary manslaughter and possible expulsion if any word of it got out.

In Andover's official record, the death of Annabelle was omitted altogether. The flames of 1891 warranted only a foot, note as being the first fire on the famed campus.

3

In the aftermath of her death, my moods swung wildly, and an escalating depression plunged me into bouts of harrowing head pains, leaving me a gaunt ghost of my former self. Speaking of ghosts, I made love to Annabelle's ghost every night, sometimes twice or even thrice, my headaches permitting. She might be dead to the world—her tombstone said so—but under my quilt, in my arms, she was always my living bride, my virginal wife. When I began my first year at Yale, my headaches miraculously subsided, and musical studies began to interest me. I found the combination of pipe organ and stained glass particularly soothing. Bach was a forest of solitude echoing with Annabelle's angelic laughter, Beethoven an islet of nostalgia, lush with her sashaying shadows. Stained glass was my darkened sun, freckled with pigeon poop.

Even though the organ stopped, the music lived on in my head with gnawing reprisals, keeping me starkly awake all night, though never away from my Annabelle. Insomnia only made a Hercules out of me and a Joan of Arc out of her. What a honeymoon it was, though it did bring back my headaches with shocking ferocity, which at various intervals pushed me as far as wanting to kill myself, but I never did.

The night always came in time, and I simply could not unlove my Annabelle.

I dabbled in poetry writing, first as a sonneteer, then as a balladeer. The narrow wards of rhymes and meters left me smothered with claustrophobic gloom. It was in prose that I blossomed. I envisioned myself a nervous diver standing atop a roaring cascade. Once letting go, I soared like an eagle. The soaring, not of me but of my poisoned pen, proliferated an enviable body of work: forty-three essays and two eclectic tragicomedies. But the gem amidst the roughs was the twelve bound volumes of letters to my Annabelle: four hundred and twenty-one letters in all. They were burned to ashes on Annabelle's twentieth birthday in a fire aiming to end it all, yet narrowly I escaped, a sobbing arsonist.

The flirt with fire was cathartic, though it did leave a scar around my waist where the letters had been tied. The windows of my heart suddenly opened; desire stirred from the base of my spine, and thoughts of infidelity tortured me. I wrote copious confessions to my Annabelle, and she wept with me under our quivering quilt. The glory of our subsequent lovemaking was worth all my penitent penmanship and conniving contrition.

4

Annabelle reigned over me like the empress she had yearned to be in life. She was formless, airlike, ubiquitous, and pervasive. She lived in the light, in the air. She was all the colors of a rainbow, all cycles of a season, and I, her lone subject, surrendered on the shrine of her glory. In my head, I could trace her thoughts forming, dissolving, re-forming, and vanishing again. In my heart a sadness lingered, not of mine but of her origin. She mourned her own death, and I mourned her grief.

My surrender simplified all my urges, for hers were now mine and mine were subjugated. If any element of me rebelled against her royal wish, headaches rolled in like an afternoon tide, threatening to bury me in the darkness of her existence. But why would I, in my rare foolishness, rebel against such a fine ruler? In her boundless generosity, she showered me with love and lust, comforted me with her warmth on cold nights, and guided me with her omnipotent wisdom, which, among other things, aided me in escaping a narrow brush with a certain sanitarium.

The dean of Yale had urged my father many a time to consult with a certain Dr. Price, aptly named for his pricey establishment where he had been known to cure those possessed. Prior to my compulsory oral audience before the Collegiate

Fitness Board, which included the renowned Dr. Price, invited by Father to test my sanity, Annabelle had me read a certain journal titled *Proceeding*, published by the American Society of Psychical Research, a Boston institution established in 1885, specializing in the research of parapsychology, telepathy, hypnosis, apparitions, and the paranormal. "The Possessed and De-possessing," a feature in that particular issue by none other than Dr. J. S. Price, showed me the ins and outs of that pseudo-science cooked up not by any scientific endeavors but by the compilation of hearsay and rumors.

I did a perfect job, acting in every minute detail contrary to the set rules established by Price for diagnosing one possessed. I was sure of myself, revealing no hint of a mental double life. I was nostalgic of Annabelle (the possessed felt no nostalgia). I was outrageously boyish, coming in unbathed for days (the possessed took on the invading spirit's personality—she was squeaky clean). In the end, I threw in some teary moments, confessing to seeing her ghost and being frightened (the possessed did not tell). Not only did I convince those graying academicians of my sanity, I also led them on a wild goose chase with my pseudo-knowledge of the dark side, suggesting the Hindu method of depossession— blowing cow-dung smoke in my face or burning pig excreta under my bed—at which time I noticed Dr. Price pull out his handkerchief and cover his nose.

The Collegiate Fitness Board members, at Price's recommendation, labeled me as deeply depressed but only slightly delusional, hanging rather thinly to a blade of sanity. Even a subsequent discovery of a silk-draped wooden mannequin taken from under my bed was not sufficient to send me packing for Dr. Price's place. But Dr. Price did, as a cautionary catchall, prescribe for this "abnormally disturbed youth" two classic medicinal solutions for my invisible ailments: group exercise (to peel away from my sorry self and rebuild a robust body, which in itself is the best pharmacy) and Oriental studies (finding the ghost's "life story" to demystify my ghost, a classic trick).

As the following journal will attest, both prescriptions by our Bostonian ghostbuster not only failed to free me from the tangle of Annabelle but also in time and in many avenues fastened my abject soul tighter to that illusion of my lost love. I, in the words of the wizard Dr. Price, advanced from passive seer to a progressive ghostchaser who would trot the globe in search of the shadow of his lost love.

5

From the beginning of my Yale years, I had shunned all sweaty sporting activities involving more than one male participant—myself. The fear of denting the delicate her in such mindless physical clashes kept me away from the likes of football and basketball, and the thought of baring my Annabelle-in-my-head to the filthy locker room frightened me. But luck was well on its way. My extracurricular activity would soon show some pink in an utterly male choice: synchronized swimming. A world champion was invited to teach Yalies how to swim pretty, and I (we) did swimmingly well in this merman's ballet. The certain female something helped me gain the only A-plus given by our miserly Olympian.

By the autumn that followed, my cheeks had regained their rosiness and my appetite was robust: I ate like a depraved, deprived prisoner with a hulking appetite for two. Suffice it to say that the rigor of such fierce sport did nothing to part me from my ghost. On the contrary, it set our sex life once more afire, with me burning through five mannequins in one summer, stolen from a fashion outlet that had gone bankrupt.

Upon my improved health, as Dr. Price had suggested,

I, with Annabelle's subliminal consent, took on Oriental studies with Professor Archer, a famed Orientalist. He was a man of few words, suitable for all vocations but teaching, yet in his own quiet way he showed us the world. The seven continents were seven white rocks strewn randomly in his own delicate Japanese garden. The ancient Silk Road, Archer demonstrated with a pair of his shabby leather shoes in which he had traveled the rugged gateway to the Orient. The climb along the spine of the Himalayas was but a mountaineer's hat, broken and goggleless, and the boat ride down the boisterous Three Gorges of the Yangtze River was a photo of three boat boys, half naked, pulling the boat by rope along the shore and a bottle of murky water fetched from the delta of the river where it embraced the sea. No one had taught us more with less.

Demystifying only mystified this hollow mind. Annabelle used to be just that angel from the quaint Orient; now her entire world threatened to swallow me, and the only escape seemed to lie in the belly of the beast.

I read voluminously under his tutelage and quickly became his favorite student. In my spare time, I begged Archer to coach me in the lilting Mandarin language, one of his thirteen learned tongues. In his crowded den where he guided me with his hand over mine through the calligraphy of those graphic words, Archer became an eloquent man with an endless flow of tales. A shot of whiskey sufficed the man for a good three hours of chat. With his sometimes decisive, at times dreamy, verbal stroke, he painted a verbal canvas of an ancient Middle Kingdom where the emperor, descended from dragons, reigned, and the empress, the offspring of swans, loved. In the collages of images knitted together by the hands of my imagination, I substituted Annabelle's eyes and body into the storied empress. Leafing through the pages of dynastic histories, I saw Annabelle sitting on the throne reigning over her golden palace, Annabelle boating in the palace pond, Annabelle riding her Gobi desert stallion galloping toward me away from the Forbidden City wall. And, alas, Annabelle nude in bed with a faceless opium-smoking emperor surrounded by countless concubines.

Soon Annabelle's Peking shanghaied my Yale. Barren New Haven merged into the quaint canvas of a fairytale kingdom complete with golden palaces, soaring mountains, and meandering rivers: my world and hers roped together in a tangle of two cities. Yale shimmered like a mirage in the sunrise of a forbidden city. Library shelves brimmed not with classics of Greek origin or Latin letterings but with imagined Chinese scrolls containing the wisdom of thousands of years. My dormitory grew curled roofs, its facade carved with nine dancing dragons. Professor Archer, in profile, vanished into the body of a scrawny Manchurian monk, his words mangled with a Chinese tongue. Everywhere I turned, pigtailed Yalies dressed in silk gowns kowtowed to one another. My specters were everywhere playing hide-and-seek with me, awakening Annabelle's pulse, and at times I returned to those golden days of our nascent love, not on the leafy campus of Andover but in a sumptuous palace where she dodged me from column to column, chamber to chamber, her giggles echoing in my heart. Oh, ghosts did occur in New Haven!

Yet in all this vicissitude, the smoldering emperor re-mained devilishly faceless. The perplexing blankness haunted me everywhere I looked, trailing in Annabelle's wake, clad in his imperial garb, a faceless ghost smoking his bubbling pipe. How I abhorred his victorious smile beaming at me. Oh, that fire of jealousy! It drove me to the brink of madness. He began to bear upon me like a nagging headache, appearing and disappearing at will. Soon His Facelessness started ap-pearing under our quilt.

"Go back to your imperial silk bed!" I demanded angrily.

What incensed even more was Annabelle's reaction to our new cast member. She giggled with her coconspirator, hiding behind His Facelessness. I had to conclude that my illusion was having a sticky affair with another illusion and that it was time I, the unhappy husband, did the husbandly thing. I adopted the tactic of separate and destroy.

I read and reread Dr. Price's thesis "Separating Reality from Illusions," the only respectable publication on the sub-ject. It was obese with theoretical assumptions and presump-tions but skeletal with effective and potent tools of practical usage. But in the footnote, our good doctor did point me to the right horizon in the form of a caveat.

Page 367 pointedly warned:

Avoid a certain Mandarin ritual named Sha Gui, *meaning "killing the ghost." The ancient rite invites the hidden ghost to surface by means of a mysterious nature; then the performer of the rite, usually a monk, sacrifices livestock in the ghost's presence, ending the viability of such an illusion. The reader must heed the severe consequences that are bound to follow. Quite often, the surfaced ghost is never killed, which, for all intents and purposes, leads inevitably to the augmenting of an existing illusion, causing one to live forever in a whirl of delirium.*

6

One muggy summer day found me in pigtailed China-town where an inky advertisement, wet in the gutter, landed me in front of a storefront hidden along Canal Street. The store sign read summarily in Mandarin: *Tell Fortunes & See Ghosts*. The one-eyed Chinaman within was picking earwax for another Peking man while the store owner's wife, a petite bound-feet beauty, embroidered a silk apron. A boy, likely their son, was slurping steamy porridge from a bowl atop a rickety table. I made my request in teetering Mandarin.

The busy Chinaman barked, "See no white ghost. Out you go!"

The boy nearly ran me out of the store when his father stopped him to inquire what price I was willing to pay. I let known my generosity and desperation by leafing through a crisp pile of dollar notes. The Chinaman hurried the other man's ear job with three deep digs, suffering the customer to depart with squeaky pain, and then bargained with me in tilting pidgin English, "White ghosts three dollars."

I said, no problem.

"White chicken cost more fifty cents."

Not to worry, I affirmed.

He gestured his woman and the boy to vanish behind the

counter, and he led me along an unlit corridor into a *gui fan,* a ghost chamber.

The wall of the dark chamber was festooned with a dozen straw men painted with ghostly faces staring down at us as we sat in a circle: the black face of a forest ghost; the green face of a drowning ghost; the red face of a fiery ghost; and the pink face of a birthing ghost. My *gui shi,* ghost master, with a beady parrot wobbling on his shoulder, wrote down Annabelle's name and mine on a piece of paper and inquired about the cause of her death.

"Fire," I said.

"That cost you more," he murmured, showing two crooked fingers.

I nodded, and the ritual started with his hitting a gong while the boy lit dozens of thick incense sticks. Smoke instantly filled the air. The gong sang like a dirge as he chanted her name in a fawning tone, calling for her spirit.

"An-na-belle. An-na-belle," the boy repeated after the *gui shi.*

The parrot mimicked the boy, their shouts forming an eerie cycle of "An-na-belle."

I squinted my eyes in the thick smoke to gain that first glimpse of Annabelle, only to have the *gui shi* scream at me, "You not cry yet? Give me palms."

When I did, the *gui shi* plunged two needles into the heart of my hands.

I sobbed.

The boy stood up and began to beat the fiery ghost with a stick as the *gui shi* burned my name and Annabelle's into ashes. Through the curtain of my tears, I suddenly saw

Annabelle flying like an angel, roped from above, swinging amidst the thick smoke. Her face was draped with a red cloth like a village bride, her waist thin and stemlike. Her shivering voice called my name, "Peetkins, Peetkins."

Oh, my heart! I leapt to my feet, lunging at her, only to be stopped by my *gui shi*, who whispered, "That your Annabelle."

"Can I see her face?"

"No."

"Why not?"

"She shamed of burned face. Too ugly."

"Oh no, my Annabelle," I cried, crawling all over the chamber, chasing after her as she swung back and forth in the misty smoke. "You are never ugly to me. Please . . . please," I begged until I felt faint from the beguiling incense, reminiscent of the flaming aroma of that summer night.

In a last desperate attempt, I clutched the Chinaman's knees, begging him to let down my angel. He replied with a stinging slap across my face, rendering another dizzy spell in my already surging head. The boy leapt up from the floor to fan the smoke into swirls, and the gong was hit even harder, rippling my eardrums. Tears trickled down my cheeks uncontrollably. Was this the whirl of delirium forewarned by Dr. Price? My delicious delirium? Then through the patches of the thinning smoke, I caught a glimpse of a rather chiseled and familiar face.

"Who is that?" I demanded.

"You!"

"What am I doing in the mirror?"

"No mirror, you white idiot. You faceless emperor in your dreams!"

"Me?"

"We kill by chopping chicken's head off."

I touched my face. So did the mirrored image. I reached over with my trembling hands, and it was gone as suddenly as it had come. The last thing I remember was the boy jumping at me with the stick he had beat the fiery devil with and the shattering pain exploding in my fuzzy head.

I don't know how long I slept. When I awoke, all the smoke had vaporized and I was lying in the barber chair back in the storefront. The boy was clinking his bowl, finishing another meal, and the woman was busy embroidering her silk apron. The *gui shi* rushed out with a headless rooster.

"I chased own ghost away. See? Head cut off. You want?"

I pushed away the bloodied bird and inquired about the fate of Annabelle's ghost.

"Her ghost here with you but her soul far away in China."

"But she's buried here."

"Not matter. Leaves fall on own roots. She return to birth-place after death so she reborn."

"Reborn?" I uttered, holding my spinning head. "Reborn into what?"

"Reincarnation. Body of another. Now you pay."

For days I lived in a hazy world reliving those moments of eerie revelation. The ghost might have been the *gui shi's* wife flown from a hidden rope, and my own image the cunning reflection of a suddenly hauled-in mirror—the boy did disappear before the act. But in my heart, in that hazy ghost chamber, I felt my Annabelle, and she felt me.

In the weeks that followed, the faceless emperor did vanish. Sadly, come the fall, my favorite New England season, only occasional traces of Annabelle were all that remained in my fragmented dreams. She appeared once as a migrat, ing swan heading south, tiny in the blue sky, barely audible in the air. Another time she was a palm,treed island lone, some at sea.

All the empresses and emperors in my books resumed their slitty eyes and oval faces, and Yale was un,shanghaied. New Haven returned to its dread of white picket fences and drab leafiness, and my Annabelle was but a swan dying, her song a thinning echo calling me from misty, ancient China.

My life resumed its tranquility, and I slept much better. A certain buoyancy returned to my youthful body though I remained alone and lonely despite the insistent efforts of my mother for me to participate in such banal activities as Vassar Night, Smith Afternoon, and Wellesley Weekend.

Dr. Price was called again by Father for a nondiagnostic consultation. A certain sheen in my eyes convinced the Bos, tonian that I was much in need of some conventional plea, sure and ready to be unleashed into the social settings where some rightful girl's affection might just be the very last nail to seal the coffin of my illusions. How wrong was he!

I made perfunctory appearances in social soirées, always that shadowy fellow alone with my Annabelle,in,my,head, rocking in a wicker chair. I prided myself on keeping a three, foot distance from all the un,Annabelle girls in attendance. There were no specific faces that I remember in those out, ings or any particular voices that I can recall hearing. It was all a blur of bubbling girls whose chatter resembled morning birdsong.

Only on one occasion did I feel nearly faint when I saw

a shadow of a girl, as blithe as Annabelle, thin ankled with blond pigtails swinging over the nape of her swan neck. Was it a Vassar Afternoon or a Smith Evening? It was a burgundy *V* that I recalled and leafy Poughkeepsie that came to mind. The sunlight was amber, soothing, shining playfully through the canopy, highlighting forgotten food and neglected drinks on picnic tables.

I chased after her as she ran unknowingly to chat with this girl and laugh with that, like a butterfly, eluding me from one tribe of partygoers to another. I raced after her as a hunter would his prey: from the garden, through a long and narrow corridor, up the grand stairs leading to the Villard Room. And there, alone, she was on top of the flight, about to disappear again into the grand ballroom when she paused, sensing my footsteps. How I felt my heart stop and breath hold. How I wished she could have stayed in that pose forever. The light from the window framed her stillness—like an angel she was. The chatter outside the window faded into the distance, and the summer shimmered in my vision. I was alone with her, three steps apart, our hearts beating in the same rhythm: such an operatic moment with music swirling on the magical waves of a full orchestra reaching for that glorious climax. Then she turned and smiled.

Her buckteeth hissed like the fangs of a wolf.

My heart broke, a thousand pieces.

If any smile could kill, hers did. I fled in flight, faking a stomachache through the dark corridors draped with the portraits of a brooding Matthew Vassar.

Was it my Annabelle that I saw inhabiting the chosen Vassarian on that miraged afternoon?

Did she not once dream of matriculating at Vassar where proper ladies were groomed? Had it not been her wish to be empress of an ancient land, and after death, a ghost thinned between the wall and its wallpaper?

If I could find her in that ethereal moment on the stairs of the Villard Room, would I find her in the chambers of the Forbidden City?

7

Here and now I open the new chapter of my life on the fresh page of my secret journal that my In·In has laid before me with red vertical lines to flock my words into the vertical order that a foreigner like me is unaccustomed to.

It was the year I left Yale . . .

Damn! The ink bled—too watery. It smeared the *Ya* but not the *le*.

"In·In?" I inquire. My ink boy's tears had dripped off his cheeks into my inkwell.

Poor In·In. The youngest of the palace eunuchs, he still misses his home, and the thirteen lashes rendered him by Li Liang, the chief eunuch, for a broken vase, certainly have not helped. I wipe his eyes, and he grinds on, making our desk squeak like a night bug.

Now that the ink is silky but not sticky, our tale can resume.

The year I graduated from Yale, I signed up with the Christian Student Volunteer Movement (CSVM). I was offering myself for service as an overseas missionary for the China Inland Mission, the very division Annabelle's father, and his father before, had been a part of. The act sent both Father and Mother into convulsions. Father immediately offered to enroll me at Columbia Law School and start me as a

32

junior partner, with the potential to crawl into the letterhead of Pickens, Pickens & Davis. When he saw no sign of Junior softening, Senior threatened with the age-old scepter of disinheriting me. Mother readily concurred, though on an utterly different basis. She felt that I was not of sound mind.

Annabelle and I would have been long gone had it not been for the oversubscription of eager volunteers to the mission. But then came the horror of two French Catholics burned to death on crosses by some inland Buddhist fiends. The scare dampened the voluntary fervor, causing a precipitous drop in numbers, leapfrogging me to thirteenth in the queue; but the scare also dried up the donations going that way, stalling the program indefinitely. A rejection from the San Francisco headquarters of the CSVM shattered both my plans and my fragile health. The headaches returned, as well as a low-grade fever, which I understood as Annabelle's punishments for my inaction.

One breezy day at the tail end of summer —that summer of horror that would change all——a drunken skipper of a single-mast boat miscalculated the wind strength and launched its bow into the Pickens yacht, capsizing the vessel. At the moment of impact, Mother and Father were downstairs readying themselves in the cabin to watch the sunset. They both drowned, coffined in the very yacht they had inherited, suffocating in the very waters they had loved. Oh, that heinous Long Island Sound, tomb of their twin caskets.

In the somber reading of their joint will and testament, Father, in his unequivocal tone, repeated his threat of disinheriting me, and so did my mother. But a later signed codicil in the flowery signature of Mother, a loving afterthought, saved the day. It stipulated that I would inherit her entire estate on the condition that I, the sole heir, agreed to marry before leaving the soil of the New England states.

A good start but not quite there yet. The legal theories and the case law precedents all concluded that a couple, when dying in the same disastrous accident together, are presumed to have died at the same time. This would leave Pickens Senior's will intact, and since my mother would not have inherited his estate, this Pickens would not receive a dime. My surrogate lawyer, Melvin Davis, Esq., of Pickens, Pickens & Davis, argued that though the two spouses expired at the same time, his wife who was junior by thirteen years (Father was quite a cradle robber) would be deemed to have survived her husband by virtue of her relative youthfulness and deceased later in time, thus giving rise to her spousal right to inherit the entire Pickens estate just long enough for her to bequeath all her estate to the living heir, me.

Thanks to the good grace of my dear mother and the esquirely acuity of Mr. Davis, who was eager to get rid of me, an unnecessary partner, all I needed was a paper bride, a makeshift ceremony, and maybe, God willing, a quick divorce. Then I could retire from the world of nagging commerce and live off my legacy—suffice it to say, it was quite substantial for my meager need—and devote myself wholly to the honeymoon of my Asiatic voyage in search of my Annabelle.

To satisfy Mother's codicillary hoop, I cast the matrimonial net narrowly among the recently minted Vassarians. The mirage of Annabelle on that Poughkeepsied afternoon still shone golden in my meek memory. My deft fingerwalk

through a borrowed Vassar graduate album aided me in lo-
cating my predestined choice, the bucktoothed misery. She
had been no soap bubble of my frolicking imagination but
the genuinely solidified statue of Susan Sanders, hiding between the pages of blond Brenda Samuels and the freckled
brunette Carroll Souter, the oldest daughter of a ceramist father, with his own collection of blue-hued fine china proudly
on display in Vienna galleries, and of a Bostonian toothbrush
heiress mother.

We were duly introduced at tea at the Plaza's Palm Court,
a place for the Sanderses to see and not to be seen (they
hid their teeth behind their teacups). She was a matronly
eighteen but still possessed that mannequin physique with
bony ankles and a blithe romping gait. There was no moment
of her frowning recollection of our encounter on her part.
All the better, for I, in the know, much preferred my desire
to be passively unknowing, though intuitively collaborating.
Her shortcomings—her hiccupy laughter, the fanglike teeth,
an upturned nose, melanic nose hair, and bushy eyebrows—
paled remarkably as long as she remained silent, preferably
standing against the afternoon sun, framed by the golden
light, letting me, without her knowing, play and replay that
moment of enlightenment. Oh, one really could fall for an
illusion.

We were soon married in a white-everything wedding
ceremony—how very summerly—all for my secret goal of
reenacting that fabled Vassar afternoon. When God lifted
the cloudy veil on the wedding day and let the sun shine
through the stained glass windows of our matrimonial
chapel, shedding a gauze of golden light over her shoulders,

the entire church ceased to breathe. It was just me and my sunned angel.

My woeful eyes saw a blank face. It could have been my Annabelle at the altar and Reverend Hawthorn in the pew looking on proudly instead of the ceramist.

On our wedding night, I implored her to wear a Chinese empress gown that I had bought for a bargain from a silk store south of Canal Street. Bucktoothed Bride was unobjectionable to my groomy whim, and she was soothed by my elaborate excuse of a certain fancy for all things Chinese. However, when I suggested a puff of bubbling opium in an ornate pipe, my Vassarian bride's eyebrows stood on their tails and her jaw dropped an inch southward. But the charming Pickens could not let such a blissful night go any way but Annabelle's way. I, as Annabelle had done to me, fed a mouthful of that glorious smoke into her ready mouth. In one brief moment that lasted for an eternity, Susan and I dissolved together with the poison.

In the candlelit bridal room, the muggy summer night materialized. I continued the steamy job at hand, lifting the hem of Annabelle's skirt, parting her legs. She moaned her sweet moans, her knees clamping in fake resistance, then the base of her hip tautened and slackened in wanton submission.

By sunrise my fresh bride was found kneeling, face buried in our satin settee, the silk gown barely draping her bare self, and the call for *charge* rang again in my foggy head. She was a living Annabelle, shy from the morning sun, begging for Captain Pickens to wake her with his bulbous baton. Oh, my submissive love slave! I crawled stealthily like a sunken-bellied leopard, eyeing my prey, adoring her in the faintest of light. Had Annabelle been alive, she would have been this creature, thin ankled, fine-kneed, narrow-hipped, sirening for a reprisal of the night gone by.

When I caressed her unadorned tailbone with the tips of trembling fingers, my pale bride did not unleash an expectant sigh. A tender thrust was initiated along the valley of my doll. But my bride played an icy mannequin. Again I coaxed her with my throbbing staff, forcing my way onward as gently as a deprived and depraved soul could bear. The interior of my lover was cold as a cave. A certain irresponsive swaying of her hips, letting throw and toss whichever way I leaned on her, informed me that she was either still deep in her opium-induced stupor or coyly playing the fiddle for the mannequin-loving Pickens, who was accustomed to squeaking domination over his wooden love slave.

It was neither. When the slobbering Pickens cease-fired in the midst of his assault to investigate her mutinous silence by lifting the empress gown off her head, unveiling his one-night bride, the sight of blood dripping from the corner of her mouth, yielding a certain malodorous stench, was all I needed to see.

Who knows what I did to her in our foggy bed, upon the shaky chair, and over the satin settee. Had I banged her head against some sharp wall corner, my hands on her long curls, riding her, taming her in the act of ecstasy? Or had it been my Annabelle, acting out on her jealousies, from afar? The ceramist father-in-law's words would soon save me from the hands of the law. He whispered her preexisting medical condition into the ears of the hulking sheriff: a rare case of extremely high blood pressure that rose in times of extreme

stress, which the county coroner explained had ruptured her
cerebral vessels, causing her, and many others before and
after, to die in the arms of their loved ones.

Mr. Sanders not only did not accuse me, as many would
in such a case of neglect (the coroner confirmed her time of
demise to have been about four hours before reporting), but
he also credited me with the praise of making "her last day
in life the happiest" and offered an unworthy apology for having promised "a cracked vase" into my hands, depriving me
of lifelong bliss as a wedded man. I was rather moved by his
generosity of shouldering all the blame that could have been
borne by me, for which I could have spent lengthy years licking the keyhole of some smelly upstate prison cell.

As I sat in the front pew, six feet from my prettied-up
corpse of a bride, a girl I barely knew, awash in the deep sorrow of her sobbing parents, I felt an extreme urge to burst out
my criminal deeds: the mouthful of opium, that sordid urge
of mine that brought us the unwanted ecstasy that killed
her. But I didn't and couldn't! Annabelle-in-my-head, now an
experienced, soothing ghost, rushed me to the door where
the departing guests were and had me thank them as she had
directed me at my parents' funeral, my wedding, and now
my bride's departure. I, newly orphaned and now widowed,
red-eyed and withdrawn, stood by the door where we had wed
only days before, thanking those who had congratulated me
as sincerely as they now consoled me, ignoring my ill-fated
bride all prettied up in an open casket display.

I felt like a thief who had stolen someone else's pearl.
Susan, in another life, could have fallen in love and married

an even-tempered, less virile Harvard Man, who would have paled in every way in bringing her the kind of ecstatic satisfaction that I must have done. She would have borne her bucktoothed brood and lived to be an adorably toothy granny, but she was gone, sacrificing her youth for me and my Annabelle.

8

I had moved into my parents' townhouse, now that I was the legal owner. Legal I might be, but was it moral? Three deaths in one summer? How summarily convenient. Jack the Ripper couldn't have ripped a neater job.

I shall say that as I dug deeper, a certain speck of fact popped up, as it would occasionally in my mental upheaval, and clarity surfaced.

On the very deadly afternoon when Father and Mother went sailing with their yacht friends, I had been expected on board as well to get some fresh air, though I had not known that I was to be matched on the fateful cruise with a suit-able girl just returned from finishing school in Paris. I had planned on going because an art curator, Bernard Hughes, who had dedicated his life to acquiring Oriental arts, por-traits, and antiques for the Astors, was the guest of honor, and he, in Mother's words, looked forward to meeting the young Pickens.

Minutes before I was to step out of the house with Mother and her company, Father had long been on board, I was sud-denly attacked by a most severe case of diarrhea, the kind that threatened to empty one's entrails. Strangely, I hadn't eaten anything remotely trigger-happy as far as that kind of downpour was concerned. Neither had any part of me been chilled; on the contrary, it was a summer day that needed chilling. As soon as I felt it was safe to go, the urge would return, rendering it utterly improper to board any thing without embarrassing the entire Pickens clan and their friends. Exactly three hours and thirty minutes later the disaster would strike, and I would be the only Pickens left dry ashore. The incessant cramping of my lower abdomen only ceased upon hearing of the boat's sinking.

Cosmic puzzlement? Perhaps. But that would not be the only coincidence of the day. An uncanny article in a newspaper that I usually never rested my eyes upon published a list of other minor coincidences stitched together by a snoopy newspaperman, fedora and cigarettes and all, I imagine. He wrote, and I quote from the article headlined as "The Eerie Coincidences Leading to New York Society's Sink of the Decade," that the skipper of the lobster boat was aged thirty-nine, the ninth child of a Great Neck Catholic clan. He had nine children of his own, and it was the ninth anniversary of his marriage (a prolific lobsterman) to one of twin sisters, who each had only nine toes. The accident took place on the ninth of the ninth month, exactly nine minutes after seven—a clock on board had stopped in the moment of the accident.

These might all sound like mindless rhyme concocted by a desperate newspaperman. Maybe the coincidences weren't so coincidental after all. Let the preponderance of evidence paint itself: that portrait of a cunning criminal, my Annabelle-under-the-quilt.

Nine, the royal digit of the Chinese emperor, was Annabelle's favorite number. She had professed to wanting to have nine children, with the little runt, a curly girlie, to be named Nina. She believed in the cycle of nine lives, each one a reflection of the previous. "Which one are you living now?" she used to ask me. She yearned to soar up to the ninth heaven where the pears of immortality and the peaches of longevity were grown. Harmless it might seem, but in the end, nine were injured, including the curator and Parisian girl: the former lost his voice, his Adam's apple slashed, rendering him a permanent mute—he, I gathered, was to talk me out of going to China—the latter lost an eye, making her a one-eyed beauty, and clipped her lip, popular not even in the eccentric city of Paris, making it an utter impossibility to be matched with anyone. In one act of genius, all paths to perdition were cleared of my Annabelle's foes. No one, I mean no one, but the devil could have done it except for my sweet darling girl.

So there you have it. I had thought of doing in my folks, but in the end it was the ghost who took the charge with the cobweb of nines. There are no laws or tenets prohibiting her from such deadly vengeance: she is dead. No hanging or beheading could hurt her anymore. My conscience was utterly clean—no bloody fingers or smoking gun. Just a snugly hidden ghost doing what might very well have been my own intended deeds.

There were moments, many moments as I roamed in my dark world, when I felt as if I was the only seeing soul among the blind multitude. I was the clear-eyed chosen one who had crossed over to the dark side, secretly privy to the underbelly of a busy loom that wove the fabric of coincidences, making them seem so conveniently and banally coincidental. Nothing happens randomly. Every occurrence is the result of much nail-biting premeditation in the mammoth cosmic game of chess played by angelic go-betweens, those butter-flies of which my Annabelle is one, as the following chain of miraculous events will attest.

9

I wasn't the only one on earth dreaming up little angelic ghosts as colorful butterflies. At the close of the previous chapter, on the point of my comparing all ghosts to butterflies, In-In, my presumed illiterate ink boy, tugged at my sleeve, picked up his little brush, and proceeded to draw a butterfly with the simplest of strokes, yet affecting such vividness, as if the little creatures in flight were futilely barred behind the red lines on our draft paper.

"You are an accomplished painter," I complimented him.

"Baba painted paper lanterns, and I apprenticed at his shop, painting little creatures on the bottom," he replied shyly.

When I asked him why he had painted me such a lively gift, he told me dead people soar up to become butterflies in China. I pinched his rosy cheek with affection and awarded him with a tael of silver for having stayed up past midnight to whet my ink.

All the little eunuchs in the palace had to work so very hard, and for what? A sunless living ahead of them all. He would have been better off, much better off, staying a lantern painter in the faraway village. But who am I to chastise him for what he had not chosen himself? It might have very well been his parents' choice to make him a sacrificial lamb to serve the palace so that the rest of the family would live forever in heavenly and material blessings.

In/In, as I observed, wasn't really the country bumpkin that he pretended to be. This wasn't the first time he had let out his secret. Upon rereading my unfinished memoir, I had encountered numerous corrections stealthily brushed in by the boy, making up a dot here, extending a stroke there. Though I marveled over his refined penmanship, I often wondered why he was hiding his literacy, and what else was he hiding from me. No matter, and no hurry, which seemed to be the pace of the palace. No one is without secrets here.

In/In's drawing had to have been inspired by a much loved fairytale that I had read during my double/visioned senior year at Yale. *Butterfly Lovers* could have been plagiarized from the Bard's *Romeo and Juliet*, except for two countering facts: it had been penned long before our bearded Brit had been fathered, and it had a happy ending—the mark of the pro/digious Chinese art of melofantasy. Two doomed lovers, who had died separately yet were buried side by side, soar away from the dusty earth as butterflies. Now and again on starry nights, a common eye could spot the lovers blinking in the margins of the Milky Way.

I dwell on our beloved flyers because this very chapter under my dripping brush could well be named "My Butter/flies." Life, if one sees closely, does take on certain themes.

For two years following Susan's death, I ensconced myself in my ill/gotten abode, barricading myself in Mother's bed/room where I was purported to have been born. I felt a certain umbilical link to that space, which promised the possibility of a new beginning. Mother was nowhere to be found, though her things, her scents, her motherly something, hung perennially in the air, mixed with the fragrance of gardenias seeping in from the garden down below.

The barricading was necessitated by my illusion that the entire house, three stories plus a little attic, were flown with little butterflies. Not your normal type but dark and white ones, choking themselves into every nook, vying for anything as a foothold to rest their busy wings. Everywhere I went they surrounded me, landing all over me. Annabelle told me that they were the nimble players of the aforementioned cosmic chess game, the undying spirits of rotten corpses and scattered bones. Without this nesting place, they would forever flutter in windblown graveyards and weedy cemeteries. Worse, at night they were hunted by ghost catchers to clock their time for a journey of finality—good men to heaven, bad fellows to hell.

In the security of my domain, in the gloomy twilight, we made my birthing room our eternal bridal suite, me and my Annabelle, as I planned our very next step with thumping heart. I penned many a letter to one Mr. Plimpton, the head of the CSVM—a goateed square fellow, a pioneer of foreign missions who had spent his formative years in the Amazon jungles encoding the Indian dialect—begging for him to give me a position in the vicinity of Peking, boldly capitalizing my offer to cover my own expenses for my tenure. My desperate tone must have gravely moved the man, so much so that he was willing to create a new mission for me in the city of Pao Ki, three miles east of Peking, on the condition that I enroll at the New York Theological Seminary as an interim student to fluff up my sermonic pedigree and that, as an additional condition, I should consider remarrying. A spousal presence was not only pastoral but also a necessity. Think windy pastures with only cliffs and sheep to gaze at.

I was all but ready to consider delving again into the dangerous waters of matrimony when I suddenly received a grave letter not only informing me of the death of Reverend Plimpton (choked to death by butterflies in his throat) but also with his death, the scratching of his original plans to open another mission for me. I still remember that rainy day. The entire city was silver and iron. It was on that very afternoon that a letter from my former Yale professor would arrive. No doubt pitying me as an orphan and widower in need of monastic solace, he informed me that a certain Chinese luminary named Yip Han was searching for a scholar to tutor the young emperor of the Qing Dynasty. Professor Archer had written a glowing letter pointing out my outstanding qualities and unblemished academic achievements under his own tutelage, sans my bout with insanity. The moment I tore the letter open, I could almost feel Annabelle's shriek of delight. Again and again she was the very one pulling all the strings, making the least possible person write letters for the least qualified candidate.

A meeting took place near New Haven. Mr. Han, the first Mandarin Yalie, sent by the palace to study modern science, had eventually fallen into the trap of Connecticut and married into the rather prominent family of Catherine Kellogg, producing a brood of modified Chinakins in snow white Connecticut. Mr. Han commented that he would have been the best teacher to teach the emperor Western things, but a subtle gesture—pointing at his short hair—told it all. He had forsaken their most telling token of loyalty to the Royal Court, cutting off his pigtail. A return home would be improper, to say the least.

An annual fee was talked about, fifteen hundred lian of silver, a thing that came rather as a surprise to me for I would have paid my own way to be inside the palace. Mr. Han, at the end of our talk, informed me that a decision would be arrived at after he had seen all the candidates. But a rare butterfly, a purple emperor, suddenly appeared near his window. He, an avid butterfly collector, chased into the courtyard, abandoning his talk with me, his net in hand. When he returned, beaming happily, the position was readily offered to me. It was a sign, he said, though later he wrote to say that the butterfly mysteriously disappeared from his collection without a trace.

I took this as a call for me to charge into our destiny. I dashed about trying to prepare for the journey of my life. After all, I was the last Pickens, and I could see no point in my future where I would be returning to this metropolis. There was only *going, going,* and *going* that I heard in my heart. Not a *ding* of coming back. The hunt for Annabelle's incarnation was the only bugle call I heeded. The voyage was more sacred than my own worthless life and the mission holier than all the gods melted together.

I put the house up for sale. An initial enthusiasm was dampened by my dogged refusal to let in the prospects for fear of their seeing what I saw—the resident butterflies. My unbending rule was mistaken—as a broker would whisper—as a sign that it was not only cursed but indeed haunted as speculated in society. It scared away a ruddy-faced English family, a social climbing French couple, and a scion of a Jewish banking family, all looking for a house with a fashionable address.

There were also stocks to sell. Mother had substantial stock holdings in a few aluminum concerns, the sale of which, unbeknownst to me, could tip a certain corporate balance among feuding families. Naturally, I was first the object of much nagging ingratiation and later, with my cold indifference, of heinous threats of bodily harm.

The tenderest care was given to the disposal of Mother's portraits of her gardenias, a girlish hobby dating back to her Smith days. I had grown up among easels of her favorite blooms, lumpy imitations on oily canvas. They were my motherly flora, which I personally entrusted to a renowned German framer, paying to have them all properly set and hung and have on permanent display in a third-tiered art gallery, memorializing a closet artist posthumously. As for Father's beloved belongings—golf clubs, a collection of pipes, and those wing-tipped white shoes—I dumped them from the shadowy pier on a moonless night along the East River, the closest inlet I had to the Long Island Sound. The exertion exhausted me. I was found sprawled, fainted, on the fishy pier the next morning by a stocky longshoreman.

Then and there Mr. Davis, my estate lawyer, had me sign all my power over to my father's sister, Aunt Lillian, a thin-lipped spinster, healthy as a horse and thrifty as a beggar, to be my administratrix. I had to be hospitalized for the remainder of the winter. Not only did I feel wobbly due to dizziness but also a chronic nausea had me heaving up everything that a dwindled appetite could hold.

When I was released come spring, good news was in order. The house had been snatched up by a titled and brazen homosexual from Hungary who donned a red cape with butterfly motif. Aunt Lillian blushingly reported the manners of the dainty duke and the whopping price agreed upon without the buyer's seeing the place, which quickly brought to my mind the picture of a pale nightwalker. Later news confirmed his unnerving habit of keeping his windows as closely shut as I had. Little did we know, the queen of all butterflies had come to town.

The stock sale, belated by lengthy negotiations, an unexpected market rise (lack of foreseeable output from southern aluminum mines), and Aunt Lillian's hatred for the squabbling clans, caused her to sell them all to the open market for double the price. Best of all, my health turned robust with Annabelle nursing me, enabling me to withstand the arduous journey ahead. My recovery coincided with the availability of the first luxury ship advertised, departing from the coast of California. By March of 1898, Annabelle and I were well on our way, languidly ensconced in a paneled train crawling to the golden coast.

10

After suffering through a month-long wait in San Francisco—every day I spent in a rocking chair on our hotel veranda, wondering about the mysterious Oakland wrapped in its blue wispy mist—we finally set sail across the Pacific battling through the treachery of the Hawaiian trade winds and the Okinawa typhoons.

In aqua April our ship reached coastal Tianjin during a slanting drizzle and amidst rumors of inland peasant riots and a southern cholera scare. I felt prone to neither fear nor fright, and I cast about looking for any transportation further inland. A timely tip from a Parsi from Punjab led me to hire the only coolies available, two strapping twin brothers of Shandong origin, who chewed scallions and tobacco leaves with equal rhythm and rigor. The twins had misgivings at first. Boxers were killing the blue-eyed, red-haired foreign heathens, and all sula in their service. But I deigned to let it be known that a triple fee was in offer if they would be willing to shoulder the three-day foot journey to Peking. The Tianjin-Peking express had ceased operation—German owners, who feared railroad sabotage, were hoarding railcars for future military use in retaliation against the murder of a certain traveling German count.

The twins were still of two minds, identically confounded,

when I proffered a folded Accord of Employment with the Dragon Throne's golden seal imprinted as a closure. To see the chattel belonging to the emperor was to be blinded into submission. The brothers genuflected and prostrated on the dusty road long after such paper was safely returned to my inner coat pocket.

For my safety, and their twin pigtailed necks, an accord of another sort was acquiesced between us. Even the roguish hands of rebels would refrain from prying a bridal veil or a rouge coffin lid, the brothers reasoned. Forthwith I was suffered to conceal my salient self in a dainty sedan behind an expediency of red drapery, playing a bride en route to her new home.

Three days of shortcuts and leeways, I alighted from my stealthy sedan in Peking.

The brawling brothers bargained for a raise in their carrying fees, having outrun bandits near Kaifan and eluding rebels in Roujiafu. I rewarded them accordingly on condition that I retain the veil as souvenir. The brothers ripped it off their carriage and gave it to me, then fled like ghosts, their pendulant pigtails swinging in the wind.

A blinding Mongolian sandstorm coupled with the lingering rebel fear rendered Peking a cascading castle of dust with its citywide commerce athwart, with inns and taverns interred in a gray shawl.

Ruefully, I accepted a meager offer of lodging from the loathsome American legation, on condition—theirs not mine—that I subject my mercenary self to a lengthy interrogation as the sole witness, save for several wretched Franciscan nuns, to the atrocities en route from the coast. Sessions lasting hours on end were conducted by a military attaché, a Colonel Winthrop of Wingdale, New York (pop. 79), with a twitching inclination of his left cheek. Such tic occurred with each death and bruising encounter I enumerated. A pro‑tracted rendition of our final flight from the hot breaths of Boxing rebels over a narrow rope‑bridge, across a ribald river, along a hill‑hugging path spiraling over several mountain waists, led our gallant interrogator into a ticcing spasm, which had to be duly doused by a shot of fierce whiskey before more was to be extracted from me.

The sandstorm raged on.

Knowing the worn credence that a welcomed guest is a useful one, I made a practice of ending our sessions with cleverly inventive cliffhangers and plot twists to ensure an‑other night of deserved stay under the legation's roof. My ever‑expanding narratives were so convincing to my host that later sessions were eagerly attended like readings of some ex‑alted writer. My audience grew to be the full ambassadorial staff, including spouses and ladies of such establishment who would one moment sob at my sordid saga, at another burst into uproarious laughter on account of a minor triumph or sly dodge of ever‑tailing enemies in a journey fitting better the duration of three months rather than the paltry three days I actuated on the road. But who was counting? An enthralled audience is a willing conspirator.

I am not singularly to blame for any factual embroidery or fictitious needlework. I merely acted on their unspoken plea to prolong the notion of my heroic roguery and their false security ensconced behind the wall of marbled prem‑ises in such time of despair, which in turn beget gallantry such as mine. Consequentially, as days wore on, my service earned me an ad hoc seat aboard the legation's six-man strategic council aiming to advise the Congressional Commission on the Chaos in China.

My reportage was begrudgingly transcribed by a secretarial officer into lengthy homebound dispatches, which made up the bulk of timely intelligence for the Washingtonian despots to decipher. My officialdom was short-lived and fairly doomed when, in the aftermath of having my account telegraphed, certain inconsistencies—dates and localities, bandits and rebels—began to emerge. The traitor was my transcriber, whom I had fatefully bumped off the inconsequential council with my own appointment—a little Indochina intrigue of sort. But it suffered me not the least.

The same colonel pleaded with me to serve as the ears and eyes in the Big Within, the Forbidden City, which I readily rejected with disdain, mumbling something to the effect that it offended the chastity of my lofty position as the anointed royal tutor to the boy emperor. The colonel then let it be known that his door was always open. I felt not the least obliged to expound on the gist and bounds of my hidden aim; a tethered man could barely glimpse a heavenbound kite, let alone the stringless one that I am.

As soon as the dust storm settled and the metropolis emerged from its veil, I hastened across Tartar City, where the Manchurian elites lived, to the office of Neiwufu, the Imperial Household Department, to present my notice of arrival, knowing well that an auspicious date had to be piously prayed for and cautiously selected by the Court astrologers before the young emperor could begin such alien education with the first ocean man in their hundreds of years of Qing Empire tradition. A prompt edict was issued to the legation informing me of such, hinting at an infinite delay, thus allowing me to start reconstructing the four corners of my Annabelle's pillared universe. A lengthy peruse within the legation's vaulted Archival Chamber, aided by a librarian named Martha, under the labeling of "Inland Christian Missions," unveiled the pebbled road map of Annabelle's former petaline whereabouts: Hua Cun, Flower Village, the seat of her father's fallen mission in the easterly outskirt of Peking.

Urgently I set out on a mule to see her former home, traveling among the country roads thronged with filial tomb-sweeping crowds. The mountainous terrain jutted and strutted, and yet I was as clear-eyed as an owl on a moonlit night, vying for the first glimpse of a fabled and dappled horizon.

Jealousy of another kind suddenly saddened me. I began to mourn not Annabelle's passing but her life without me. It was emptiness I felt. How I yearned to retrace every single step back in time into her enchanted childhood with her leaning on my arms, *oohing* and *ahhing* over every tree she had climbed, every river she had waded across, every breath she partook, every bird that had shadowed over her in her long summer days and cold winter nights.

Village lads in my wake, I entered the courtyard of her childhood home—Hawthorn House, presently guarded by a blind village man and his seeing son, the former sunning himself, the latter kicking an empty tin cup afoot.

If only the dimpled courtyard bricks could talk, dimpled by a certain pigtailed former dweller's rope-skipping footfall.

If only the sunken well, dried now, could unleash her muffled echoes, return all her rippled shadows. But such a plea was in vain. It was but empty walls circumventing an empty court, yard, fronting empty rooms, three in number, a faded Jesus portrait still hanging askew in one. The only life attesting to its prior vibrancy was the titular hawthorn tree singularly thriving in this drab watercolor of decay and abandonment, though it having lived would affirm an episodic fable once told me on a long ago summer night by my Λ.

The Hawthorns delighted in sipping their spring tea under this very tree, betting on whose cup the blossom petals would fall into, the chosen one beholden to brew the next pot. Thrice, Annabelle had said, the petals had blessed her cup.

I fished out a petite silk bag and dusted its premeditated contents—ashes from that fated fire—onto the courtyard ground. This ghost-calling ritual of the Orient—though savagely lacerated by the likes of Dr. Price in the West and his imbecile followers, whose usual tools of crafts ranged from clumsy Geiger counters to oscilloscopes—imminently blurred my vision. Hardly had the last of the gray ashes set, tled than the ensuing phantasmal vista emerged.

The holes and gaps in the drab, decrepit Hawthorn House were suddenly filled and brushed to life by a rush of greenery of a lively pasture. Sounds and motion of this bygone life came to be.

As if called on by a hidden stage master, upstage walks in a handsome, straight-backed Father H calling dearingly to Mother H, who looks out of her kitchen window with the most adoring expression. Then from the third room, with its gate facing south, strides in my Annabelle, her tiny former self, white skirt hemmed with green, matching white socks over her trim ankles. She looks nine, if that, skipping her frayed rope toward the courtyard, pigtails swinging to and fro over her shoulders. One glimpse of her and all was gone. Life, as an ebbing tide, was sucked out of the courtyard quad‑ rangle. The sun waned, leaving only the reality of a tree fas‑ tened to my mute mule.

"Annie! Annie! You are back," cried the blind man, his trembling hands touching my nose and my ears. "Finally, you are here."

I pushed away his fingers, but the crooked digits kept coming back.

"Annie . . . Annie! Where did she go? She was here only seconds ago," the blind man persisted.

"Did you say Annie? Reverend Hawthorn's daughter?"

"Of course. Who else would I be referring to? Her hearty laughter . . . who could forget?"

"Did you just see her?"

"I saw light shining on this cursed courtyard. Tell me, foreigner, are you a seer? Why is Annie a ghost now? Is she dead?" The old man seemed greatly agitated.

"Yes, burned to death."

"Dead just like her infant daughter."

"Her daughter?"

"If you don't know of her daughter, then you know the Hawthorns not at all." He spat on the ground.

It was one thing to have a blind one tell you that he saw what you saw, but it was another when he, standing outside your picket fence, could see more than you could from within. In haste I dropped on my knees, begging him to tell me more.

"Are you kneeling?" he asked, his hands brushing over my face and shoulders. "On your feet at once, foreigner."

"I am merely paying respect to you."

"If the village Boxer chief smells a whiff of what we saw here, he will behead you," he warned, dragging me to sit with him on the stone veranda after urging his son to shut the courtyard door, chasing away all the peeping lads that came in my wake.

"You must wonder how I saw what I saw, blind as I am," said the old man.

I made a murmuring assent.

"I am the gifted one. I see things that ought not to be seen but have to be dealt with nonetheless. After each death of unnatural course, such as hanging, drowning, killing, the ghosts must be chased from the village to the wilderness, to the mountains, or into the water where they belong, depend- ing on the cause of such deaths and the birth sign of the deceased. Some tell the truth as I do, while others tell the people what they desire to hear, making a mockery of our trade. I am pleased to meet one of my kind, albeit an ocean man. But gift I saw and gift you possess."

"This is a gift?" I shook my head. "It is more like a curse."

"I was given the gift as one is given a soul upon birth. Al- ways able to see with my inner eyes the ghostly and the dark. If the world hadn't told me that I had been born without eye- balls, I would not have known what blindness was all about: I am as sighted as the next man. Now do share with this petty blind one how you came to the power."

Like a shy pupil in the tutelage of divinity, I recounted the death of Annabelle. The old man sagged with sadness, claiming a fondness for her girlish voice and kindness. Then I talked of my ensuing waves of headaches and swells of dark moods, which led mysteriously to this affliction, and failed attempts to rid myself of her ghost.

"Pray do no such a thing; it would only taint your power, and in some incidences, endanger that shrine that is your person."

"How do you mean?"

"Can't you see? It's not her death or your grief that has led to this power; they merely aided you in bringing to the surface what is innate and inherent in you. Such power is the gift from the divine so that you can shed light on what is dark and murky to the eyes of the ordinary, the souls of the unenlightened populace. It's your second soul, pressed upon you from the very first breath you partook, a double seeing from the womb of your mother and seed of your father."

The blind man was a poet. Perturbed, nonetheless, I deigned to ask, "But why can't I see more, such as other ghosts, other etheric aura, other phantoms in limbo?"

"Because your hostess, the first ghost that you have ever seen, holds you in her captivity. You see, a ghost or its spirit is viable only through you, the earthly host, to effectuate its needs and its urges, and carry out its task left undone on earth. Conversely, you need Annabelle, the initiator who pierced the darkness, to widen the narrow breadth of your window into the other side. My hostess held me in her bond-age for the first ten years of my life. It was my very own grandmother's ghost who did such, only that my young eyes would be shielded from the gory and unsavory. Maybe Anna-belle intended the same for you, or maybe she was being her ghostly self, binding you solely to her service so you would let yourself be ridden hither and thither on errands for her and no others."

Such commentary jabbed like a needle into my heart. My Annabelle enslaving me? When love was premised upon with lust as its able architect, I delighted in following my sweet‚ heart's every whim; to be told that I had the seer's eyes all along and that she was merely a ghostly nymph who had con‚ fiscated all that was endowed upon me was another matter.

What is one, Pickens or not, to do with such burden, such weighty premise? How did this threshold‚sitting vaga‚ bond know anything about a white man who might be crazy enough to be labeled psychotic? Did he know that to make such an overall declaration about a soul, fragile as I, was tan‚ tamount to dousing more oil on the flaming fire of madness?

I was about to inquire into the validity of his claim when I heard him intone, "It is faith with which you came. It is con‚ viction in the cause not of your choosing that you must de‚ part our village with. But before you so do, please explain to me why there is no ghost of the infant buried in the backyard where all have claimed that the infant daughter of Annabelle was laid to rest."

"Annabelle had a daughter?" My head turned suddenly into a hive of buzzing bees as I palely asked the question.

The narration trickled out from the bearded mouth. "Annabelle had just turned thirteen when she went on a short excursion with other church girls to the neighboring town‚ ship of Lord Wang Dan to give away Bibles and sacks of rice. Other girls returned at sunset but not Annabelle. Sunrise the next day, she returned. She brought with her sacks of silk. There was no trace of any wounds, no claim of torture as had been rumored, or any ransom sought. She claimed to have studied the sacred book with the warlord that night, and that was all. But little did the Reverend Hawthorn know, in his chambers, that that warlord had made a woman out of her that very night. Such ill-gotten pregnancy soon evidenced itself, much to the shame of the good reverend, triggering the bloodiest battles that this region has ever seen. Annie was later said to have borne a stillborn; the stiff bundle was buried in the backyard."

In the aftermath of such a tale, fablelike but gruesome, I stumbled around, following the blind man, who followed his seeing son into the weed-grown garden. A cloud of sadness seemed to choke not just my heart but also my vision.

In a narrow shaft of sunlight I perceived the small tomb-stone that bore the words *"Nina Hawthorn, Loved in eternity by her Lord and family."*

I did not remember when I finally found my way back to Peking, though I did recall a certain tael of silver changing hands from my purse to the seeing blind, upon the urging of the blind one's son, who prodded me to pay for the story his father told. As an afterthought, I'd given them another tael in the hope that they would continue to guard the house for my loved one, and as a throw-in the old blind seer slipped into my pocket a folded page with some writing on it, with a whisper to the effect that if one is inclined to go full circle as a ghost hunter, such printed words were to be heeded.

II

In patience I waited for the royal summons to arrive. Cicadas sang from morning till night. The mosquitoes from the stale moat buzzed fatly. *Wutong* trees along the narrow alleys turned immodest green, swinging like the pigtails of rickshaw boys. Occasional thunderstorms slanted their lacerating rain at my windowpane. The humidity from the meridian sun suffocated Peking into a prison of lethargy and inactivity, grinding the city and the Neiwufu, the Imperial Household Department, into a dozing stop.

Boredom, insipid poker games with other legatine staff, drove me to finally open the letter thrust into my departing hand by the blind seer. Under a weak lamp was laid bare before my eyes the densely scribbled passage, unpunctuated and rendered in archaic Chinese:

> *Each ghost serves as a bridge leading one gifted along the passage of knowledge toward his final endowment. Seek him so you will be led to the next door. That would in the same manner cause one to arrive at the next in this maze of puzzlement. Seek him as if he were a friend; know him as if a foe. A seer's vision is limited by an earthly* bagua *compass, cosmic* feng

yun—*divine arrangement of wind and cloud. A full enlightenment will be bestowed on the gifted only when he surrenders all his earthly urges and submits himself to an irreversible* chu jia, *becoming a monk, falling into the bosom of nature, a calling of high mercy.*

Such spare words. Such clarity.

To gain entrance into the vastness of my power, Annabelle was merely my first door.

Who is it that shall be my next, and the one after, so that I would be guided to the splendor of my widened vista? Could that bestial warlord, Annabelle's initiator, be my next? Was he the ghost impersonating the faceless monarch in our former threesome encounter?

Seek him as if he were a friend; know him as if a foe.

Coincidentally, or maybe not so coincidentally, a certain moodiness evidenced itself on my gaunt face, causing the kind-hearted Mrs. Winthrop to introduce me to a poker mate, Martha Plume, a spinsterly librarian with long stilted legs and a pair of big-knuckled hands that could choke the life out of a book or deck of cards. I thanked Mrs. W for her kindness and let it be known that the pending hermetic Court life would inconvenience even the tritest of an attachment. Such rejection, unbeknownst to me, was taken as a token of my shy nature and modesty, bespeaking of well-bred propriety, making me, who now was on the verge of moving out, even more desirable to a persistent admirer. As I sat waiting for the summons to be issued by my employer, a lengthy storm further rendered any departure moot.

Finally a midnight knock on my door left me, the shiver-ing Pickens—she arrived scantily wrapped—no choice but to imbibe in what little warmth a cold night had to offer. A handful of ensuing trysts with Midnight Martha left me gasping for life, while she, her spinsterly self boasting a pri-mal glow, kept diving more deeply for more, as a seasoned pearl-diver would with long and hearty breath. Spinster she might be, but naïve she was never meant to be. The tables quickly turned in our ritual of coition: a certain manliness leaped out of her, anointing her the domineering one of us two. Her assertiveness with certain positional demands and familiarity with all her vital organs and mine alike, shocked me, as did the boldest and the most sodomistic acts she sug-gested, which sadly only emboldened my dominatrix to re-sort to even raunchier devices, of which I shall deign myself from inking.

The affair, as you might expect, didn't outlast the storm. In one outburst of youthful whim following a rigorous co-ition, the Iowa-bred book-duster dragged me into the wet courtyard, wishing to relive a wintry girlhood something.

In her first attempt at rope-skipping, warning prof-fered, her left foot slipped while the right one was caught sideways by the loop, causing her to fall backward, breaking three lower vertebrae, necessitating her to be sedated for the foreseeable future in the renowned Rockefeller-built Union Hospital.

A brief visitation to Martha's hospital ward, and a bundle of Peking peonies as long-stemmed as she, was the last I saw of her. Later reportage from the legatine confirmed her slow recovery and eventual marriage to a jealous and, might I add, vindictive Harvard man, thusly freeing her, at least temporarily, from the urge to prey on future guests of the meager accommodations that offered little accommodating comfort except her own cold frame.

12

For all that I had nightly contributed to her unsplintering, Martha fulfilled my petty wish, lending me the key to a file merely labeled as "Rape of H's Daughter." (Oh the fire of anger was aflame already!)

The legal memorandum to the office of the ambassador drafted by Bernard Buchanan, Esq. (Columbia, LLB), to find legal ground to initiate the act of war, outlined the barebones known facts: innocent A abducted and raped by a thugly village lord named Wang Dan, who was a scion of a tea trade fortune who forfeited the chosen path of his forefathers to take up the sword and form a hedonist sect with its members numbering in the tens of thousands and who had anointed himself the son of God.

Our buccaneering Bernie went on to paint with valiant strokes the sparring feuds, predating A's rape, between Reverend H and the self-made messiah over provisions, parishioners, and properties.

H (Phillips Andover, Yale) was no cowardly man of the cloth. Impinging on the principles he held steadfast, guns were secretively requisitioned from a British supplier, Dunhill, Moore & Bro. of London, via the stinking port named Fragrant Island. His flocks of Rice Christians were immobilized, and skirmishes were had with Wang Dan's hooded swordsmen and robed arsonists, making the regions southeast to Peking into a present-day crusaders' Holy Land. Bloodshed, not quite, but battles galore. A series of diplomatic and governmental interference—Americans asking the Manchurian Court to calm its subjects down, which was duly regarded as an insulting and inciting gesture—only heightened the stakes and worsened the hostility. H's unbending commitment to his daughter's honor made him a hero, making the Hua Cun Congregational Church of northern China a stronghold of sorts among other foreign fanatics deadly bent on saving Manchurian souls.

The lone Brit merchant of war supplies no longer sufficed. In war, all churches and chapels were brothers. An arsenal of Italian bullets, German rifles, American grenades, and Russian sabres was stacked behind the towering H.

On the opposition, Wang Dan, H's crusty counterpart, a prior anti-Confucius atheist in the eyes of his countrymen, now stood an icon of patriotism. More hooded swordsmen swore their legions, and robed arsonists aided Wang's ascension. It was war or nothing, fingers on the trigger, swords unsheathed. But on the day of the planned confrontation, upon the testy abutting ground that would soon be soaked with blood, in walked my pubescent blonde, my Annabelle, a Bible in one hand, a basket of freshly picked wild flowers in the other, singing hymnal songs in Mandarin. She wore white that day, a token beseeching peace and a symbol of hymenal purity. The shouts of men at war poured forth from opposite camps, H's command being most audible, but undaunted was my angel of faith and dove of goodwill. Buchanan's narration understandably faltered under the weighty import of such a moment forthwith, but the scribe rose up to the occasion as a good sergeant would do, albeit on paper, and penned with gut-wrenching acute vividness the following thematic passage, which I must quote verbatim in order not to undo the gallantry of the scene to follow:

Imminently guns were lowered on H's camp; swords and daggers were sheathed on the other. In the golden wheat field the battle cries suddenly quieted into a silence of disbelief. When Miss A reached the vast middle ground field, the Christians, at least some of them, broke their line, dashing after her, guns in hand, aiming to recall her into their ranks. A handful of Wang's camp also raced toward A, swords and spears in hands.

A paused in her advance and stood still as she beckoned them with waving hands, inviting them to join her in singing hymns. Those who witnessed this recounted seeing her twirl, sway, and jump with her thin arms swinging, as if performing her favorite rice dance, a Manchurian ritualistic art to celebrate the seasonal bounties.

As the combatants narrowed around her—men of thuggery righteous in their own minds, arms ready, eyeing each other with ancient hatred and disgust for one another—A threw herself suddenly prostrate on the ground, her hands clasping her precious Bible after casting away the basket of flowers, shouting or rather singing out her prayers to God.

The soldiers of souls reached over, pulling on her four limbs, to clear the path of war. One eyewitness recounted that Miss A brandished her family Bible, a treasure given upon her birth that she placed by her pillow by night and carried in the silk jacket handmade by Mrs. H by day. The corner of God's book caught on a corner of a soldier's eye, causing him to let loose a scream of pain in that vital moment of vulnerability. In the next fleeting moment, Miss A snatched the handle of his sword out of his gripping hand. The sword in one hand, Bible in the other, posed no threat to anyone. They shouted her to depart this focus of contention. The walls of men came closer to one another. Among the encroaching men was Reverend H running among his followers with a bayoneted rifle. From the opposite end came Wang Dan astride a Gobi stallion, his right hand pointing a sword, in the other hand holding a red-jacketed holy scripture of his own invention, with thousands of his footmen guarding his flanks.

The meeting of hostility was imminent. The sound of galloping hooves shook the ground and the fury of men raced the wind.

Miss A appeared, holding her gleaming sword blade to her thin throat, shouting the words, "Leave this battleground now or I shall kill myself with this sword!"

A Christian scout tried to approach her, which only caused her to throw her Bible in the air and slice it into pieces with her sword in warning. She ran barefoot down the line to separate the men ready to kill, from south to north. Then again she ran, widening that belt of peace until the soldiers were safely apart. A few stubborn Christians, our witnesses included, who were slow to retreat, nearly had their toes cut off by her sword.

Now in view of thousands, she turned, sword still to

her throat, and bowed to her father, then turned to face that stallion in the distance, rearing on its hind legs, and walked past Wang Dan's parting men, looking to the one commanding them. She began to run, heading toward the archnemesis of her own father, of her own God.

Mr. Wang climbed down to help her onto his saddle, holding her from behind. The horse galloped away, trailed by his men, leaving behind an empty field and an army of disheartened and much-puzzled Christians.

At this conjuncture, Reverend H, instead of calling his army to arms, collapsed. Weak and delirious he begged to be taken back to his home. All his will and fortitude seemed thwarted, thus ending that day bloodless.

The fate of our Joan of Arc, a true heroine, in the aftermath of her captivity, was kept unknown, except for rare glimpses by the paid spies who occupied the inner sanctum of Mr. Wang's township. Such scouting was, at best, sketchy, speculative, and second- or third-handed, gleamed from the maids and manservants toiling within Mr. Wang's ancestral estate.

One account revealed the sight of red lanterns being hung on the very night of said failed battle, hinting at festivity of uncommon significance. Only weddings and Lunar New Year deserved this lengthy protocol. The rest of the year those silken-clothed, bamboo-ribbed symbols of liveliness and tools to drive away the presumed evils were carefully wrapped with long sheets of fabric and retired to storage until occasion would call on their use again.

Could it be that Mr. Wang, who had been known far and near as a married man many times over, had *taken another bride, this time of white skin, the daughter of his enemy?*

The other account, this one from a nephew of a butcher within the estate, claimed that ever since the Ocean Bride's arrival, the lord's meals had secretively taken on an aphrodisiac flavor prescribed by a famed doctor from the inner city of Peking to shore up his dwindled libido. Additional food items included daily supplies of oysters to be sucked raw with a dash of vinegar and soy sauce, four sets of mountain goat testicles simmered with ginseng roots, and blood-curd spilled from virgin pheasants weighing no more than nine lian (less than a pound).

Another more serene and soothing account originated from Colonel Winthrop's own cobbler, who had a widowed aunt serving as an amah, *a tea lady, to Wang Dan's third wife. Our* amah, *on several occasions, reported seeing the foot masseuse rubbing oil onto the Ocean Bride's bare feet and thighs to warm her up for the coming night with Mr. Wang.*

The above observation suffices to negate the unfounded claim that Citizen A was the object of torture and that her abduction was impinged upon her rather than a volunteer act.

All the above witness accounts unfortunately could aid us no further in our evidentiary exploration into the matter at heart.

Buchanan's memorandum ended abruptly. The entire legation was reluctant to engage me in this subject matter or tell me what had become of Buchanan. I shunned the ambassadorial staff who had long deemed me an insufferable creature lurching about their domain, overstaying my welcome, and instead I tried to befriend the kitchen staff. They were a sweaty bunch: a sous chef of Swiss descent, who after downing several shots of U.S. government issue whiskey, confessed in his Franco-English to having heard of Buchanan's sudden discharge from legatine duty, and later his hush-hush tragic end aboard the Canton Express to Wu Hang, a central city of rebels and warlords, with assassins still at large and unpursued. I aimed to cajole the chef for further disclosure, but the single malt had kicked in and all he could do was cry and talk of his childhood spent in a Lausanne orphanage.

The fate of my Annabelle eluded me at each step. But fate shall alter—it always does, mine and hers. Alive or ghostly, the myth and the mythology were to unveil themselves within that forbidden life awaiting me. All these entanglements are but precursors of what is to befall me.

13

That day of my entrance into the royal palace, I was met by the High Prince Yun, the birth father of the emperor, at the Gate of Valor. Prince Yun was a man of average height, with a pair of bushy, slanting eyebrows hanging over long slender eyes. After pleasantries were duly exchanged, Prince Yun read me a lengthy royal decree of things that were to come my way. Among the listings, I was to receive the fourth highest rank of officialdom among the Court personage, allowing me the privilege to ride on a four-manned sedan and be gifted with an apartment within the palace grounds. The offerings were long and tediously delivered, detailing such trivialities as the meals and petty household upkeep privileges.

Though the outside world was only a wall away, the isolation seemed complete upon the closing of the tall iron door. A sense of suffocation and longing overwhelmed me. This must be what a convict would feel facing the mighty facade of his destiny.

Eunuchs draped over my shoulders an embroidered silk robe in the color of blue, with elaborate piping and patterns of dragons and phoenixes, and they put upon my head a hat with a peacock-feather plume: symbols of my rank. Henceforth I ascended into a four-man sedan. The foursome members of the palace eunuch corps—maroon gowned, thinned-voiced men—carried me through the Gate of Valor, a northern back entry reserved for familial affairs, its casualness hinting at a heightened degree of privacy.

We passed Mai Shan Mountain, a slanting manmade hill piled from the soil dug from nearby Bei Hai Pond back-ending the palace outside its wall whereupon a Sinned Tree still stands, accused and convicted of providing a conniving branch, enabling another boy emperor, not this one, to hang himself in despair. The historian in me cherishes this nugget of factual reminiscence. A full Court trial was held to con-duct a three-day proceeding wherein the tree was the defend-ing culprit, with a charade of sobbing witnesses. The Court trial was necessitated by the need to find a killer because suicide would be impious to heavenly intent and purpose, making human and fallible what is loftily of gods and ages. The tree was uprooted to stand trial, possibly the first of its kind, only to be replanted back as irrefutable proof of a noxious growth, a sinner to be viewed by all and to suffer the insufferable, of having done in the one who could not be so undone. The tree, old it might be, blossoms annually with gusto, attesting not to its innocence but to a certain absurdity inherent in this monarchy or the next. Who, least this author, is equipped to critique an establishment that had outlasted many other empires?

Where am I, in the procession of my entrance? Oh yes, we passed beyond a canopy of old pines, expectedly gnawed and knuckled, skirted ponds and lakes, turtles and goldfish. I was passing the back palace—you see the historian in me never quits working—the notorious dump for those of the hundreds of neglected palace women. All legal wives of the young emperor, they were chosen yearly, selected for their talent in needle, medicine, nursing, singing, dancing, or culinary skills: essential workers living at the Royal Court. A lucky one might one day catch the eye of the emperor and engage with him in a ritual known as *de fu*, getting lucky. That seed she carries and the child she bears, if she survives the envious saboteurs who hope for her death or disappear-ance, will bring fortune or misfortune.

My apartment was a gift from the emperor himself, a two-storied elegance deftly called House of Deference and Tranquility, renamed and redecorated for my use, much to the protest of the old liners, whose paws would, as you will come to know, impinge upon every fabric and inch of this city within a city: the nation within an empire.

A thin boy was kneeling at the apartment door awaiting my arrival in the dappled light of a noon sun, maroon gowned as all eunuchs were attired. All palace women naturally were to be watched over by the men in the house, the unique eunuch corps, thousands in number. Men they might be but manly they are not. This shy boy was my endowed vassal, an ink boy in name, though his chores varied. He was, foremost, to be my little lantern, shining the way in my initiation into the dead-end lanes of my palace existence. Without him I would go nowhere and accomplish less.

"What's your name?" I asked after the sedan carriers departed.

The boy hesitated and said quietly, eyes downcast, "I was

bestowed the palace name of In/In, though I was known since my birth as Cow Penis in my home village, a fortnight's jour/ ney from here."

"Cow Penis?" I smiled at his endearing pronouncement, tinted vastly with a Shandong accent, one of many varieties made known to me thanks to my teacher, Dr. Jeffrey Archer.

"Father saw our neighbor's cow's penis while it was taking its piss when Mother bore me in our pigsty, in the midst of her chore of feeding a litter of thirteen piglets."

"You could have been named Piglet then."

"But it was what Father saw that counted. So Cow Penis I was called till the day I *yian ge*—cut off my penis. Uncle Ting of Lung's original clan would not wish to let anyone know of this name: it would render my service here improper and disrespect the Heavenly One."

"Why did you tell me then?"

"You are to be my protector to whom I shall enslave my/ self. No secrets are to be hidden from you because a secret would be a genuine act of disrespect. Please tell no one of this secret, and many secrets I shall hide for you."

"Shall you?"

"That is the only way one stays safe, out of misfortune . . ." He stole a glance at me, trailing off. "I have already overspo/ ken, haven't I? From now on, I shall be mute with what I say, deaf to what I hear, and blind to what I see. I am your wind and its shadow. I am here, but I am not here. I will carry out any chores you please. I will keep clean every inch of this apartment and replenish it with fresh goods acquisitioned and gifted to you from the Heavenly One. In the morn, I shall be up before you making the early tea and fetching breakfast for you. Lunch you shall have in your office together with other royal tutors, and supper is to be served from the servant's kitchen with a special menu you shall select at daybreak so goods of your choosing can be secured and the bill be written for the Neiwufu's review and approval."

"Their approval?"

"It's merely perfunctory. There will be no full board reviews, save for the seasonal one conducted by the Fu's royal trustees and assignees. Have I spoken too much already, master?"

"You have not. I have much to learn from you. Will you be my guide?"

"I have many rules to adhere to, as stipulated by the chief eunuch. If my service to you fails in any manner, punishment awaits me."

"What rules do you speak of?"

"Many that I have had to commit to my memory since the day of my arrival, speaking of which, I should not be having this conversation with you, as you are new, lofty, and . . ."

"And what?"

He stole another glance at me and whispered, ". . . alien and vastly strange and different from us."

The boy's utter candor caught me off guard, contradicting the rumor of the perversion and corruption of the entire eunuch corps surrounding the titular emperor. I gifted him with a Döbereiner's lamp, a lighter, so to speak, that I bought off a legation staff member. When flame ignited the contraption, In-In's face lit up. He kneeled again and rose only after I had departed the hallway and entered the room I was to dwell in for the foreseeable duration, leaving the scant luggage I brought to be dealt with by my new boy servant. That night, after a meal of rice with four dishes and a soup were served to me—each officialdom is ranked by the count of dishes served per meal; four dishes with a soup put me, much to the anguish of Neiwufu personage, among the ranks of royal tutor—I retired for the first time to my sleeping chamber, the location of future sins and later shame.

That night, I dreamed of her, my dear darling Annabelle; it was the longest duration we have been apart. She came in a blur of angst, not in any physical solidness. In the background, there were sounds of waves. Amidst the hushing whisper of the sea, I heard her say, "Find her," and repeating such till both her presence and her voice were no more.

14

In the graying twilight, In·In led the way along the walled lanes, our footfalls echoing down the courtyards, a lantern dangling from his hand casting our diminished shadows against the walls. I had endured an unbearable audience with the Queen Mother, a painted and bejeweled dowager in her full glory, who had acquired her title by way of an infamous arm·twisting adoption, wrangling the emperor at the age of two from the bosom of his own mother. After a thorough inspection, she dismissed me curtly with a wave of her silky handkerchief. A fan would have been more fitting, but she was being fanned by two young maids, sweeping away the morning flies buzzing over her painted veil.

I next met four fellow tutors, old scholars who, though toasting me with hot tea, greeted me coldly. Such guarded·ness was to be expected, adhering firstly to the belief that relations among educators are to be thin and pale like water; true affection would dent the thin walls of one's intellectual sovereignty and demean the honor of a genuine scholar. A true intellectual should be scholarly about his own pursuit of knowledge, unbiased by his personal likes, thusly raising the bar of general scholarship. I also expected that the tu·tors would all bear a collective grudge against this slooped ocean man. They had all, without exception, ascended this far not by chance but by academic achievement, earning the highest marks in the civil service examinations held every six years, based on which the palace selected their officials. Such achievement was then assiduously followed by decades of devoted service. Only then could one be considered for the lauded position of a royal tutor that would endow sumptuous estates and unparalleled prestige to be enjoyed by not just himself but all his offspring.

I offered each three deep bows of respect, which they returned. In the gloom, the morning hours trotted on. All the other tutors came and went like shadows in a puppet show in muted sequences, their gowns swishing, hats lifted passing one another, and chairs squeaking. Then my turn came, with a eunuch leading me to the royal study quarters. It was deep in a mansion quieted by tall walls, eunuchs pass-ing and going, feet light, hovering, busying themselves, birds perching on willows seen through fan-shaped wall windows, blades of grass secretly poking up in cracks and seams be-tween bricks and smoothed stones.

The emperor himself was on the porch, a fine-boned, thin-framed creature dressed in a white western suit and necktie, head tipped with a round-brimmed crown, and wearing a pair of black leather shoes.

"I wear this in your honor," the teenager proclaimed in hesitant English, reaching over his right hand, ready to shake mine, when I heard the servant order me to kneel. *"Xia bai huang shang,"* he said harshly. But the young emperor was quick, grabbing my hand with his, shaking it health-fully. I was ready to attempt a kowtow, as required, when he pulled me up.

"Mian gui," he said, granting me pardon. In the same instant, he ordered curtly for the eunuch to leave. *"Qu le, qu le."*

The eunuch bowed, not daring to look up at his master,
though his reply was firm, claiming a higher order from the
Queen Mother, whom he called Grandpa, to watch over
the teaching ceremony.

"Qu le!" The emperor's voice rose with severity.

Off the servant went, mumbling, casting me a low men-
acing glance. *"Yang ren bu shou ting fa."* Translation: "That
ocean man didn't kowtow to the emperor."

Heads would have normally rolled for such a slight, but
not on this day.

As soon as he was gone, the emperor hunched his back,
stiffened by his starched collar and snug suit, and bowed to
me; his hands still held mine in a tight grip. The gentle manners had no doubt rubbed off from the obsequious eunuchs
who had surrounded him since an early age, playing guards
and angels, friends and teachers. Gratefully, I returned the
favor, bowing back.

"Come see my house," he said, resorting to his English
again, urging me indoors.

I nodded.

"But you have to be a blind first."

"A blind?"

"Close your eyes, if you will," he amended excitedly, and I
realized he had meant to say "blindfolded."

I did, entering, his hand guiding mine, his gold rings cold
to my skin.

"Now open them," he urged.

When my eyes opened, it was not the somber schoolhouse

my mind's eyes had foreseen—one desk, two dull chairs, his facing north, mine east—but the sight of his crowded collection of foreign artifacts: longhanded clocks, stubby snuffboxes, and bicycles, all in multiple numbers and disorderly display.

"They have all been gifted me by foreign kings and queens, princes, and female princes."

"You mean to say 'princess.'"

"Pince . . . ass?"

"Prin . . . ce . . . sses"

"You can't begin my lessons without my permission," the young man said with a giggle.

"But learning is everywhere and anytime."

"Let me write that down." He quickly whipped out a notebook and pen from his inner pocket. "Now who is it who says that?"

"I did."

"You did." He nodded, scribbling on his page, wrinkling his nose in all seriousness.

How could I stop such a zealous youth!

"There are many more, but they will illfit my chamber. Someday I shall show you the collection in its entirety. That clock is from the English queen . . . have you met her before?"

I shook my head.

"This vase is from the Emperor of the Sun—that would be Japan. The bicycle is a genuine Raleigh." Upon which conjuncture he discarded me and leaped onto its saddle and pressed its bell, causing three rapid *dings* to echo the space. Then off he leaped. Led by the emperor through an open rear door, I suddenly saw a wavy mirage rising in the summer heat. In a green-lawned backyard, a dazzle of a nymphet blonde, thirteen and no older, was straddling over a beastly motorcycle, sun in her face, goggles in her hair, thin thighs apart, one long and booted leg resting on the gas pedal, the other on the ground.

My heart instantly caved in.

She gazed at me, long lashes blinking, head tilting to one side as Annabelle had been prone to do all those years ago. Her eyes instantly enlivened my abysmal darkness.

A muted, gagging frog leaped out of my parched throat. "A-A-Annabelle."

"Isn't she a beauty?" the emperor asked.

"Beauty indeed," I replied foggily.

"It's no Annabelle, sir, but an original Hildebrand & Wolfmuller gifted me by Emperor William of the German Empire."

My mind was awhirl.

"And the girl riding it is my empress, Qiu Rong."

"Empress Qiu Rong, of course," I said. Though dazed, I still possessed enough comity to bow.

Qiu Rong—Oh, my Annie in blood and flesh! Where and how?—didn't bow back. Instead she blew a kiss, forming her meaty lips round and then parting them wide on an airy smack that bared her whitened teeth and tip of serpentine tongue.

The motor roared and smoke puffed, not by diesel or its throaty cry but by magic of its phantasmal rider clothed in a yellow robe and yellow silk scarf. She shot into motion: a bee blurred, buzzing around the girthy yard, round and round, bumping a hedge here and denting a branch there, screaming in trilingual gibberish—Giddyup, *jen-ta-ma-ban* (a Pekingese curse), and some undeniable Germanic fricatives—while the hem of her robe fluttered and pattered afore and asunder, bare thighs showing.

Cloud-thick fumes transformed the dappled yard into a New England night in June, in May, aeons back—muggy, frothy, with faint sniff of haystacks and horse dung. Circling before me no longer was a bethroned empress but my very own virginal incarnation.

"You like it?" asked the emperor, mistaking my spell as enchantment.

I nodded dizzily, phantom perfume of opium clouding my judgment.

"You ride it then. Qiu Rong, come here." He waved her over.

"I . . ." Circle one. "Am . . ." Circle two. "Not . . ." Circle three. ". . . . Finisheeed!" she screamed as her tires scratched near my toes. "Get your own bike, you Amerrrican mannn!" She pronounced the syllables with a German accent, *man* twisted to sound like *mon*.

Casting her bike-handle outward, she suddenly threw herself between me and her consort to be caught, her budding bosom snug against my chest and tiny waist in the emperor's hands.

"You are quite naughty, you know," the emperor teased lovingly.

"I *am* a naughty child of yours, aren't I?" his empress said, blinking her long lashes, her feet still tangled in the saddle of her bike.

"Oh, big man you are. Feel his arms." She clutched my

upper arms for support, her long fingernails digging my skin, her eyes studying me with childlike indolence.

I remembered little else but Qiu Rong's laughter. I recalled even less of my initial tutelage with the emperor, yet her absence cut a garish gash in my heart.

15

In the gloaming, as I was dining alone in my apartment, the cursed eunuch reappeared, gazing at me with disdain, cunning in his cold eyes. I offered him a chair and a cup of tea. He kicked away the former, which movement knocked aside the latter, spilling the tea on my delicate tablecloth as he sat with arms folded, one hip on my dining table and one foot on the fallen chair.

He minced no words. With a heavy Shandong accent tainted with garlic breath, he demanded an immediate financial remuneration to keep his silence about my earlier dereliction: failure to bow. I was rather amused. Agreeing to play along with this clown, I lay my bulging money pouch on the table like a gambler, causing his eyes to gleam with greed and foot to stop rattling the uneven chair.

"What else have I done wrong? Tell me and all shall be yours," I said, caressing the bulge of coins.

His hip nearly slipped off at my pronouncement. Standing, he paced the room, tapping his knuckle on the polished windowpane as if inspecting its firmness, rubbing the tablecloth between his filthy fingers as he fondled the silkiness. He reasoned that I would be well served to appease the entire eunuch corps, the palace's cogs and screws. What offended him the most in our earlier encounter, he recounted with the

rather generous openness of a paid counselor, was my inclination to turn the young and temperamental sovereign against
him, thusly against the entire eunuch corps. He paused for
effect, recalling having been rashly sent away, costing him a
day's pay and three whip lashes by the chief eunuch.

He leaned over my plates—sautéed celery; shredded
chickens; three-layered pork of skin, fat, and meat; river escargots deftly shelled and pungently spiced—and picked up
a shred of poultry with those same two grubby fingers, feeding it to his big-toothed orifice, chewing it noisily and unevenly, his lower jaw moving horizontally like a mule. Wiping
his fingers on the chest of his robe, he preached on.

Any corporeal punishment or monetary reprimand that
resulted on his behalf meant that offense was taken by all
eunuchs against such outside agitator. They, he added, as a
whole, had a long memory, which in due course could serve
to do or undo anyone within any rank in the palace. Pleased
with his logic, he pinched three snails in a four-fingered pillage and dropped them down his throat, causing him to gag
with spasmodic contortions like a rooster choking on a kicking frog. All Shandong men were pepper men, but not this
one. The sideshow went on a bit with him coughing up a
storm. I was more than ready for his breathless death before
he was himself again, aided by a douse of my neglected tea.

"A palace girl was knocked up by the emperor once. It
should have been a joyful occasion, but her nipples were cut
off, and the infant gouged from her womb; she was left to die
in isolation at the back palace. The service was not rendered
by ghosts or spirits, which this palace boasts many of, but by
us eunuchs. Why?" he asked rhetorically, helping himself to

another pinch of my food. "Not that she was unkind to us, but that she was envied by a friend of ours. Vital it is not just to be good to us but more important to never be a friend of our foe or foe of our friend. Simple as that." He picked up my soup bowl and chucked several mouthfuls before licking his lips with satisfaction and wiping his mouth with his sleeve.

"So how much will it be?" I asked.

"The whole pouch as you have pledged, of course. And it would be worth all your while, for I have seen not just one item of dereliction but many."

"Enumerate them all."

"Well . . . you did not walk behind Him, you spoke without being asked, you didn't kneel or bow to Her Honor, the fourth empress of his throne, and you were intimate with Her by touching and grasping Her in your arms," he said, scolding me with his accusations like a cross governess. "I might not have seen it all, but others did from a tall tree outside the backyard, and more yet peeping through hedges and fences. Now part with your coins."

He was about to pounce on my pouch when I stole it out of his reach.

His face reddened with rage. "Why are you withholding it?"

"Allow me now to count the list of *your* derelictions ever since you entered my apartment."

"*My* derelictions?"

"Yes. You stormed into the royal tutor's residence without cause or permission, attempted to graft me for ill gain, stole from my dishes, ate with your dirty fingers, and chewed with your mouth open: all actionable samples of inhospitality and foul manners. Do you wish me to report all these to your emperor?"

"You dare do no such a thing."

"Try me." Our gazes locked.

"No, no. Please, no." He dropped to his knees, kowtowing fiendishly.

"Leave at once!"

Gratefully, he leapt to his feet. About to run off, he hesitated. "Perhaps you could spare me three tael of silver so I will be kind to your servant." At which conjuncture In-In pushed open the dining room door. The left corner of his mouth was bleeding and his eyes glimmered with tears.

"I shall only part with my coins if you can write me a receipt for such remuneration."

The dome-headed eunuch fled like a ghost.

✦ ✦ ✦

After cleansing In-In's bloody lip with a dose of vinegar and sending him off to his quarters with a handful of candies, I burned three incense sticks on the windowsill facing a gray and ceremonial moon: one to bid farewell to my dead lover, another in gratitude to a certain ethereal hosting spirit, the last to the epochal ascendance of a long-promised mirage, my reincarnated Annabelle—she in flesh and blood, reborn on the other side of a forbidden wall, exhumed from the ashen bones of Andover.

As the incense burned, permeating the night air, a fistful of butterflies suddenly flew in dashes and shafts of moonlight as if let free from an invisible fortress. They fluttered their wings, flying in pairs, dipped low, then rose high, appearing from and disappearing into a languishing bamboo grove like living spirits.

Finally I sighed, dipping my finger, ashen from a new burn, at the fallen ashes: fallen on a fresh eve from which a new life would begin.

16

Glimpses of Q from the schoolhouse's ajar door were dizzying. Riding the dinging Raleigh, a white pigeon on its front bar matching the color of her stockings and pleated skirt but not her schoolgirl shirt, which was blue in hue and cut low in full glory.

Every so often she would run her front wheel into our study chamber, ringing her bell, *ding, ding, ding,* and inquiring, "When are you going to finish? I am so bored." She dragged her syllables, punctuating each with great impatience, face sweaty.

"Soon, child. Go ride some more," the emperor would cajole her, waving his fingers.

Peeping in another time, she asked, "Why can't we ride our horses in here?" as she put one leg up on her front bar, skirt riding up, her pubescent thighs thin and lanky. Not even the copious and dubious geography text could douse my longing, causing me to lean forward as if nursing a bellyache or an intestinal rumble.

"Grandpa won't allow it, you know that. Off you go." Her husband dismissed her, anxiously returning to study the antique desk globe that I had spun off a Tartar City pawnbroker.

"Grandpa, Grandpa, Grandpa . . . that old hag. Why can't

we just call her that?" Q kicked off one shoe to bare wriggling toes, the pinkie poking through a hole in the sock squirming to its own tune.

What I wouldn't do to lick the little runty toe, stockinged or not.

"Not another word about her, darling. Can't you see I am busy?" He spun the globe slowly, frowning with puzzlement. "Our empire isn't big *at all.*"

Intrigued, Q rolled off her seat. Leaning the bike against the door, she strode into the small schoolhouse, rude feet thumping the oak floor, one shoe missing. "Hah! I told you so. You wouldn't believe me. You are but a pithy chieftain, not even a minor warlord like your cousins. Henpecked by that dying bitch and surrounded by stupid half-men!"

I noticed her inward gait, toes in and heels out, typical of sandal-wearing Japanese girls.

"But Britain is even smaller," I interjected, pointing at the sorrowful isle surrounded by a raised sea.

"Let me see!" shouted the Asian deity, crowding his head toward mine.

"Indeed, it's tiny—no bigger than our Formosa Island." The emperor pinched out a monocle, a Western affectation he had picked up. "How dare their queen send her armies to my shore!"

"It's got nothing to do with size, you dope." Q pushed my head aside and inserted hers between ours, puffing her rattling fricatives into my left ear a thousand beats a minisecond. "They've got iron ships. What have you got?"

"We could have built iron boats ourselves."

"Too late. Your auntie embezzled the navy's money to

build her own palace, which she hardly summers in." She draped one arm over my shoulder, the other over her consort. "She must die and die soon or we'll all go to hell." The *h* in her *hell* was coarsely Parisian.

"Qiu, darling! Mind your tongue before my tutor. He is a guest."

"A robbed and blackmailed guest, at best." Q slyly rubbed her right cheek along my left ear as she huskily hummed, "You won't mind telling us the truth, will you?"

"What truth?" I asked.

"Robbed and blackmailed?" The emperor put down his monocle.

"He was fleeced by your eunuch last night."

"You were?" the emperor asked in concern.

I remained mute, merely shaking my head, wishing to forget the ugly encounter.

"Say something, you big wolf," urged Q. Turning me to face her, she shook my shoulders with her twiggy hands. "Please, Pi-Jin the Pigeon. Last night, an order to swindle you was given by the chief eunuch—my maid said so, and she never lies to me. If you don't tell us, and these half-men are not duly punished, what you will see next is the cover of your coffin."

"What pelf did he demand of you this time?" asked the emperor.

"It was nothing," I demurred.

"Be truthful with me. Otherwise you are not fit to be my tutor."

"What would his punishment be for the offense?" I asked.

"Can I answer that?" Q raised one hand like a schoolgirl,

eager for attention, covering my mouth with her other hand, commanding, "You be mute, Pigeon."

Mute I was, her hot palm sticky on my quivering, helpless lips.

"Your eunuch didn't get anything from him."

"Why not?" asked the emperor.

Q pinched my nose bridge painfully. "Because Big Nose here demanded that he write a receipt for the sum of three silvers as proof of record, scaring him away."

"A receipt? How brilliant," the emperor declared.

"He should run this palace for us," said Q. "Do you have the, shall I say, testicles for it?" With a gamine grin, she sank her bottom onto her husband's lap.

"What are testicles?" The young emperor turned to me expectantly.

"These," said Q, grinding her rump deep into her husband's lap, a sly smile curling her lips, "are your testicles."

"You mean, I believe, to say *courage*," I corrected.

"In German we say 'testicles.' It means the same thing, you prude," Q said.

"Worry not, I will provide you with plenty of testicles if you will agree to accept my decree and help manage my affairs here," pronounced the young emperor. "It's so very chaotic at times that I think there is a conspiracy against me within my very own palace."

"Of course there is a conspiracy here against you, and me, and now, your new court jester is included!" Q gave her man a peck on his lips, her eyes slanting at me. "And you know why?" she asked, turning to me. "Because my husband loves me like no emperor has ever loved his woman before."

"No," I protested. "I am here only to teach."

The emperor shook his head sternly. "No one is to say no to me. I will assign you your new tasks in due course. Now it is time for punishment. In-In, go fetch Elder Li and Dong Shan, and don't forget to bring the squad."

The comedy had just turned tragic, I realized, as the boy flew out the door like a ghost.

"No, please," I begged.

"Told you he has no balls. Be calm," Q said playfully at me. "You will enjoy the spanking. It's such a spectacle." Whipping out a pack of Rothmans cigarettes, she tipped one into her mouth and lit it with a Döbereiner's lamp.

Elder Li, the toady chief eunuch, with a set of muddy eyes hidden under bushy brows, led the dome-headed Dong Shan and a squad of four, bamboo poles in hands. The squadron knelt on the courtyard stones awaiting their master's orders. Blurred words were exchanged tersely, an order given. Dome Head, knowing his fate, pulled up the tail of his gown and peeled down a flimsy wretched undergarment, baring his bony buttocks. Silently, a squad member struck him again and again with a supple pole. Red stripes instantly marred his skin, and blood soon oozed, streaking his bare thighs. After a short spell, the whipping ceased and Dome Head collapsed face down, too exhausted to gather himself.

Then another order was given, this time not by the emperor. It was Q's words, high-pitched and thrilling like the jingle of a silvery bell. "Now you, Elder Li. It's your turn."

A fleeting puzzlement clouded Li's face, a glint of sinister hate that darkened his eyes as they darted the span between the emperor and me. Then he undid his ready robe, a saggy ass peeking at the shining sun.

This time, it was not the silent squad but Dome Head who took the pole, whipping and spanking his superior. First gingerly; then, after being scolded by Q, savagely, as if in wretched retaliation, one heavy strike after another, engaging his act with the utterance of one losing a grip on things, maddened by certain rage, not against the one under his painful pole but at his own hands, which had been cursed by a devilish spirit, beating his very own master for which he was bound to receive another bout of punishment. His strikes threw Li left and right, an old frame in jeopardy. The old skin broke seam by seam and bled reluctantly without the chief eunuch crying once as he buried his head on the ground, digging his nails into cracks along the paved yard. Then it was done.

The two limping and aching eunuchs had to be carried out of the courtyard by the squad.

The palace doctor would be summoned, I was assured by my pupil, but the lesson was taught. Very well taught, I might add.

17

A pouring rain ruined the prospect of a noon picnic the next day. My pupil and I were ensconced in my apartment playing chess behind a rain-streaked window. Two mosquitoes had been pelted against the pane. The bamboo grove was rendered gaunt with leaves down and branches felled. Wet birds chirped forlornly from damp nests flooded by the downpour. Outside Q was climbing a tree, calling to a pigeon dozing on a lone twig, nursing a big belly sickened from a meal of squirmy worms.

"Goo goo gooo!" she coaxed impatiently, her thin limbs tangled palely against the slippery tree. "Come back or you will die."

"You're going to fall, Qiu Rong, and wet yourself," my pupil urged without looking up from our chessboard of jade. "Checkmate!"

"Are you blind? I'm already dripping wet," she shouted back, waking the bird for a moment, but the pigeon soon resumed its nap in the rain, swinging with the windblown branch.

"I'll kill you with arrows, you hear me, birdie?" Q threatened her pet, which moved the creature not at all. "You playing deaf, huh?"

She produced a pebble and threw it, missing the pigeon.

97

"You cursed bird. Now I'm going to kill you with cannon-balls. Yep, I've got cannons all lined up in the barracks. I will crush you into a bloody mess—"

"Come on down," the emperor urged again absentmind-edly, pinching my king away before resetting a new game. "And you called yourself a Yalor."

"Do you mean Yalie?" I asked, as I surrendered two sil-vers into his waiting hand.

"Should have gone to the other school—Harvard, isn't it? I've heard it's much finer." The emperor was a jokester at times, befitting the reputation of what other tutors called *fu*, a streak of frivolity in the character.

"One should never bring about the cursed H before a Yalie," I said.

"A rivalry, huh? Just like those English schools, what is it . . . an Ox and a Bridge? I know things, you know. I had firstly requested a tutor from them."

"Did you?"

"Grandpa detested their queen, especially disliking her beaky nose. It was that unlucky nose, Grandpa said, that be-widowed her early in life."

"How wise of her. What made Grandpa a widow her-self then?"

"A poisonous arrowhead killing my predecessor instantly."

"Tell me about your empress."

"Darling, isn't she?" he said, his eyes full of delight look-ing out of the window at Q. "Native born, foreign raised, but all mine now."

I tilted my head, a frowning inquiry.

"She used to be Grandpa's favorite company—rare, exotic."

"Not anymore?" My frown deepened.

He shook his head. "She's all mine now. That's all that matters. You know, she is really a cousin of mine."

"A cousin?"

"Well, not in blood or flesh. By adoption at her birth, which, of course, is never to be talked about per Grandpa's strict order."

"Why not?"

"Shameful. She lacks a blood lineage from the original Yellow Banner Clan."

Looking away from Q, he glanced my way. "Do you fancy her?"

"I . . ."

The emperor could be quite sly.

"It's no crime, really. Everyone else does, initially at least. Five silvers this time?" he asked, shoving a pawn forward across the drawn paper river.

I followed his move with that of a leaping horse, diago-nally. "You're robbing your tutor blind."

The emperor—let us for brevity's sake call him S, short for sovereign—paused in his next move. "Want to make it interesting?"

"How so?"

"You win, spend the night in my chamber. I win, I will spend this night here." He raised his brows in anticipation.

I shook my head, protesting, "You can't lodge in this hum-ble dwelling."

"Of course I can. It was my very intention that I spend some nights with you here."

"But where would you sleep?"

"I could sleep in this chair or that sofa. It's quite all right. I've always wanted to do that. I have been sleeping in the same bed all my life. But no one has ever invited me as a guest before."

"Defeat me then."

"Defeat you I will," said S cheerfully.

A gust of wind blew Q's pleas to tickle my ears. "You cursed bird . . . Please, please come back. I will never feed you worms again, I promise."

Though she sounded in tears now, the bird remained forlorn and unaffected.

"I will make you a new nest with feathers—goose feathers! Not good enough? How about silk or cotton? I will feed you only the sweetest fruits. Please, I will make you a mother. I will buy you a man pigeon with white feathers like yours . . ."

Only then did the imperial pigeon reply "Coooo . . . coooo." It spanned its tips, fluttered its plume, and flapped wetly to perch on Q's left shoulder. With the slight weight added, Q's branch snapped and gave, landing Q in the mud. But she was unhurt and only had attention for her pigeon, like a mother with her fledgling, her chest heaving with gratitude, unstirred by neither the thunder's roar near nor S's pleading afar.

I raised off my chair, seeking S's approval. "Might I?"

"Suit yourself," said S, busy with his move, swiping a horse and a pawn with one leap of his chariot.

Umbrella in hand, I rushed across the dimpled courtyard to her side. Rising to meet me, Q leaned against my chest, a wet child. With a towel, I tenderly dried her sweet cheeks, puddled dimples, matted hair, reddened earlobes, and angelic neck—Oh, my heart!—then her pet, which beaked back and cooed defensively.

Q's giggles vibrated the thready rain pelting the oil, papered umbrella. "You tickle, big man."

"Shall we go inside?"

"No." She pouted. "Lookie . . . I'm bleeding." Skin was broken on her hand, a tincture of red forming, nipped by a timorous twig.

"I know just the cure. May I?"

"Cure it then."

I lowered my lips onto her pale palm, licking her cut with the quivering tip of my tongue, one eye glancing at her sideways. Her palm coiled in a fist then relaxed. She blushed before letting fly a series of curses in German or some other Balkan lingo, faking anger.

"It is a Cherokee Indian's favorite remedy. Manly saliva."

"You savage man." She kissed me on my left cheek on raised toes, minty breath, leafy tobacco.

"Your neck is bleeding, too."

"Really? You twit." She pushed me away with a throaty chuckle, then slipped away from my arms, my heart, ankle thin, slender calfed, child slick. "Awful man!"

Oh, my dearest Annabelle, is she the one you pledged? Is her arrival your departure? Who is she to you, to me, to us, to your dying, to your sustaining within me? Am I to be her savior or ruin?

Faltering, I followed her back to my living room. Barely did I pay attention to him, preoccupied with the image of

Q curled up in my sofa, wet as a drowned cat. Her pigeon flew tentatively from bookshelf to desk to armchair, then to my bedroom and back, in transit dropping her poop whitely on the chessboard.

"You ruined our game!" exclaimed S.

"All you care about is your chess game and yourself, Husband!" Q admonished. Seeking her cigarettes and finding them wet, her anger rose.

"I am inviting Pi-Jin as our night guest. It is settled." He looked at me with the confidence of one who is rarely contradicted. "Tonight, six p.m. sharp. Isn't that joyous, my dear?" he asked.

She shrieked back, "Give me a cigarette or something. I'm freezing to death, can't you see?"

"I am not your servant," replied S mildly, "and you should quit smoking, among other things."

"You are the virtuous one, huh?" Q lunged at S, who nimbly dodged out of the way.

I caught her, falling, in my meddling arms.

"What can I get for you?" I asked, not knowing what was amiss.

"Big wolf, you don't have what I need. He hides it! He is the one who has to pay. Get out of my way." Q picked up an inkwell and threw it at S, missing him but knocking down my collection of history books. The jade well, undented, fell on the posh carpet.

The crisis only ebbed when eunuchs, without warning, as is the rule herein, appeared and carried her away, with S sinking diminished into his chess chair. Onward he complained in a manner that was remorseful and teary, generous on the part of his wife but critical of himself. "One day," he said, "this would all be over. She will be undone. And I don't know what will become of me."

Here was the tale that flowed out of S's mouth.

Q had been a lively child bride who had caught S's eyes in their first encounter when she had been presented to Grandpa upon return of Q's father's foreign service. No one had been more enamored by Q's easy charm and quaint beauty than the dowager herself, who fancied herself an arbiter of all arts and tradition and who daily surrounded herself with talented and artistic personages. Among the dowager's close companions was a noted Peking opera singer named Yu Fang, a diminutive man who played a woman's part (singing and dancing being the rarefied trade of men), winning the hearts of both female and male patrons. Another favorite was a famed calligrapher whose style of calligraphy the dowager herself mimicked with great success.

Qiu Rong, however, was a novelty, trilingual and white-skinned, the latter being seen as *gui*, which meant noble, versus dark and lowborn. All the Chinese nobility painted their faces and necks with powder when seen in public to appear "pale as jade," a phrase worth more than the value of the stone itself. Q also possessed musical talents, playing the *oomphing* organ, which her father had imported from Frankfurt.

Q became the favorite of the dowager's daily companions. Her days were filled with Q's music. The dowager even sponsored a soirée for all the foreign diplomats' wives at the Summer Palace for the sake of Q, who acted as an interpreter among the attendees, much to the dowager's pride.

It was at the height of such buoyancy that the dowager

had decided that S should be married a year earlier than previously intended, as required by the Manchurian law of royal matrimony. He, S, would conduct an abbreviated bridal search to round up the rest of his empresses, the first, second, and third consorts, giving the fourth designated position to Qiu Rong, notwithstanding the blemish that she was of mixed blood and an adoptive offspring rather than an inherently born girl of the Yellow Banner Clan. The dowager took it upon herself to advocate it against the naysayers of this matter as a sign of the Queen Mother's being advanced in thinking and progressive by example, though she pointedly made clear that no one was to ever discuss the pedigree of Q outside or inside the palace. The only thing the dowager mentioned was the prospect that the coupling would produce, if any, the finest-skinned heir to the throne, thusly reducing the darkness of S's skin and adding further purity to the Qing tradition, which the dowager believed was tellingly manifested by the color of their paler skin in contrast to the darker tan of the inferior Han nationality, the bulk of the Chinese citizenry under her rule.

The emperor himself was the most joyous, for he not only fancied the blue-eyed blonde as his consort but he also cherished the bridge that Q would span across the cold shores between him and the dowager, whom he had regarded with fear since a young age, and who had subjected him to many torturous disciplinary acts whenever a deviation or dereliction had been committed. At one period between ages seven and eight, S had trembled whenever coming into the presence of the dowager. Q, in sum, was to be the sunlight that thawed all the rigidity of that cold frontage, and warmed his desolate chambers with her beams of light.

The beginning months of their matrimony were music and talk—talking till night had long faded and strolling along all the ponds and lakes. She took up nearly all his nights, including those rationed to the first, second, and third empresses, the latter two a twin set of beauties from the southern province of Fukien, chosen for their beauty and talents in calligraphy, which won the dowager's heart, and their ability to sing throaty Hing Hua opera melodies. But soon a certain light began to fade in Q, and boredom seeped into their married life. The lakes seemed dry despite their clear water; the ponds, rich with fine memory, seemed sour. Q became an insomniac, staying up nights, slumbering away days, forsaking the trivialities of many a Court ceremony, most vitally the Sunrise Homage to Grandpa Dowager, resulting in her being alienated from the dowager's inner circle, which resulted in more petty dereliction on Q's part that the dowager increasingly blamed on Q's bastardly seed. The alienation did little to lessen Q's deviation. She resorted to that which he now had to hide. "Tonight at six," he said curtly. Peeling himself off the chair, he dragged his leaden feet in chase of his beloved Q.

18

Dancing in my head, awake or in dreams, was nothing but Qiu Rong, my empressly fugitive, not of this earth but of my soul at large, largely waiting to be marshaled and tamed.

Oh, her legs apart, her calves inwardly plump. A memory of a mole gradually surfaced, right under her left ear along a blue vein. And that smile . . . sisterly to Annabelle's, rightfully all mine.

Had my Annie patently given her likeness to Qiu Rong's keeping? Had my old love finally given way to the new?

I bathed myself in the tub. To dull my urges, I drank a shot of single malt while phantoms of the past flew around me, the scent of muggy hair, of Annie and Q, the fragrance of summer weeds all mixed together.

Upon arrival at his royal dwelling, an enthused S met me, wearing a mysterious smirk. Q, my piquant gadfly, was nowhere to be found, though her faint shrieks and silvery giggles lurched amidst us deep in an adjoining grove, an iridescent yet muffled hide-and-seek, hidden and sought.

A certain emptiness drove me to down with S toast after toast of my own brew, ignoring a supper of steamed hairy crabs, simmered bear paws, stewed leaping rabbit, and braised fatty goose, to name but a few. Dim prospect dulled all things around and above but not my fiery urge. More shots of whiskey finally emboldened me to inquire S about Q's absence.

"It's not her night here per palace rule," he intoned solemnly. "This night belongs to my first consort. Q, being the fourth, my last empress, has few rights or honors that way, though I will have more say after an heir is born of my first empress, per Grandpa's advisement. It's the bargain agreed upon when I was granted permission to take Qiu Rong as consort."

"Intriguing."

"Indeed, it is. What you see here is not what it is. Few things here are of my own will, except Qiu Rong, and now you." He sighed. "I endured much to have you here for her."

"For her?"

"Much melancholy she has. Palace life hasn't been easy. To you." He raised his cup, downing it before refilling it with my bottle. "One thousand cups of wine intoxicates this host not at all."

I followed readily with the closing verse of the famed and much lorded couplet composed by Li Bai, a Tang Dynasty poet. "Ten thousand volumes would pale against the depth of my gratitude."

"Well versed you are." Emptying another shot, he challenged me to a poetry contest and alcoholic consumption. "Gin Shi, you and I?"

"Rhymes and meters?"

"Style and polish."

S called out to Dome Head, hidden behind a teak screen. "Servant, bring more wine and four treasures."

A battalion of eunuchs appeared, some adding plates of fresher food, others bringing jars of fine brew, still others carrying in an oblong writing table, a jade inkwell, rolls of rice paper, and quivers of wolf-hair brushes. Rice ink was circularly ground in the inkwell by In-In, the palace's finest, his hands as soft as bird's feet, ensuring the silkiest fluidity. Risen sheaves of paper were smoothed out and settled by a jade ruler.

The tawny wine of Shaoxing origin was only to be served in a silk-thin porcelain ware and sipped carefully and slowly. But imperially, S tilted the earthen urn and took a big wincing swallow before handing it over to me for the like taking.

A game of poetry making ensued with each brushing a worse entry than the other, producing an array of limericks, sonnets, and stanzas filched somewhere, ranging from quasi brilliant couplets—*"A drunken poet wades deep into a river, foggy; he wonders if it pours asunder from a sky, high"*—to frivolity— *"Three monks sit side by side nude in the bathing sun; six heads swing right to left without a stir of peeping wind."*

Ink bled and brushes flew, soiling rolls of rice paper. Jars poured and cups emptied, filling full the throats of fools. It was then when the muse of poetry possessed us both.

Haunted, drunk, and self-absorbed in his glee, one was prone to act in roles of his invention. Gripped, one could reach the moon, climbing the lanky ladder of darkness: many prior poets had perished falling off bridges and cliffs, their heroism lauded by similarly inclined souls. This state of airy consciousness was likened to a state of transcendence by monks and poets alike and deemed a glimpse of the Isle of Bliss promised by Guanyin, a lotus-leaf dwelling deity.

S slipped away, only to return singing Peking opera arias rather expertly, costumed as a woman in a trailing gown, vivid with soft hand gestures and supple with a hippy gait.

Eerie? To be sure. Alarming? Not at all.

Noble-blooded and augustly descended he might be, S was no more or less than an odd elk of my very own ilk, a novel chip off the aged and rotten block; madness and singularity were twins conjoined, inseparable. He bloomed into a full blossom, as a peacock would fan its tail.

Absorbingly, S inched toward me, singing a throat-swelling number while dancing a notoriously arousing routine known as Floating Lotus Leaves with his feet squirming forward, toes touching, heels gliding like a silkworm, other body parts unmoving. His hand faked a porous fan as he swiped a subtle wrist, urging a wordless breeze. Lyrics strained from his pursed lips smeared with red. Sorrow and anguish—the melodic widow's remembrance of her dead spouse—were arced and raised between his freshly painted brows in the slender shape of two willow leaves. Genuine tears trickled down his faltering cheeks as he clicked his teeth and smacked his lips, enunciating each and every weighty word of widowhood, singing a requiem ending with his slowly falling forward, reaching to grasp my left knee with his trembling fingers as if holding onto the ghost of that sung operatic hero crushed under a rock rush from the Great Wall of his own ancestors' making.

S remained in such posture long after the last note was voiced and my applause receded. Then feebly he raised his head, gazing forlornly into my eyes, and uttered the closing lyrics of the aria in a singsong tone, "Don't take her away. She is all that I've got, and all that I will ever have in this life and the next. Please . . ."

Since the Mandarin language makes no distinction between a *he* or *she* in sound, when he uttered the above plea, I mistook him to be restarting another musical stanza, complete with the gesture of falling, weeping, tearing, and knee jerking that was unfinished from his last solo act, taking *he* to mean a flat *he* rather than a new *she*, a suddenly ascended syntactic phoenix.

Sensing no reply from me, he shook my knee some more and this time cried out the following: "You do fancy my Qiu Rong, don't you?"

"No, I don't!"

"And she fancies you. I saw it—her kisses, her hugs. It all means nothing. She is all mine, do you know? I will conquer her, that wild child, just you see. I saw the way she looks at you—*Big Man*—that nonsense." He sneered. "You don't think I could be a Big Man, do you? I'll show you."

"What are you talking about?"

"I could kill you with this silver stick." He picked up a chopstick, pausing to examine it.

"But you won't!"

"Servant!" S shouted.

Dome Head availed himself, bowing before S.

"Bring Qiu Rong here for her bedding duty this very moment," S ordered.

"The first empress has been readied for you. It is not Qiu Rong's turn," Dome Head said with head lowered. "It's by Grandpa's order."

"I am the emperor, can't you see?" S demanded, looking

hardly imperial: his makeup was soggy, running down his cheeks, one brow blurred into an enlarged olive leaf big in the middle.

"I shall speak to the chief eunuch; the set order is not to be altered," Dome Head replied, bowing low.

"You are not to tell another soul. Out you go, you useless rat!" Rising on his knees, S lunged at him, chasing the eunuch out of the dining chamber, leaving In-In standing behind a marbled column, his shadow thin.

"I, too, can be a Big Man," S said, shuffling along, his feet heavy.

Leaning on my In-In's bony shoulder, I was just as clumsy. The length of a long corridor seemed to wiggle. Hung lan-terns gleamed like monstrous eyes, flaming with hatred, flick-ering at our passage.

S stormed into his sleeping chamber, modest in size, dull in decor, lit poorly by chandeliers of candlelight hanging from the pointed roof. He rushed to one end of his chamber where a boat-shaped bed stood draped under a red mosquito net. Forcefully, he lifted up the front of the net, finding noth-ing. He searched the back end, leaning feebly on the bedpost. There, with a girlish yelp of fright, leaped up a thin figure, frail and slightly hunched, her hair loosened and bony shoul-ders slanting, not a shred of clothing worn, rendering her pale and tender under the lights that flickered with the rus-tled net.

"Your Eminence, pray forgive me," cried the girl pitifully.

"You lowly servant, how dare you come in here for favor without my permission!"

"But this is my night. I am, after all, your first consort."

Shaking with plea, her hands covering her budding chest, the girlish figure squatted before the enflamed S.

"Tell me who it was that let you in here! Tell me or I will pull out all of your hair." He reached for her loosened coif, grabbing a bundle, which he yanked with great force causing her to let out a yelp of fright and pain.

"It is Grandpa's will. It is all her doing. You cannot blame me for wanting—"

"It's all Grandpa's fault," he sneered, slurring his words. "None of your own flesh-and-blood base wantonness and greed."

"It's your fault as well!"

"How dare you accuse me of any fault?" It was enough to stop S from yanking her hair and pause to hear what she had to say.

"You . . . you haven't even mated me, not once since our wedding night. Am I that ugly? Is Qiu Rong that pretty, taking up all our time?"

"How dare you speak of me—of her—this way!"

Grabbing a palm-leaf mosquito sweeper, S savagely slashed her bare back, along her chest, down her thighs and buttocks. The sweeper cut through the air with whipping sounds, each lash punctuated by her fearful cry.

The scene nearly incensed me to leap forward in defense of the damsel in distress, when the petrified consort, sensing no reversal of fortune or softening of his manly wrist, fled out the corridor, a frightened child.

"How I detest that girl," S said, teeth clenched. "Someday all will end." He sank his thin frame onto his wooden bed, batting away the languid net, a dazed stare in his eyes. "I will make her a woman. Take this." He reached under his pillow, producing a folded silk bag tied with string, and passed it to me. "Now go fetch Qiu Rong. Tonight is the night of happiness of flesh and blood, of legacy and heir; tonight you will see this. I want you to witness my manliness. I am not what she claims. I am capable of doing my duty. I will make good that promise. The Qing Empire will have its own heir from this man, and no others. The legacy is mine to uphold, the dynasty is mine to prolong."

"You shouldn't have beaten your empress," I snarled, and I hurled myself at the prone S, only to be thrown aside with his easy left elbow, a glimpse of his warrior art on display.

"You know not half of what I am enduring. Now hurry." He threw the silk bag at my side. Readily I was helped up by In∕In, who led me away in search of Qiu Rong's residence, several high∕walled courtyards to the west.

"What is this silk bag for?" I inquired, leaning on In∕In like a blind's cane.

"It contains silver ingots, marital favors of Ru Fan—entering chamber," In∕In explained in a low, rattling voice.

"Enter what chamber?" The liquor, fine or foul, was dancing in my own dwelling now.

"Her chamber."

"Why can't you take this favor while I rest my feet?" My knees were buckling, my head bobbing, as we neared a set of stone stairs. "I'm exhausted."

"I am not allowed to go in your stead. Such task is a sacred and secretive one," said In∕In, yanking me forward by my hands. "Only those high in ranking and trustworthy are allowed to carry it out."

"What is to be done besides delivering the silk bag?"

"*Bei dai.*"

"Carry a sack?"

"Empresses are carried in this body sack by a chosen eu-nuch to accept favors from the emperor, and they are allowed to crawl under his quilt into his august bed."

A shadowy sentry of three night guards armed with spears and daggers passed us quietly by. Ten yards later, they hit a bronze gong—one, two, three—three beats intimating the depth of night.

Her residence soon came to view under a pale moon, an elegant house fronted with a garden and surrounded on all sides by a roofed porch from which *guan hua,* the leisure of appreciating flowers, could be pursued by the dweller, and *pin cha,* tea drinking, could be brewed and brooded upon for her visitors.

A puppy came running and jumping up to sniff In-In's hand as he knocked on the door, announcing our arrival. In-In, to whom the pet seemed familiar, fished out something from his robe pocket and threw it. The puppy trotted away, munching fiercely. A bone it must be from the feast, uneaten and ignored.

"Who is it?" Q's voice was heard, though it was her ser-vant, a girl named Lin-Lin, who answered the door, sticking her head out for inspection.

"We are here to take the empress to the emperor," In-In replied.

"How can it be? It's not Missy's night . . . and what is he doing here?" Lin-Lin asked, giving me an eyeful.

"It is the emperor's wish that Pi-Jin carry over his bride."

"Is he drunk or smoking again?"

"Both."

"How about him?" Lin-Lin asked, pointing her finger at me. By now I was leaning rather feebly against a column lest I collapse onto the dark rosary bed.

"They were feasting together. The emperor, in a rage, threw the first out, giving silver back to your Missy. It is a favor. Be quick to wake her."

"Favor, my foot. He hardly does anything to her anymore."

"Who says that?"

"Missy. She is all restless, smoking more every day."

"Here, take this to her and get her ready now," In-In urged, passing her the silk bag, "or the emperor will climb the chimney, the way we left him."

"See," Lin-Lin pointed out in disgust, "it's even embroi- dered with first empress's name."

"Speak no more nonsense," In-In said curtly.

"Wait, then." Lin-Lin shut the door, sending out a puff of fragrance that could only be opium, which the rich and powerful all indulged in as a favored pastime.

"The silver is given, what shall we do now?" I asked, in- haling the minced air, a mirage of a narrow-laned bordello swimming in my head.

"We wait for her to be ready, and then you carry her to our master." Holding my right hand, he pinched the web between my thumb and forefinger. A surge of sharp pain charged up my shoulder, leading me to shake off his grip.

"What was that?"

"An acupuncturist's trick. A single pressing of this nerve hub will make your head alert and feet steady again."

"Come now, Pi-Jin," Lin-Lin said, opening the door for me. "Empress is ready to enter the bag."

I stumbled inside under dim light, amidst hazy smoke. Q sat nude on the floor, her clothing strewn all around her while a pipe dangled from the corner of her mouth. Her thighs were long, skin jade-like, and shoulders bare and bony, a still por-traitist's dream. Her breasts were peach-round and nipples upturned. Her hair was loosened, cascading down one shoul-der, shadowing over her left bosom. Smoke spiraled, contour-ing her face, rising along her forehead to linger among her hair roots like summer hay caught up in a smoldering fire.

"Have you seen enough, Big Man, or should I remain this way for you?" she asked, blowing a puff my way as she turned to face me, her thighs parting as she spoke.

Oh, you evanescent Eve, my pubescent siren. Another moment of truth and I would be condemned per palace laws or just layman's conscience.

It might be the wine or a sniff of O, but this Pickens presently felt no fear or remorse, for she was for my taking. She was that promised reward, that pledged pavilion in the wind, upriver on the narrow horizon. I wanted to drop on my knees, submitting to certain, eternal death just for a lick of her sweat beading down her left breast, but before I could do so, Q's servant slapped her mistress's thighs together and yanked the pipe out of her lips, rendering Q to roar with anger, "You will be punished, you worthless maid!"

Minding not her mistress's curse, Lin-Lin squatted by Q's side, lifting her up by her arm. "It's time to go accept the favor. Get into the sack." On the floor was spread the bag with string loosened around its mouth.

"Favor? I want to see if he can get his *diao zi* hard enough for me, or I'll have to cut it off next time he teases me."

"Never mind her gibberish; you really shouldn't take what she says to heart. She means no such harm. She is just a little bubbly. Please tell no one of her state, Tutor Pi-Jin. Had we known she was to be called on, I would never let her have what she desired," said Lin-Lin, pressing a bag of said herb into my robe pocket.

One foot at a time, Q stepped within the fallen sack to sit at its bottom. Slowly Lin-Lin pulled tight the draw string then passed the end of the rope to me.

Like a thief, I swung her over my left shoulder and stumbled along the path shone bright by In-In's lantern. Q's softness warmed my back; her shallow groans rhymed with my gait. Fate tempted me every step I ferried; destiny urged me on. How I yearned to leap away from here, my loot in tow, vanishing from this seraglio, usurping his as mine—mine in celestial design, foretold by that puff of urgent summer flame in the long-ago land where initial love sparked, was kindled and ignited.

Under a low moon the palace was icy, though heat hung still in the midnight air. The sovereign lay stiff and flat on his back, his mouth murmuring Buddhist psalms to calm his own nerves, his nebular mosquito net shielding his secrecy and shame. Loquacious red lanterns were lit, feigning festive cheer. S, however, looked the part of one dying, shivering in fear of his imminent demise.

All his servants were out of sight. I could, in one swipe, knock akimbo the walled lanterns and set the chamber aflame via the burning mosquito net, trapping the despot in his bed surrounded by heated fury, ending this fiasco before it could ever begin.

Gently I lay down my supple ward at the foot of his meager bed, so that she, by strident etiquette, could duck low and crawl humbly under his cold quilt. It reminded one not of a congenial congress but some tunneled and testudineous thievery.

Q stirred slightly when I untied the sack.

"What took you so long, Pi,Jin?" the sovereign uttered from his bed. "Did you take the first dipping already?"

His acrimony needed no reply.

I peeled the sack down Q's sleek form. Lamely, she leaned against the bedpost, her eyes half closed, head drooping to the side, a dazed daffodil.

S pointed to a partitioned screen. "Sit behind there and watch."

Casting a final glance at her, that urge rose again. All I had to do was leap on S leopard,like and I could muffle him to a baffled death with his own quilt.

Discreet, Pickens.

I sulked to the seat assigned me behind that folding screen, lacquered and ludicrous. In darkness, I watched them through the cracks as S rose up, gourd and thistles swinging, to tower over the supine Q. He shook her shoulders till she was awakened, muffled shouts were exchanged.

Q struggled to her feet, facing the discourteous cuckold, slapping him across his cheek. "You spineless child. Look at you. You want to be a Big Man? Where is your MAN? I can't see any, can you?" She ducked her head, faking a search of his midsection.

This time it was the emperor who empowered his bare palm, delivering a forceful pair of smacks across her cheeks, throwing her rustled blond hair awry, nearly bringing her off her feet.

"How dare you slap me!" she cried, covering her face with both hands. "I am not your other whores, you filthy drunk."

"And you, *yan gui,*"—smoke ghost or addict—"your breath reeks of opium." S sneered. He lifted her up like a caught fish and threw her onto his tumbled blankets, before assaulting her with mad thrusts while shouting curses of royal variety. "You are useless womanhood! Good for nothing but this! Where is your . . . ?"

"If you have to ask!" Q screeched.

"I'll punish you . . . till you bleed to death!"

"If you know how," she taunted.

"Where is your thing?" He paused to investigate, peering between her thrashing, upright thighs.

"Even a blind bull could find his mare's cave," fumed Q, letting him fumble some more. "Why are you doing this? To impress your tutor?"

"No, to show you what I got!"

"You haven't gotten much there or anywhere, believe me."

"You are an ill-bred whore!"

"The way you like it."

"Don't you tease me!"

"You're making a fool of yourself trying to do what you cannot."

"Don't you want me to sire an heir so you could be a legita— . . . Ouch!"

"Why don't you ask Grandpa to show you how? She knows

plenty such tricks. Enough to get herself knocked up as a lowly palace concubine."

The emperor suddenly paused, lying still on Q's bare belly, panting. "Did you have to utter her name? See what you have done. I am weakened."

"Why are you crying again?"

"Why? I can't . . ."

"It's no sin or crime."

"But how I adore you."

"I know." Carefully Q rolled him off to lie limply by her side. Gently she wiped his tears as a mother would, with her palms and a gibberish of affection and tenderness. When he calmed, she climbed atop him, and he reached for her with arms raised. A wrestle ensued, entangling them in the lumbering thrall of the mosquito net, rendering it impossible for this one-eye witness to grasp it all save for a here-and-there glimpse of bare limbs and partial bodies resembling a game of tumble-in-the-hay between two ungrown and un-initiated in the matter of man-and-mates in some lonesome palisade cliff, where men wrestled their teary goats and foaming foals out of necessity and a pithy dose of painful pleasure. The mosquito net was soon ripped and torn from the ceiling, tumbling voluminously over Q's loosened hair. Straddling his bare back, Q pulled on his long hair, bending his neck backward while locking her gaze my way into my cleaving heart.

She shook off the residue of the fallen net, revealing her back, slender and V shaped. With her gaze still on me, she spun him over and sat on his face. Then she rode with gentle-ness, as if the horse beneath her was trotting on a soft path;

her rosebud breasts heaved and her hair tossed with each motion.

In such coupling, he let out a string of muffled groans, ode of the beridden. She loosened a spread of spasmic utterance, not dissimilar to a chuckle, a giggle, or small cry.

This was not some fancy horseplay of Q's Germanic upbringing, nor was it some banal theatrics. It was a page off an ignoble volume, namely *Yin Gong Yan Shi,* a handdrawn pictorial of coital poses and positional perversions long cherished by emperors, and equally treasured by their concubines. Yale's collegiate library boasted a rare copy, which I had copiously abused during the yellow days of June, July, and August, and all the seasons in between while cocooned in Connecticut.

Literally, S was involved in a ritual bearing the poetic caption of "A thirsty man drinks from a sweetened spring." Straddling her emperor with her tailbone affixed on his eager lips, and her own head bent over his miserly growth, Qiu Rong was performing none other than the manly favorite known as "A virtuous girl blowing on a stiffened bamboo flute."

Oh, the edacity of one and esuriency of the other!

The riding and the beridden lasted for long minutes before Q raised her head from her task, lips smeared and face sweaty, to reach under his sallow pillow. She fumbled out his *ru yi*—a smoothly polished wristthick jade stick, the emperor's good luck vade mecum of Buddhist import and potency—and drilled it cold and hard into his anus, engendering a thrilling yelp of pleasure on the part of the delighted monarch. His engorgement firmed and then limped as Q gained her rhythm and probed it further in its depth.

S moaned in staccato hiccups, arching his knees, begging the enchantress to rekindle his waned wand, but such act of desperation only roused her tigress's wrath. She unstraddled the fugitive, rolled him over and mounted him from the hind position as a raunchy gutter hound would of its yelping bitch, her jade stick sawing.

Never have I, in all my sordid years, encountered such sparks and spirals of eruptions. Thrashing beneath her, S was thrown sideways, headlong, every way and no way. Slowly his moans of pain sedated into whimpering groans and muddled gibberish of love and loving. Candlelight flicked its last buoyancy and bedposts ceased their shaking and squeaking. All was calm.

"Take me home now, you foreign pervert!" So saying, Qiu Rong rose from the emperor's slain carcass, casting away the silk cloth I gave her to cover her body and throwing in my face a timely towel to dry her sweat.

"What about him?" I inquired, eyeing S, lying face down with arms sprawled and mouth foaming like a dead frog.

"He won't die. He's in heaven, if that's what you are asking." She gazed at me with her vivid blue eyes. "But I am not, can't you see?" Without warning, she flung herself into my arms, sobbing and kissing me over my lips, my mouth. Oh, my ape heart, thawing and melting all in one monstrous beat and phantasmal rhyme! The saltiness of her probing tongue, the gentleness of her succumbing breasts . . .

"Take me home before I gouge the pervert's heart out. What he needs are no wives but man-whores from Europe with all their palatial debauchery. I'm dying here from suffocation. You are the only one to save me . . ."

"Say no more!"

"Take me away from here—the further the better." She leaned into my chest, her soft arms draped over my shoulders, kissing further down my neck, setting all my chest hair abuzz and my nether bulge to ache so. I could have had her, bare and whole in the dying glow of red candlelight, with utter impunity. After all, her husband's fouling had already oiled her path, and her barren oven had heated to its hottest. All it would take was a devilish prick, a gentle lift off her feet sinking her carefully onto my lap, and heaven would be mine, and bliss hers.

Rather, I eased her into the waiting sack and swung her over my shoulder, heading for her chamber without In-In, who had been frightened away by the bedbound upheaval. Only when clear of the emperor's chamber did I inquire of the cause of her utterances of escape and refuge.

"Why? Can you not see? Every breath I take here is fetid and foul. Don't you know I was born to be a free-willed princess? My father spoiled me so. He let me learn Japanese and their art of flower arrangement when we lived in Tokyo where he was an ambassador, even though it was taboo, for Japanese was considered the language of our enemy and their customs barbaric. I even got a certificate for skill. . . . You know you should never put chrysanthemum in the same vase with anything else, ruins its purity.

"While in Austria, where he was next stationed, he had Vienna's finest tailor cut all my dresses for all four years that I was to live and grow there—my happiest years. How I adored Vienna!

"A stubborn officer, Father's first secretary, a pawn of

his enemy, protested Father's indulgence of me. Another devious courtier even wrote secret letters back to Court to impeach Father as a traitor of Manchurian culture and customs. But Father heeded them not at all. On the eve of our departure he gave me permission to hold a farewell ball for my foreign friends against Mother's protest. How I adored that evening: the beautifully dressed guests from all walks of Viennese society, the orchestra music swelling . . ."

Upon which I skipped down the steps of Tai Hong Palace.

"Stop tossing me around like that! Anyhow, I could never forget the very moment when I appeared at the grand staircase of that sumptuous residence, the grandest and most fashionable. Hundreds were awaiting me there in the ballroom, Father and Mother among them, my friends, friends of my father and mother—the entire diplomatic corps was there. Even their king sent me a token: a silk embroidered tapestry of the Blue Danube that ran across the girth of Vienna. How I adore that city.

"When I asked Father why he allowed me to hold such festivities, he said with much sadness that the moment we returned to China, all my fanciful ideas and free urges would have to be put away for good, for no one would allow any of my capriciousness back in China. Father threw that party for me at the risk of losing his office and of being labeled a traitor to his nationality and his Manchurian ancestry. It was just as Father had forewarned me. All these things he had done for me, all the love, and he isn't even my birth father. I was passed into his wife's arms not long after my birth by a foreign countess of unknown origin besoiled by a Chinese merchant. My birth mother was young, forfeiting me to their care before hemorrhaging to death at Union Hospital. That swine Chinaman father of mine was nowhere to be traced, probably crouched in some *hutong* gutter puffing his opium, waiting to waylay other young white-skins of their innocence and naïveté. Cursed bastard that he is, he's the only one I have left now. I wish I knew who he was, but I never tried to find him: I was afraid my lordly father would chastise me."

"Did your adoptive father ever mention the facts of your birth to you?"

"Only once when I was still in Tokyo. Lady Dominic, the wife of the Portuguese ambassador, called me a mixed-blood in Japanese, which Father didn't understand, of course: he never learned to speak Japanese though he is fluent in German and English and some French. When I told him about Lady Dominic's words, Father was incensed and wanted to retrieve the dinner invitation he had previously sent her for the occasion of the emperor's birthday. Mother was so upset that she suffered a headache for three days, refusing even to talk to me, which is a sure sign that I was not to broach the subject ever again; that Manchurian pride of fatherhood was not anything anyone could dare broach, and thinking herself barren was Mother's everlasting sore spot. Now that I am all but abandoned here under these old trees in the cold palace, forbidden to be seen even by my father and mother, with a husband weak as he, that wish has again and again come back to haunt me, to seek out my birth father. Can you help me?"

"For what purpose?"

"So I can leave this place."

Before I could give my reply, the courtyard door swung open and the maid Lin⁄Lin appeared like a phantasm.

"Is that you, Lin⁄Lin?" Q inquired.

The girl nodded.

"Were you listening to what we said?" Q asked.

"I heard only your voice but not your words," Lin⁄Lin replied, eyes lowered.

"Stingy bones! You are lying again, aren't you? Take me inside now."

Her servant took the silk sack, swinging it over her shoulder before kicking closed the door in my face with a curt, "Good⁄bye, Mr. Pi⁄Jin!"

19

Summer solstice fell on the following day. The school-house was closed so S, the son of heaven, might lie prostrate in prayer to his forbearers at the Ancestral Shrine, to thank them for a good year gone by and new one to come.

All palace concubines and eunuchs were restricted to a vegetarian diet while shunning the venomous sun, and all impure secularities were stalled, save for what was to befall my abode.

It was near daybreak, semidark, and my senses were keen and lucid, still indulged in a continual dream, in which one thinks of genuine occurrences as a dream with sleep an inter-rupting agent breaking its sequential order.

I shaved, urgently wiping the wick of red blood off my upper lip, trembling hand to blame, before dousing it with a dash of Clubmen, the patented pungency of muskiness and man. Bathrobed in a silk gown of Kyoto origin embroidered with a giant butterfly on its back—its wings extending onto my arms, causing a backward onlooker to see not its wearer but a metamorphosed monarch motioning with life—I sipped first tea, which In-In had brewed and brought upstairs. Slowly blowing its jasmine steam, I gazed out the eastward window whence my angelic darling would materialize, if not to soothe the ache of my apish self, then to round up the dipping arc of the perpetuating dream. Like the dream, the meandering mood was pastoral in tone, dim in hue, with a deafening qui-etness sans morning birdsong or early leaf rustle, clear of the harried footfalls of eunuchs long gone beyond the palace wall accompanying their master to the Heavenly Shrine. Human-ity stood evanesced within this planetary consciousness, save for that tinny, tiny caress of my beloved pet's feet, courtyards away yet only heartbeats apart. The dimpled courtyards were rattled by the summer rains, and the pelting raindrops were like the palpitations of the *di hua*'s heaving heart—a mythical flora believed to hold aloft all locality, big or small, in prosperity or in despair—and mine as well. It was along that petal-strewn path, rustle-less, through a grove of bamboo trees, their leaves rain-laden, that she came, her feet bare and hair wet.

I heard an exchange of hushed words downstairs, and In-In was dispatched out the door into the rain, re-entering the mossy path she had trod. Leaves stirred, and petioles and branches swayed apart like the entrance to an enchanted for-tress. Resultantly, the circumference of the current dream was upheld.

She stomped upstairs, running into me on my way down on that narrow curving flight: it was a flicker of a moment but an unending eternity. She had on a red *qipao*, a bewitching dress hugging her pubescent shape and tart nipples. Heav-enly she smelled of wet soil, crushed leaves, and a stale sweat. Morning light showed the delicate down on her forehead, the asymmetrical dimples shallowing her cheeks, and long sloping earlobes that paled against her russet summer skin. She was caught, weak-kneed by the moment, with lovey-dovey symptoms of an enraptured youth: a held breath suspended midchest, slightly parted lips, softening almond eyes, and an acknowledging blush tiding high cheekbones.

I put my arms over her lean shoulders.

"Behave, you ape. We've got work to do," she said, dodging out of the rim of my hands. "And what is that awful odor about you?" Before I could lower my arms to contain her, she slipped through, climbing to the top of the stairs, leaving me just the sight of her small back, boyish hips, and in-turned toes. I could have thrown myself at her, ravaging her, again and again on the steps, but the moment passed, though not the ache of my groins.

"What, might I ask, do you mean by that?" I was barely able to uphold my crumpling self by adjusting the belt around my slick waist, ill-hiding a certain protuberance.

She sprawled obliquely on the top steps, elbows on the landing, wet dress conforming to her bodice and thighs, thin legs apart, sloping calves naked, bare ankles bent in the most juvenile of manners.

There, before my gorging eyes, as I followed her upward, were her unshod feet dangling over the edge of a step, mud on her soles, blades of weed on her toes. Feet to pleasure, feet to torture: an erogenous paradise, a provenance of obsessive fancies. How I yearned to suck on every digit from her innermost lanky big toe to her littlest pinkie, an afterthought of a toe. Did I mention that she had a case of syndactyly, with her second and third toes stuck together by a meaty web? But all the more suckable and succulent. Feet, mind you, were no mere parts of functionality, but sensuous condiments in lovemaking in this culture tilted for perversion, preferably bound, the tinier, the more alluring. A corseted foot arched to resemble a horse hoof was poetically potent, known as a *three-inch lotus;* the faltering hippy gait it engendered was a tingling object of lust among all flat-faced and sunken-nosed Chinamen.

"What are you nosing about my toes for? Sit down here and cover yourself, Big Man." Q's hand patted the carpet to her left, breaking my reverie. Tamely I sat on my assigned turf, my legs crowding hers, yanking down the left front of my sleeping gown to cover myself. Frankly, I was sick of this Big Man business. One moment she could be so stricken by her crust-thin emotion, and the next, vulgar like a mercenary street waif off some Boston wharf. Relief came readily when I garnered a peep at her tender armpit, rank with a tiny shock of curlies when she raised a short-sleeved arm and parked it over my shoulder.

"Now listen, Big Man," she cajoled. "The whole palace is a ghost town: everyone has gone to the shrine. We've got things to do." She dug her fine fingers into my upper arm while over-lapping her thin legs in a stack.

"Today is the day," she whispered conspicuously into my ear. "Let's pay a visit to Union Hospital where I was born. There must be a record—if not of my adoption, then of the death of my mother. I've been there once. It's run by foreign doctors with foreign head nurses guarding each ward."

"How can I be of use?" I asked, her nearness tickling my nerves.

"You are one of them," she said with wide-eyed certainty. "And you're a sweet talker and a handsome man. The old nurses there will open anything for you."

"A sweet talker?" I faked a frown, questioning.

She nodded, her long-lashed eyes downcast as if bemused by her own toes, so that I could see her profile and the tiny mole on the center of her left lobe.

"How handsome?" I asked, leveraging on her sweet mood.

She nodded a second and third time and bent her head lower, showing a shaded nape whereupon her hair changed to blond down. So utterly fragile! I could almost fracture that slender column to pieces with one robust snap.

"Quite handsome." She turned her face, nose tip to my ear, and lifted a strand of my hair, draping it over my ear, blowing with tobacco-scented breath another filament away from my left eye. My hair roots went atingle at her breeze, my head dizzied as if fondled by seductive fingers, sending a thousand little caresses up my scalp and along my burning temples.

"How sweet?" I urged dreamily.

"Lozenge sweet!" The wench wrenched my spiculated nose-ridge hard between her knuckles and gave it a fiend-ish twist followed by a hammering blow with her other fist. "That's how sweet it is, you foolish man."

"Where did you . . . ?" A hot rush burned down the sep-tum of my nose, reddening my upper lip. I cupped my nos-trils, blood seeping through my fingers.

Q flushed with pity, her puerile almond eyes darkening with worry.

"Oh, I'm so sorry." My helpless child cupped her lips as if in like ache. "I was just playing the Russian sickle and ham-mer game."

I uttered nasally, "Now you have to—"

"What can I do, you poor darling?"

Before she finished speaking, my crimson paws had for-feited the bleeding nose and inserted under her hairy arm-pits, lifting her lithely to plant her rump on my sighing lap, her vaginal mound a mere fist away from my aliquant ap-pendage. Had she writhed one inward inch, or giggled a half-ticklish breath, she would have autumned a windfall to last me a fortnight, a forever. But heaven had to wait . . . though I couldn't.

My child sat in stillness, astraddle my mutinous thighs, examining me with impenetrable attentiveness, a trait per-versely privy only to the young. Her tilted eyes squinted into one conjoined eye; her upturned nose, as turned up as her ancestral A's, wrinkled with frustration, and her nether lips grew lax.

Diagnostically pleased, she pushed my chin up, then lifted the frontage of her silk dress to wipe clean the red residue while nursing me with another pinch on my nose, this time to stop the bleed. "You are a naughty man asking me those silly questions. You deserve to bleed to death."

"Hmmm." Before I could open my mouth, she had brushed her lips over mine, sealing the words within; another brush of her soft lips and I would tremble in tatters and shreds, but she wasn't to repeat. I nearly fainted. But quickly I reas-sembled my fallen self and slipped my hands along her waist to finally rest them on her slight hips. How I now detested round matronly hips, thickly constructed like those of my original tutor, the quiet Mrs. D, and some expedient others of her breed in between.

Tightening my grip, digging my nails into the soft rise

of her buttocks, I thrust her hips toward me, aiming her nether protrusion—that final cliff wherein dives the man. She unleashed a *hah!*—an airy issuance halfway to its final formation as an utterance, the plea of meek surrender. On my part, a certain after-rain mushrooming had long flamed in a mushy forest, tented and canopied. I was squeezing her hind cheeks, readying for another deathly blow—mine, not hers—when Q pulled her slim elbow sideways like the sling of a catapult and levied a numbing slap across my face, throwing my cheeks to flop and lips to flap. New blood spurred from my already bleeding nose.

"You rascal, now see what you have done." She cursed prettily. "Be still. I'm trying to stop you from bleeding to death." Her attentiveness was a marvel to witness, having just struck a jaw-slacking blow. This time my spillage gushed onto the white of her dress.

She kept my nose tip pinched, aiming to cease my discharge, which, as long as she was busy with her enterprise, I minded not at all. I pivoted my heels on a higher rung of stairs and gave her a bit of a toss, hopping her bottom just an inch off my skin, letting her concavity sink directly on my tortoise's head; each hop brought home an abject awakening deep in my heart.

As I tossed her some more, letting my toes do their kinetic tricks, she gyrated her tiny waist. Such circular gyration only incensed the heat in me—I was nigh fainting again. My darkened eyes saw a dusky bonfire on the New England prairie burning with sizzling zest.

She mopped my blood with one hand, pinching my nose with the other, suffocating me. I closed my mouth, stopping my breathing altogether. The resultant delirium was to die for, causing a hallucinatory mirage to appear: in my lap was my Annabelle, not Q.

Such evocation caused a sudden halt to the entire business at hand. I searched around, sensing one angry and awry vein engorge on my forehead. I was not going to succumb to threat by *mi amor* with my oven heating a near boil, ruining what I had so long craved and was so near to attaining.

"If you get caught doing this," Q said, without cease in her circular gyrations, "we all will be hanged."

"Doing what?" I asked, resuming the hopping of my lap, panting for that goal that was nearing.

"Doing this." She sank down her tail, letting me feel her softness, the warmth from her inner groove a thin undergarment apart. My hardness lengthened and rose, standing obliquely to face its headlong onslaught, peeling painfully with each of her forceful glide: it was then and there I reached that delirious state where one clung to nothing, and everything around me, above me, and under me ingratiated itself toward reaching that finality. As I accelerated my urging, I was blinded by a numbing sensation rising en masse along every cell, along every tiny man-hair, every porous inch, every yielding yardage.

In the distance I heard Q say, "Please come with me . . . to the hospital . . . and help me . . ."

"I will!" Slipping one cupping hand from her waist down to her bottom, I poked one single deviant digit, the middle one, into her parted crevice, slipping it tightly into the unknown, followed shortly by her pained convulsion, triggering my own deathful cry as I let loose a monstrous deluge that soiled the front of my robe.

Through my glassy vision, I made out a slender form slip-ping off my tattered lap, blushing possibly and dashing down-stairs, leaving me to die alone on the steps.

20

After cleansing myself and consuming a beastly breakfast of dried sweet dough, buttered cornbread, and coils of lamb sausages exceptionally rendered by my prodigious young cook, I secretively appeared, suit wearing and hatted, at a deserted eastern gate where I was met by a four-man sedan. Behind the drapery was my pubescent mate leaning on her side of the cushioned seat, powdered and coiffed, dressed in the hunting attire of safari pants and knee-high boots. Her eyes were downcast, staring at her own knees, with a pink blush that even her white powder could ill cover.

"What took you so long?" she asked, slanting her eyes to peep out the tiny sedan window.

"A meal and a bath," I answered while taking my seat, gazing her up and down. Those slender thighs under the manly wear stirred me; she clamped them closed as if sensing my stare.

Outside the drapery, the head of the foursome gave orders, and our carriage went aloft and mobile through a side archway; the main one was reserved for the chosen, and no one else. The glow in my heart animated me to reach over my paw, yearning to touch her.

She slapped the encroaching hand away with her ringed

fingers, an inset green jade denting my palm. "Be proper," she snapped, pasting herself to her sedan wall.

Three willow-lined streets later, she sagged and sighed before leaning her head on my shoulder. I cupped her hot hands between my sweaty palms; she dug her nails, lightly denting my skin. After a silent ride down some leafy boulevards, she tilted her swan neck and hungrily kissed my eager mouth, one long leg swinging over my lap.

By noon—a bound-foot granny could have outrun our hoofed foursome!—we alighted under the awning of Union Hospital. A turbaned concierge of Indian descent chased away the scattered paupers before greeting us with his shiny, white-toothed smile.

Among a cluster of nurses and doctors crowding the white-walled corridor, Q followed me, as a minor would with a father or uncle. Beyond that fortress, outside the maroon wall, she was but a helpless child.

We were courteously greeted by the hospital administrator, a jovial old chap from the coast of Maine, Blue Hill to be exact, a peninsular hamlet south of Bangor: a predial digit dipping in a pellucid Atlantic sea whereupon I had once swum in a quarry pond with some local lads. Colonel Putnam, the hospital administrator, a crippled soldier of the Spanish War, refused to grant me privy to the underground vault of the hospital even after I hinted of my tacit liaison with Colonel Winthrop of the American legation. The one-legged letch kept leering at my escort sitting in the corridor, whom I merely introduced as a lady of enormous means and whose concern over the lineage of an invented friend would, when adoptive identity known, lead to a possible future donation. He only yielded after planting a prolonged wet kiss on the back of Q's hand. His cursed lips lingered inappropriately long for an initial encounter, or any encounter for that matter. The curative effects Q had on the lame duck engendered a rare pang deep in my groins, but I kept my quiet, though inwardly I shouted, *"Lick my blushing bride's hand one more time . . ."*

But calm I remained. Life is marred with wrongs.

We climbed down dusty stairs, Putnam wobbling alongside Q, iron key in hand, an obvious bulging in his treasonous trousers. He had to lean on her thrice down three short flights, pushing away my aiding hand.

"These documents would have been condemned, but I kept them," sighed Putnam, unlocking a rusty chest labeled by dynastical reign and its Westernized calendar year.

Before letting us browse the aged contents, our pugnacious Putnam hinted at the neediness of the crowded wards and the stinginess of the nurses' quarters. Q frowned at his plea, and on the spot dropped fifteen tael of silver. Ownership of said coins brought a gleam to his eyes.

The probe through the meager month of April 1885 produced ten births under the midwifery of Nurse M. Mead. There had been an outbreak of plague that year at the hospital, scaring away expectant mothers from the maternity ward. Among the listed were a set of twins to a French couple, one caesarean birth to German merchants conducted by a surgeon initialed as M.H., and three consecutive boys to respectively productive Russian railroad engineers. The three boys were trailed by a succession of four baby girls to three Londoners and one Yorkshire veterinarian.

There were no offspring of Manchurian ancestry or Chinese parentage.

"Where is my name?" said Q.

"Are you . . . ?" Putnam's shiny forehead wrinkled in puzzlement before slowly breaking into a grimace.

"No, she is not," I said emphatically.

"But this much silver and your obvious mixed blood . . . You have to be—"

"It proves nothing," I opposed adamantly.

Barely before I ended my words, Putnam was on his knees. "Your Excellence." He grabbed Q's honey hand and abjectly kissed it again and again. In between his canine breaths, he uttered, "I had long been an admirer of your regality and your pedigree, having dined once with your father. You were young then, six or seven, having just returned from a diplomatic tour to the Empire of Japan. It was at the Hawthorn Bloom Banquet that your father hosted annually. I was freshly discharged from the army hospital in Manila, having just taken my present post. What a grand host your princely father was. What a darling hostess you presented, standing beside him, greeting your guests on that unforgettable spring day when hawthorn trees were in full bloom and butterflies were alighting upon their nectar."

"You were there?" Q seemed smitten by the man's charm and faulty memory. Had he really been there at the soirée? Did he falsify the incident and the chance meeting to gain footage into the cockles of my queen's heart?

"I was. I even shook your little hand. For a brief while I mistook you as a Japanese girl." The man of Maine was bubbling over like a lobster in a pot.

"Really?" Q seemed more enchanted than ever.

"You were wearing the most delicate Japanese kimono—"

"I did! It was my favorite that I still keep in my possession. So you really were there. How marvelous."

So, he was there. So were a thousand others! I wanted to give him the proverbial boot sending him upstairs, but he must have evoked something fatherly in Q, for she squatted down as no empress would have done and helped him to his feet.

Putnam shook straight his wooden foot, undoing a mechanical kink, and he dragged Q along across the dim room to a spider-webbed corner. On a dark shelf, Putnam fumbled and found a bound volume.

"Margo's Confession!" the man said excitedly. "A beloved nurse who has since passed. What isn't recorded often finds its way into Margo's entries, may the Lord bless her soul. She had always wanted to be a poet, you know."

Putnam opened the diary to the pages of April in the year of 1885. The first few entries were dry accounts of the diarist's busy days shouldering her responsibilities as a ward nurse at Union Hospital. Then came the pertinent entry:

> On this bleak night, I was awoken by our young doctor pounding ever so hard on my flimsy door. Though I had just returned from a thirteen-hour shift, with my heels sore from standing and running, I leapt out of my bed. The young doc told me he had an urgent case of a dying woman, this time one of our own, the daughter of a Congregational Church pastor.
>
> I ran as fast as my old feet could along the hallway.

One cannot imagine how much running we do here, from bed to bed, from one ward to another. Union is only peaceful from its outer white facade: nothing is at peace here except the departed in the back wing.

It was crowded in the triage room. Armed clergymen guarded the hospital's front gate, and grim-looking women chirped like morning birds, flitting about, crowding corridors. Amidst it all was a tall and handsome man, the pillar of the congregation and my dear and darling H.

On the gurney a young thing was covered with her own blood soaking her dress. Her father stood holding his begrieved wife, a pretty woman of little charm. Acrimony would seem untimely for one in despair, but she deserved it. She had once given me a cold stare and curt words after I had fainted in her husband's arms during a citywide rally to condemn the Chinese occultist named Wang Dan, who had abducted Reverend H's only daughter. We had been protesting, also, against the American legation and the Manchurian Royal Court for having done little to intervene in this matter of life and death.

I am already blushing as I compose this entry, seeing Reverend H. You see, we were lovers, thrown together by chance and loneliness. This town could make your heart so hollow at times.

That particular noon rally, while he had been freshened by our rendezvous, I had become weak-kneed and wan after the sweaty exertion, thus falling faint in his arms to be witnessed by his sour wife. The wife dressed me down with her sharp tongue by uttering, "Next time find someone else's arms to faint in."

But enough said about H and me. The word was that
H's daughter had not just been abducted by the Chinese
occultist, but raped and impregnated by him as well. . . .

Upon reading these words, I nearly fainted.

Could this be the same H, as in Hawthorn, the progenitor
of my darling Annabelle? Could this young patient on the
gurney, under Margo's pen, be my very own heart and soul?

My bleeding Annie, my wounded Annabelle! I trembled
like a shaken sieve while urging my dewy eyes further along
the rows of scribbling ink. Even though Q and the incapacitated hospital administrator were near and reading the pages
as avidly as I, it seemed as if I was alone with this vital account
recounted in this precious volume by one sinning nurse.

And for that duration of time before the eventful night
in the hospital I am describing—dark wintry months—
H suffered much and alone in the confinement of his
attic. He became a fugitive of delirium and despondence.
He was never whole again no matter the tenderness and
love I offered. The few times he sought me, as he always
did in times of trial and uncertainty, he seemed lost, not
in ways of our intimacy but in ways of his soul.

He was vengeful, brooding over an ugly outcome—
his daughter's pregnancy. He was bent on purging the ill
seed of Wang Dan from his daughter's young body, and so
anguished that he even dared suggest that I slaughter the
bastardly life, concocting a scheme to have her drugged by
a devout herbalist parishioner and dragged down to a crypt
beneath his chapel to have me cleanse her young womb

with a knife or pessary. Bitterly I rejected his request. But today, as I watched H's daughter nearly die on the table in the pains of childbirth, I wondered if this had been the right decision.

The young surgeon was able to do what needed to be done. A cesarean birth was skillfully conducted, and mother and daughter were saved. Before the young mother opened her eyes again, fate was decided for the newborn: she was to be declared stillborn and the secret kept from the mother forever. The child was to be given to no other than my old friend, Prince Qiu, whose sterility has long deprived him of an offspring. Such arrangement would not only resolve the headaches of H, who knew nothing of the infant's placement, only knowing it would be rightly taken care of, but it would also dissolve the knot of international political intrigue. Yet for days and days afterward, guilt consumed me so, until I could no longer contain myself. In a moment of weakness, I sent the young mother a secret note laying bare all the facts about her child. . . .

With that, ladies and gents, my damnation is complete, and the circularity of Annabelle's curse perfected. There is no hell hot enough for my ruffian self.

How could you have entrapped me so, my Annabelle, dangling me by such a thin rope of entanglement? How could you have misled me so in the path of my passion and lust?

As our sedan squeaked in this fading light, I told the child of your heritage—of you whom I had so loved, of whom I had sought near and far—of her father, that rebel who had sired her.

I had anticipated a rash reaction, but Q took it as facts of life, myth or not, blaming no one, cursing none. She was as open as a clear sky, as accepting as a quiet sea.

"You are a madman, are you not?"

I nodded.

"Are you glad you found me?"

I nodded again.

"I must find my father," she said as if to herself, before leaning on me with her eyes closed.

As darkness fell upon the silent city of Peking, I realized that Annabelle was my captain, I her ship. She had brought me here, but for what reason?

Oh, Annabelle, what am I to do with your forsaken heir, loving her so?

21

For days I languished in a gray mood. Fog surrounded me even on the clearest of summer days, and all senses and sounds were muffled and blunted. I felt detached from all that held me whole, living in a cocoon, owing no one, owning nothing.

Such mood was worsened by the absence of Qiu Rong, that girl fathered by my fate. How I longed for her, though with a new kind of love dawning on me, an unfamiliar kind, not of lust but perhaps fatherly.

All her previous seductiveness became memories of childish charm perceived not from the prism of a perverted eye but of a doting yet possessive parent. Her giggle was no longer a cooing love call but the call of a bibbing tot, her coyness that of a teething infant. I was sorrowful for that forsaken child, mournful of her motherlessness. In the fog, a path was cleared. In the gray, a sun broke through.

No one has stood as I did now in this far fringe of time and apogee of space serving as that which binds man to heaven, acting as a conduit between real and ethereal, light and dark. And so I am the seer, chosen to answer that heavenly call.

This was neither lunacy nor madness. I had found her, my dead lover's lost child, without a map, a lantern, or a fancy occultist's torch. All that led me to my find was my pitiable and improbable love, the air and water sustaining this bedraggled interloper, and nothing more.

When Qiu Rong returned, summer solstice anewing, she came to me with a lilt in her gait, the surrounding palace all hushed. In that tunnel of silence, in she strides, my jade princess, pale in a tangerine dress like a wedge of sun in motion, the hem riding her abstemious calves. Her hips were fuller and shoulders rounder, no doubt the consequence of rich food and inactivity: seven days of opera watching with the dowager and her Court retinue. Her eyes were darker and deeper with angst and anguish. Could you have been love stricken too, my child?

She halted briefly, her swan neck tilting adoringly, blond pigtail swinging over one shoulder blade. Then she hopped over the threshold, running through my hallow atrium, her gait lithe like a deer's, before flinging herself into my trembling ape arms. Wretchedly she weakened me with her parched lips and quivering hot tongue.

In broken murmurs, she uttered, "You horrible big, big wolf," as she wolfed me down. Mutely I held her, my treacherous hands caressing her nymph buttocks, my desperate fingernails unable to help digging deep into her taut and silky skin. She stood barely to my chest, her hair smelling of summer crushed weeds and morning fresh leaves. Her neck tasted of stale sweat and coarse fragrance.

Carefully I lifted Q up, leaning her face over my shoulder as a father would of his napping child. My toes kicked up my squeaky stairs, my footfalls, lithe like a thief's, echoing faintly along the empty villa . . . In-In had bargained for a leave to tend an aging, ill servant of his village. Gently I put her down on my bare bed, enshrining her within the white mosquito net.

I was about to fetch tea when she gripped my hand and asked, "You do love me, don't you?"

"You have no idea," I whispered, my voice trembling.

"Then don't leave." She pulled my pajamas off, discarding them at my feet, and imbibed my scepter in her quivering mouth.

22

My imperial pupil donned a green suit, Q's wedding gift to the groom two barren years back. It was of Austrian tailoring, with a broad chest and pinched waist and a short collar, making him look the part of a Continental esquire, complete with wingtip shoes.

"I have important matters to discuss. Can we have lunch in your study?" was all he said before our class in geometry. It was one of S's favorite lessons, after the "Introductory Parliamentary Politics" course, which had only been allowed after a lengthy array of approval and disapproval among many an invisible imperial adviser, and after three changes of course title.

The emperor was quite excited when I showed him the drawings I had rendered in my spare time of a circular lily pond, bricked squares, triangles of curvy roofs, and the octagonal Taoist compass, linking learning to reality. He rubbed his hands, as if seeing these objects for the first time. "You mean to say that all these sciences are inherent in what surrounds me right here under my roof?"

"And more. Your ancestors excelled in making things that have long been imitated and mimicked by all abroad."

"Name one such mimicry."

"Cannons derive from the basis of Chinese fireworks. Also compasses, which came from China, now needle north on all ships. There are many other things."

"Such as?" S's eyes shone with an intense light so typical of youth, the kind of light only possible when the early morning sun was shining at its best.

"Noodles, what the Romans had borrowed and remade into pasta."

"Yes, yes, the trade of that monk named Marco Polo. Qiu Rong gave me pamphlets explaining his exploits, her very first present to me among the many she brought from the ocean lands of her father's diplomatic tour. That Marco fellow, though much noted, I found to be a self-grandiosing trumpeter of sort, who touted himself as a friend of the Court though there were no traces of his presence or record of his involvement in any of our Court proceedings. I have searched all over, spending days in the Treasure Wing myself, searching for proof of his claims, any which would have pleased me so, but there is none. A fraud he must be then, writing books about land he possibly never set his Roman foot upon, telling tales he must have heard from those who made them up in drunken stupors on ships that once docked far off our land. Fairytales they all are. He is, for my worth, a fraud. Now what do you say about those noodles?"

"I, too, have read his writing in his original Roman language."

"And you are impressed by him?"

"Not at all. I, too, have found him to be stretching things a bit, only for the purpose of making others believe."

"Stretching things a bit." My pupil laughed rather shrewdly. "You mean like those noodles he had purported to have imported into his land, which anyone with flour could think of making? No one, even the most foolish of men, would eat the wheat or barley raw rather than making them into some shape, some form. All I am saying is this man is a fraud: Romans had no need to learn noodle making from our ancestors, as our ancestors had no need to learn such from another land, another race."

"I am sorry that I brought him up."

"No, I apologize. I meant no offense."

"We are having an academic debate."

"Then noodles we should have for lunch to end this debate."

His anger, as it turned out, wasn't triggered by any hearsay about the secret trip to the hospital with Q, which I had little doubt was within his knowing. What I knew about him was that he picked his battles, as dictated by his moods and fancies.

While waiting for the meal, I wrote a poem for Q, whom I missed, whom I craved.

Pond is dry
Save for its tears.
Tree is dead
Save for its roots.
Dripping . . .
Rotting . . .
Dying . . .
Wishing . . .

A little North Soong Dynasty verse, pensive and nearly feminine, but every bit Pickens, dripping with foolishness.

When ready, the team of chefs and servers who, as usual, accompanied His Augustness for the sumptuous lunch, were sent away. Lunch customarily encompassed one hundred traditional Manchurian dishes and plates symbolic of status, mostly serving as sacrificial food, as if he were a deity needful of daily prayers and offerings. All such dishes— fatty goose, fried pigskin, leaping carp, et cetera—were to be made fresh, and the uneaten or half-eaten portions were to be ladled out to this servant or that official as gifts that cannot be refused and must be eaten, giving the receiver an unspoken ranking of favor to be gauged by the day and seen by all since such list of giving is routinely recorded in the *Daily Gazette*, the Court daily.

After sending away the traditional retinue, all we were left with was the service of In-In, who carried a tray out with two bowls of ginger noodles garnished with two pieces of fatty duck breast swimming in chicken broth.

Among the slurping sound of consumption, S began, "There has been an enormous deficit in our coffers that I was informed of by the palace Neiwufu, which is their way of spurring me to increase provincial taxes and terrestrial levies. But knowing of the famine going on in my ancestral Manchurian land, and the plague sickening the south, and the floods drowning half the farmlands along the southern coast, and the warring southwestern regions bordering Burma and Laos, how can I?" He twirled his lengthy noodles around his chopsticks before feeding himself such, swallowing quite delicately with his mouth closed. A burp was suppressed to impart his next sentence. "I need to augment your duty to supervise over the Neiwufu, that den of thieves, with an increase of this sum of wages." He shoved over a piece of writing authenticated with a red seal. The sum of six thousand tael in total. Sufficient for a ministerial secretarial post at Court, bearing the second degree in authority, namely, the rank of Mu Yan.

Anyone under the sun, the Manchurian sun, that is, would have forfeited his firstborn for such a salacious fortune, whether he was of the elite literati and someone who had jumped hurdle after stringent hurdle to prominence, or he was just an everyman with a litter of ten to feed . . . but not this bloke. The duty to supervise such a group of imbeciles would be tantamount to suicide. I remembered the story of the concubine, with her body violated and her baby cut from her bleeding body. If the Neiwufu didn't kill you, you would soon wish yourself dead; just being near the Neiwufu, who made their living on ways of deceit and trickery, would make any sane person fill with suspicion and doubt.

A selfless official had previously vanished from his home only thirteen days after his assumption of such supervisory duty. Another had died of fatigue and inexplicable ailments, coupled with advanced age. But the emperor made no mention of such.

When I pointed this out, he explained it away as follows.

"You are different. You are not one of us. You don't have much to lose"— Besides my life? —"in the way any subject of mine could be subject to."

"How am I different?"

"You are an ocean man, with your legation only a wall beyond."

"That doesn't make me feel safer."

"You will have as many guarding you as you deem proper."

"I haven't come for this—"

"But you have come, and I am in need of your service."

"I will have to think about it."

"You will have plenary power," he added.

"Power isn't—"

"It's an order, sir," S said in a firm voice. After a pause, he added, "And you shall have Qiu Rong at your disposal to aid you."

I lowered myself to my knees, taking the honor few deserved or desired.

23

I was ensconced inside my silken quilt, nursing inti‹
mate thoughts of just and reasoned encounters with Q for
the days to come when a bedside candle flickered without
any trace of a breeze, its flame imminently snuffed as if some
stealthy fingers had intruded pinching it dead.

In the darkness, my hand was suddenly twisted as if a
mighty claw wrenched my palm; another yanked at my dig‹
its, giving me excruciating pain.

"For heaven's sake!" I rolled off my bed in a haphazard
manner, trying to untangle myself from this invisible invader,
tossing around the floor, cursing and pleading all at the same
time as if there were a genuine foe. Such disturbance inevita‹
bly awoke my faithful servant, who dashed up the stairs with
lantern in hand, inquiring, "What has befallen you, Master
Pi‹Jin?"

I yelped, shaking my right hand, the one still caught by
this invisible strength. "Let go of me, you cursed devil."

"Is it a ghost you see?" In‹In asked. Undaunted, he shone
his lantern around the chamber while spitting my way and
stomping his feet, his spittle cool on my skin. "Go away, ghost.
Go away or I will burn you to death." He swung the lantern
wildly at me while spitting another wet mouthful my way,

landing its stickiness on my forehead so that it hung on the cliff of my eyebrow.

The pain only worsened as the unseen hand bent my arm behind my back, thrusting me to a kneeling position while the other invisible hand savagely slapped my buttocks with a bony and cold palm, throwing me left and right like a pitiable altar boy.

My pleading ceased. The cold hand had done it right in front of my boy eunuch. What affront!

"Whatever you are, I fear you not, you devilish ghost." I uttered those agitated words while being swayed impishly and slapped limp, but my boy, In·In, wasn't in the least afraid. He went to do what, in his finest judgment, would be the ablest thing. Pulling up the hem of his maroon robe, with feet apart, he let loose a squirt of hot urine, dashing it all over me and my floor.

My invisible foe uttered, "Cloud onto your path," then fled, traceless, whipping out the window.

"Your urine?" I asked, lying limp, gasping gratefully.

"The village monk taught me so. The purest to douse out utmost evil." In the process of tying up his robe, he gave a glimpse of his undone manhood. No tree, just a field, plain and yielding.

"Did you hear her voice?" I inquired.

"No. What voice?" Laying down his lantern, In·In picked up a blanket to wipe me clean.

"A woman's voice. She spoke in Mandarin."

"Did she?" In·In asked calmly. "It must be Empress Jen, the one who comes off the wall painting within the Tenderness

Chamber. She hanged herself with her silk sash." In-In swept a glance around my chamber as if seeing her trace. "The one whose appearance always carries ill foreboding. The last time she appeared, our oldest stone bridge collapsed over Willow Pond, Grandpa's favorite of all Summer Palace bridges. The tragedy wasn't the collapsing bridge but the ten young eunuchs crushed and drowned to death while passing beneath it in a boat."

"Take me to the mural. I must see her face."

"But it is nighttime."

"We must go while her trail is still hot. Hurry." I clothed myself in a rush. I could still sniff a certain foulness or decay, a certain otherworldliness as if some raw corpse had been exhumed, not intentionally but by hands of theft; a certain dankness, thick with ghostly urge and degradation.

Two steps at a time I ran downstairs, following In-In's boyish figure made ghostly by his dim lantern. The darkness was complete: occasional lightning far off the palace wall charged the sky with fright; dogs barked as if joining a capacious earthbound symphony, dark and deepening in an earth devoid of melodic frogs, insomniac cicadas, and rancorous nightingales. We passed a peach grove, leafy with spiderwebs, entered a bamboo forest dampened from night fog, surpassed some squeakily perturbed pond-dwelling bridges, then ran along meandering cobbled paths.

"Where is this ghost chamber?" I asked, between shortening breaths.

"The back palace," In-In confided. "Don't you see the threads?"

"What threads?"

"It's trailing the ghost."

I strained my neck, quickened my feet, and caught a glimpse of a firebug-like drawing, as if the tentative hand of an aged and freckled watercolorist had sprinkled bright hues diluted by night. It encircled the roofs of the back palace, that dwelling of palace rejects: hundreds of chosen palace concubines who were to prime and perish within the walls where they squandered their short lives awaiting succinct days of glory when the lordly emperor, in name and in law a husband to them all, would be pleased by their womanly ways enough to salvage them away from misery by the gift of a son through their dark wombs. Some did indeed have their moment in the sun, noticed by a flippant emperor, but the shine of such attention could be a double-bladed sword causing them to die by way of poison or hanging rope: poison concocted by a devious empress; the rope noosed by a conniving eunuch's hands—the servile superiors outranking even the earthly lord himself in subtle power.

In pursuit of that flock of elusive firebugs, I scaled a stout wall after In-In's bidding lantern. Bugs and mosquitoes fenced the ill abode. Along the ivy-covered wall, In-In led me by the hand, passing one window after another until a doorway was found and its lock undone with a ready key hanging among others from his waistband.

The swollen door grudgingly opened into a tea chamber. A cloud of chilling air nipped at our toes like a multitude of hissing tongues, and the train of illusory firebugs broke into chaos, scattering and scaling over dank murals, curtained windows, and pale watercolors in scrolls and hangings. Suddenly the insects regathered themselves, this time onto the oil painting, canvassed and framed, forming them-selves into the shape of the mistress portrayed and then van-ishing into her, traceless and noiseless. In the shine of In-In's lantern, the canvas returned to a portrait depicting a gaunt mistress of ocean origin, toothy and mirthless.

"The Duchess of Vienna. A gift from Empress Qiu Rong to the dowager from her childhood days in that ocean land," In-In intoned.

"Why is the painting here in this chamber?"

"The dowager abhorred it and dispatched it here to be viewed by the palace women."

"Why did the bugs all vanish into this frame?" I asked.

"Look up." The boy servant raised the lantern. There, under an arching roof, was a ceiling beam with ferocious sym-bols of phoenixes and riling dragons. "See the groove?"

It was like a scar, roughened and chafed along the girth of the beam.

"The Hanging Beam, it is called. Three hangings in the four years I have been here in the same spot nearly always at night in spring: some sort of angst, beauties faded and glory ignored. Years in and years out, the only way of escap-ing palace life is to step onto the chairs stacked atop that tea table. All it takes is one kick . . ." His voice trailed off as if eulogizing his own end.

"What does it all have to do with this ghost? This chas-ing? The firebugs?"

"The dead here are truly undead, some living through the muralist's strokes on the wall, others crying through the cracks along the tiles; still others on the Tomb Sweeping

Festival have been seen swinging from this beam like frolicking children on a swing." He shone his lantern along the
length of the wall.

Murals wrapping the chamber depicted a daily scene
within the back palace of palace women in all manners of
domesticity: bending over needlework, cleansing crockery,
minding stone grinding, brush-painting scrolls making wishes
of longevity and good health, and in one, feeding an infantile
sovereign, the only child face drawn. Outwardly the faces
were all content and their postures without peril; inwardly
there was ennui and death.

"Their ghostly spirits have all sought solace through the
painted figures. By coincidence each of the dead possesses a
striking resemblance to a matched face in the mural, which
was said to be cursed from the outset. They say it seeks those
resembling living to die one by one in this very chamber. No
one knows how many more are to die under this roof."

"A chamber of ghosts?" I said with soft query.

"Though bothersome, none dare suggest having the chamber torn down or the wall recovered with other wallpaper."

Tenderly I touched the yellowed paper with my fingertips.

"What is intended is destined. It is better to let evil find
its way, venting the path."

"Who taught you to be such a seer, young man?" I asked.

"I was born with the gift. It would have made me a fine
fortune-teller or a monk, but palace life suits me just fine: one
lives in shadows. But this firebug vanishing was the first I encountered. Ghosts have come out of their respective portrait
but never as outward creatures."

"Is there a way to go inside this painting like the fire bugs?" I inquired.

Taking his lantern, I ran along the mute mural shining the light on the four walls seeking a hole, a dent, or a dimple, however narrow, to climb into or squeeze through.

"Master Pi Jin, we must go."

"No, I must . . ." I fell on my knees gazing intently into the portrait of the Viennese Duchess through which the iridescent insects had sought to nest.

Were they the incendiary spirit of that encroaching ghost who had flown through my window, invading my dwelling? What was it the ghost aimed to impart? Was it tragedy to befall or good tidings to ensue?

"Put out the light, Master Pi Jin. We've got to run: night guards are here," In In warned, dashing to my side to blow out the lantern.

"Why are they here?"

"It's the nightly ghost chasing so the palace will be calm. Our lantern must have alarmed them to come earlier." With that he hauled me out a back window before a guard's lantern could shine our way.

Was this my *gui su?* My tomb where, should I die, my Annabelle would relive? She had all but utterly faded since I came to know the truth. Don't ask me why. It could be the ill reasoning of this warped soul, an answer to an insufferable urge, an urge deserving death, for only death could end it all, without which I would pain forever. Or it could be that in the minuscule moment, while I was kneeling before the canvas of the Viennese countess, an ancient fragrance had infused my nostrils, permeating that inner tunnel, dizzying my head. What I sensed could be nauseating, a tad foul by a dull nose, yet dear and familiar it was to all my consciousness. It was a scent alike no ordinary scent, unique only to my Annabelle.

24

This day couldn't have begun more crookedly. First I sent back a four-man sedan for my use to assume my new post as Internal Inspector of the Neiwufu, choosing to walk the four courtyards west from my abode. The vehicle's sender was none other than the outfit's bulbous governor, the dean of the thieves' den—an unfair description for a helpless man at the helm of a hellish outpost. Yen Su, the governor, was a scholar in possession of two incongruous flaws: dedication and honesty. One could be afflicted safely with one or the other but not both.

The governorship had always been a nominal role, an empty pocket as it was known, with little power and less authority. The system of graft and grease was an intricate and delicate one, a grinding mill running on its own wheel that one so posted is less to govern than to be governed by.

Upon meeting Yen Su, bowing was the only formality I would stand for. Even a simple tea ceremony was refuted, pure and plain though it might be. Yen Su was a meek man with unsteady eyes, always searching, with a hunched back belaboring under an invisible weight. His diction was laborious and tone humble. His official costume was threadbare, his boots even showing traces of mending stitches. He was a man of frugality and timidity but futile and ill posted at best, the kind that immediately evoked my sympathy.

"Long I awaited you," was his sincere welcome. Profusely he apologized. All the while his eyes darted left and right as if minding the puppeteer shadow of his master behind a gauzy curtain. A man of his gutlessness should seek the serenity of an old temple rather than the business of ruling over the rulers.

A glimpse into his dossier would later reveal the choice and deliberation of his appointment: a handpicked man with a ninth degree of familial relationship to the chief eunuch, a shadowy man of power. Yen Su was an agent lured in intentionally to calm all waters for the thieves of the dry-land piracy. But meek though he might seem, Yen Su would turn out to be that agent of change and a thorn in the iris of his dispatcher; the meek man's revenge, one should say, for in the end that last grain of humanity, pride, always tips things over. Such was the case in point before us.

The initial meeting was only to be tea for three—me, Yen Su, and Q—to look over records of inventories and outlays. But trying to intrude among us was the jarring presence of a middle-ranked eunuch, Gong Sing, who insisted on sitting in for the duration. When I sensed his steam of hostility and discharged him, the hippo-headed nonman dared spit in my direction before stomping off muttering curses. Then and there I effectuated the first missive of my officialdom: ten planks of bare-ass beating.

Three days we spent reading files, cloistered within the suffocating archival chamber, elbow to elbow in utter absorption of our own perfumes; such heaving intimacy was a requisite to blindly deciphering the unintelligible scribbles done so as to mislead. One quickly concluded what was amiss. The palace, opulent as it might be, was running on empty, teetering on ruination, already drowning in insolvency.

Here is the simple arithmetic. The overgrown house⁄hold, numbering a staggering ten thousand, was outspend⁄ing its income by the ratio of one to ten. At such a rate the golden tiles up on the palatial roofs would have to be plowed down for auction just to survive another season of mindless consumption.

The left⁄hand side of the ledger, assets—perennial taxes and levies—seemed daunting, figured in millions of tael of silver and hoards of rare jewelry. But going down the same column, one detected numerous deductions at various ranks and levels of the empire: skimming by various and guberna⁄torial fiefdoms, which were all explained vaguely in more vol⁄umes of notations and annotations and charges with archaic references of debts owed and loans accumulated, which were buttressed further by boxes and boxes of loan agreements and debt pledges all readily signed off with the emperor's own seal. One searching for any clue and inkling was to cease at this regal point, and many before me probably did, but not this ocean man, who bore no affinity to the sacredness to this symbol of supremacy. Browsing through the yellowed and certified loan contracts, I quickly discovered the traces of trickery: the closing pages with the emperor's seal never matched the preceding pages of the said documents in color or in texture. It was certain that the majority of contracts had been falsified and fortified, with the pages bearing S's seal from utterly unrelated matters that the young ruler signed daily in the discharge of normal court business. The old practice of numbering those pages bearing the seals had long been abandoned. There was no telling what other mighty duties and authorities had been signed away in this manner. One shudders at such dereliction and treachery.

Inevitably, the intake would reduce itself into a trickle like an exhausted river, roaring initially but drying itself up traversing the deserts that drain the plains. One gazing at the dwindling course would only nod, not in agreement of such variance but in pity of the taxing length and rotting bends. But that was only the one-sided folly; the other was no less sinister.

The right-hand column listed outlays and procurements. The number had outgrown its counterpart of income by such a margin that it should have toppled over, head-heavy, long ago. The superfluous entries were sloppy and the falsehoods apparent, singularly prominent being the item succinctly labeled as a "legacy fee" additional to the price of products procured.

A verbal inquiry to Yen Su was tactfully referred to be answered by the head of procurement, a womanly eunuch with round shoulders and meaty lips who claimed that such a fee had preceded the current reign, thus was beyond the spur of inquiry or probe. Hence I ordered another round of plank beatings, which this hippy hippo bore silently, though blood seeped down his sockless ankles and bent toes.

Per the Court's procedural manuals, such refusal could be followed only by a written inquiry, which Q drafted and I duly certified and registered with the Neiwufu's Documents Chamber, an act that consumed three hours, no less. Three more days went by without a slip of explanation or affirmation. When I stormed into the chamber's courtyard, the door was shut with a notice hanging on the doorknob noting the incumbent having gone to greet the ruler, a cause that no man could question or doubt, for doubting such would be like doubting the pious, and doubting the pious was heresy to the sanctuary of this heavenly court thatched on this earth.

Q, my pigtailed empress, who always coiffed herself this way whenever passionately absorbed in matters demanding her full attention, ran this reported errand to the Court historian's chamber, finding no name of this document's officer at or near the emperor's chamber for daily briefing or court events. She found a terse note, however, from the Court's tool house indicating said official's use of a ten-foot-long fishing boat with fishing rods and nets on board.

The man had all but gone fishing, per order of Li Liang, the chief eunuch.

The court might be floating legless in clouds of inertia and the palace full of dereliction, but it lacked not scribes nor bards to record what tiny events took place in all the rat-holes of officialdom. It was the mandate that the palace be roamed with scribes, highly educated scholars who spent their days putting to paper whatever transpired. Powerless they might seem to be and prickly though they all were, that scholarly something prevailed no matter the locality. Partially it was their duty, a duty of allowing the world to see through their brushes—recording such for posterity and perpetuity, knowing well that no sane man would ever get to see what needed to be seen—and partially it was pure scholarship. They might be shadowy figures, slow moving, lurching along the

foot of the wall, carrying a satchel over their shoulder containing the four treasures of gentlemanly study—brushes, an
inkwell, rolls of rice paper, and a weighty ink ingot, which
an ink boy would grind to the purest satisfaction—but they
were the only creatures here with any self-respect and dignity. They were men of words upon whose honesty and truth-
fulness the empire lay. Such men were often threatened with
beatings by those who wished a certain recording erased or
a certain course of events posthumously altered, yet such
beatings, or threats of such, rarely daunted this class of thin-
framed men. Little doubt, such was the case from the first
dynastical history when it was always the poets and philoso-
phers who were said to possess the liver and gall, not the mercenary generals or dictatorial rulers, heavenly though they
might be.

Why the sudden ode? I am merely one of them, brush
in hand, truth at heart. Always the truth: it's what endures,
what lasts.

That little footwork of Q's led us to take an excursion to
a puny pond where the document official was said to be fishing this drizzling day. The northerly pond claimed a calm
boat but not the derelict fisherman. A lesser man would have
ceased once the trail grew cold, but the stirred gossamer only
added fuel to my burning stove.

There were wet footprints fanning off the shore, and some
trampled weeds, dandelions, and forget-me-nots, pointing
mute fingers at a mystery to unfold. It would surprise no one
that he had been killed one way or another, but to drown in
this lake wouldn't be a wise choice. Grandpa wouldn't care
much for that. More would have to die for the pall it would

cast; therefore no one dared die within the Forbidden City. Someone was playing a game here.

By noon I had eased up to the office of Yen Su, the dean of nothing, an officialdom of nil, and found him asleep, snoring in his armchair, much tea drinking wasted on the dozing man. I meant to yank his moustache, waking him, but his eunuch took a step ahead of me and rocked the frail man to his senses. Yen Su's ignorance was unmatched, failing even to recall the name of that absent inferior, though he did aid me by obtaining the address of the official's residence in Tartar City.

The door to the documents office could be smashed. Q suggested such—we were quite a pair, Beauty and her odious ogre. But what was locked couldn't be unlocked through oak or mahogany: it was his mouth that we must unclench so secrecy could be spilled and frauds traced.

I sought a rickshaw off the obscure western gate, sharing the ride with my courteous Q. The rickshaw boy, head shaven and bare-chested, mistook us for an envoy belonging to the legation boulevard and bargained for double fare: an ocean man was a devil's man deserving to pay a devil's due in this metropolis. To be here was to endure. Double fare I paid, and in return I urged the boy for a speedier run not by the broad streets but via the venous lanes and meandering fareways among dilapidation and ruination that abounded in this city of decay.

Tartar City was the residential enclave of Manchurian nobles. Each avenue was lined with mansions surrounded by tall walls, hawthorn trees, and poplars. The residence of my current pursuit was an object of beauty and grandeur. North

Road 13 was located three houses down a leafy lane across from the residence of a French artillery merchant, a Monsieur de Segur, which Q recognized from a prior visit, bachelor Segur being the heart of gaiety for all occasions among the condensed expatriate crowd.

Balefully I eyed the document official's house. What bountiful reward for employment that paid an annual wage of three hundred tael of silver, which, while a substantial amount, would barely put the roof on this estate. The wall was made of green stone from far mountains, and the arch gate featured two prominent columns, formerly the trunks of some ancient redwoods, flanked by two sedate stone lions carved with the most exquisite craftsmanship and liveliness. The green wall of secrecy allowed one to see a glimpse of some garden peonies in bloom and a partial view of a pond floating with lotus flowers. A knock on the door begot no reply.

The rickshaw was stepped on as a ladder and the wall climbed. A tree connived nearby, and with a nimble lunge and hop I was on the ground, noiseless as a neighbor's cat. Rare was the sight of a mansion without a fashionable Indian servant, turbaned and stiff; even rarer was the silence of the manse, no servants charging forward or barking dogs afoot.

The door to the main hall was ajar, the fragrance of incense seeping through. A soft nudge later I was in. Greeting me was a dead man hanging from an ornate roof beam, rope taut and slender. His tongue had slipped out and the rope had cut beneath his jowl. His blood was still fresh, dripping down his broken neck and white-shirted chest, but life had departed: there was serenity to death gained only through finality. Beneath his feet was a toppled chair and a ring of incense burning, ashes aground.

It seemed like the parting rite of a man in despair: the circle of incense representing the cycle of lives, leaving one to reenter another in endless ripples and rings enlarging one's soul. But such a rite would entail much forethought and surely requisite fasting, for one never was to enter passage to the beyond while intentionally carrying what was disdained and to be forsaken in one's intestines and bowels. Our documents man seemed to have consumed a bellyful of meat for lunch or breakfast; some had upchucked onto his shirt, evidencing the residue of lamb sausage dotted with red pepper among the splashes of his own blood. The blood under his finger‑ nails bore the signs of struggle, and that wincing door ajar confirmed my claim. No genuine suicide would be conducted with an unlatched door, giving way to a possible middeath foil. I would know: I had tried a handful of times.

I had intended to shield my child away from the gore, but Q slipped by me. "He's dead. Finally!" she said, circling the corpse.

"Why 'finally'?"

She picked up the fallen chair, and stepping on it, leaned forward to examine the dead man's eyes, squinting her own. "He was good at deducting my monthly stipend, stealing a tenth of my share. I had to threaten him with bodily harm to get my share back."

"What are you looking for?"

"They say a dead man's eyes capture the image of the last person he sees."

"See anything?"

She frowned, sticking out the tip of her tongue. "No, nothing."

"Who would want him killed?"

"Many." She spat on the ground. "This rope was never far from his neck." Q spun him around like a slab of slaughterhouse meat and hopped off the chair. "He simply knew too much."

Being a eunuch was a lifelong devotion entailing one to serve his master until his last breath. Many did indeed accumulate much wealth and even mightier power, but rarely did they win the privilege to use it. They were the sacrificial lambs, chosen by their clan, and taken in upon the recommendation of a palace eunuch related by blood.

I had once glimpsed a page from In/In's diary tucked under his pillow in his absence to tend to an ailing servant, a distant uncle from his village. Therein he had jotted a line that illuminated it all: *"One pearl, a hundred acres of rich land; two pearls, an eternal glory to all but I."*

Pearls, in this reference, pertained not to jewels but the treasures of men. In/In had, in rare revelation of a true self, boasted of having an uncle, his father's youngish brother from the third wife of his octogenarian grandpapa, who had attained the rank of eighth grade officialdom in the basaltic country of his origin because of In/In's Court service. Such, though, was to be dwarfed by the august post held by the cousin of the chief eunuch as an inspector general of salt trade within his province, salt being white gold from the endless sea that would reward the cousin with a staggering monthly income of ten thousand silver tael, of which three quarters entered his uncle's pockets.

A quick search around the dead man's echoing chambers yielded the only piece of evidence that at first had eluded my eyes.

"What fragrant theft this is!" Q asked, pointing at a silk scroll hanging on his bedroom wall, consigned not to the lowly official but to Yong Le, the beloved early emperor of the Ming Dynasty, by four famous calligraphers.

"They are still the only four styles to be imitated and copied by the most adamant of learners hundreds of years after their originators' passing." Jumping off the stool, Q carefully took the scroll down from a rusty nail. "It was dedicated to Emperor Yong Le on the fourth anniversary of his ascendance, a fete much lorded in the annals of Court celebrations, shaming all that came afterward. Even Grandpa still mentions it as the yardstick to adhere to. *The fourth had this and had that,*' she would say, alluding to this event. Thousands of guests were invited, among whom were generals and officials, but more important, painters and calligraphers, poets, and even some poetesses. It was a fine autumnal day. Long stretches of desks were laid out on vast courtyards, and thousands were urged to wet their brushes and spread their rice paper putting their poetry to the scrolls. This scroll of four seasons, with each artist's brushing in the characters of such, was the brightest gem from that day, and here it is in the soiled hands of a thief."

"With this we'll singe the entire rotten Neiwufu," I declared. "Let's return to the palace so we can seal and search the Treasure Chamber immediately."

"Why the hurry?"

"Once the word is out, they will try to cover their traces."

Q produced an expedient dagger and cut the hanging rope, letting the dead man fall. "Never leave a hanged man hanging. His ghost will haunt us all."

The sun was setting, and the city of Peking was all gray shadows, urging onward the throng of people heading south before the city gate closed. The punctuality of the gate closure was notorious. Those locked within would be torturously inspected and put away in the night jail as thieves or rioters. Such stringency made no exception for Court workers or royal affiliates. Even the dean of the potent Neiwufu was not exempt, riding his sedan bent on the path home. It was under the Valor Gate that we detected his sedan and intercepted him. The scholarly dean was not the least stirred by the death of his inferior. All he cared for was beating the closing gong: the first strike was for warning, the second strike announced the gate's closing, and the third and last strike marked its locking; then night ensued with the city sequestered.

Unwittingly I ordered him to return to the palace to hunt for the killer.

"Killer?" He learned toward me, frowning. "What killer?"

"The man who ordered him hanged."

His anger was sudden and surprising. "How dare you utter this ugly inflammatory word in my face? Here is the key to the Documents Chamber, a thing that I have always kept close to my chest: something you should be careful not to misuse. You have one night and one night only to clear this matter or indict the dead man; then all ugly and unsubstantiated talk of murder shall cease when I return in the morning."

Onward the harried man vanished, dusk in his wake.

25

It surprised me not at all that word of the death had outrun our feet. By the time we reached the Neiwufu's outer gate, a pair of Court marshals were waiting for us, their hands clutching an order from Grandpa herself demanding our presence in her chamber immediately.

Grandpa was bent over her writing desk, brush-painting calligraphy onto a rolling scroll, accompanied by her ink man, Li Liang, the chief eunuch. Having risen from the modest rank of palace woman—over five hundred of them—she was uncharacteristically known to have mastered the high art of ink and brush, having a special penchant for painting such characters as *longevity* and *harmony*, gifts that she doled out generously to admirers and visitors alike. The brush painting was, to her and others, a mental tai chi one does for relaxing tense nerves and sore bones, akin to a warm cup of rice wine or a doleful puff of opium.

Without stopping the brushing at hand, she said in her thin-throated piercing voice, "I heard of that official's hanging. You need not burden me with the details. It's unfortunate he has done himself in. I heard that you have been poking around the Neiwufu's offices and chambers and that was the cause that drove the man to his unfortunate death. Do you know what you are doing?"

When Q asked to be allowed to reply, she was duly hushed by Grandpa, who cast her slanting gaze at me and continued, "Tell me, what are you trying to do? To disturb the nests of all the birds here?"

"We are merely acting on our great ruler's direction," said Q rather timidly.

"I heard of that too. You know his words are not to be relied on. He has his good days and bad—you should know better. When I first met you, you were far wiser, taking my advice to aid him, acting as a bridge between me and his Court. That's why I made you an empress, hoping you would give me a roomful of heirs. But no, you changed your colors like a chameleon, leaning on your own whims that at first seemed rather charming to all. Then you began to mislead him, knowing him to be gullible and foolish. Did I blame you? No, I let you do what you two wished. I can only watch and hope, praying to my ancestors for wisdom and enlighten, ment." She dipped her brush in the inkwell, then returned back to the scroll, crafting a perfect dot to end the stanza of Tang Dynasty poetry she was copying.

"But that man did not kill himself," Q persisted.

"See?" Grandpa uttered with annoyance. "There you go again with your foreign tongue when I'm not done talking. Didn't your adoptive father teach you anything at all in those barbaric ocean lands?"

"Yes, Grandpa, he did."

"I would not say so. Now tell me, why would anyone want to kill that cursed man? And why would you try and blame someone else when no ground was found for your assertion?"

"He left no note about killing himself, and the door of

his house was left ajar. There was also blood under his nails though no scratches were found on his person, hinting at a struggle with those who concocted to have him killed."

"Nonsense, you fool!" Grandpa set her brush down and pounded the desk with her fragile fist, making the inkwell and rice paper leap. "How did you come up with such absurdity? First, you accuse the entire Neiwufu of stealing. Now you call them murderers? No one is a killer here except you two. Your inquiry pushed him to his death. You two are the murderers! A man can endure only so much. You gave him no way out."

"We only asked to see the files and ledgers."

"Files and ledgers? Don't you know those files and ledgers contain essential palace secrets? How can we let this mere ocean man see such contents of confidence? The world would soon know." Grandpa cast a cold glare in my direction.

She did not mince words, that old witch!

"He is acting only upon our ruler's order, checking on the Neiwufu to sort out the reason for this great deficit. This palace is running on empty, far outspending its intake. I was schooled in Austria in the science of mathematics and was involved in the bookkeeping at my father's embassy. I want to help our emperor account for things that may or may not be the fault of anyone so that this palace might have a healthier fiscal well-being."

"Gibberish! Your foreign schooling may have been good, but you have put it to the wrong use. Our young emperor is not better off because of your education. I would say he is worse off because of your wild influence. As for the deficit within this Court, much of it has to do with your free spending: *your* horses and foreign motor bikes. The blame should start from the very top. You should put a stop on your expenditure. You used to give me gifts of things you fancy. Now you don't even think of this old lady who championed for your admission into the palace."

"It was your sour words of criticism that have driven me away."

"Sour words are only words that are true. They are sour and biting because I speak wisdom that glided by your ear-drums unheeded, which failure for certain would have you endure the bitterness of my wrath. Don't you know the em-peror is, after all, my son? That soft-hearted deviant of mine wasn't even weaned off my breasts of wisdom yet, and there you came along taking him away from me while I had wished to bring him closer to me."

"I shall do my best to right the wrong," Q said, stricken.

"So you have said many a time. You break all pledges easily, shaming yourself again and again. I have my eyes and ears—your trip to the Union Hospital and other things. I am watching you two; you had better be careful."

"Yes, Grandpa." Q bowed deferentially.

"You must cease this investigation this very moment," Grandpa said, resuming her writing.

"But what about the death of this man? Someone killed him!"

"Self-killing is a way of peace and resolution. It's nothing new. Talk of 'murder' will stop immediately. I am giving his family a sum to soothe them and a plaque of honor for eter-nity. He died not in vain but for the palace. It is an honorable death, self-imposed or not, a worthy death—something that you have yet to learn or understand. This is called devotion, utter devotion. Now I need to retire. You are excused. No more probing until further words from this chamber."

"But here, look at this." Q presented the scroll confiscated from the dead man's house. "This is the most precious scroll handed down from the Emperor Yong-Le. It was hanging on the bare wall of this eunuch's residence, who you said had taken his own life."

"Now you see? He *did* have reason to hang himself. He was a thief."

"Thieves are everywhere here. Can't you see?"

"Cease on this matter. Such is my order." She waved her wide sleeves, and the chief eunuch saw us off with his cold, unblinking eyes, a de facto husband to the old and frail dowager, trusted to the point of impunity, giving the man, or rather, the partial man, utter license for abuse and misuse. His words became her thoughts, her urges his action.

The death of the documents official didn't stir our emperor a bit, though the news did cause a wincing tic on his left cheek. He fumbled for his sea-tree smoking pipe, and a pinch of opium was produced from the velvet bag that he kept at his bedside. Only after a puff was drawn deep into his lungs did he look up to gaze at us with a thoughtful stare through tusks of fortifying smoke. "Don't stop now," he said, "or death will come our way. You have the night to look through the books. For sure, it'll all be sealed off by daybreak tomorrow." Another puff down his throat and he continued. "You know what I found out?" he asked whimsically. "A cousin of mine is secretly being groomed. Another court is being set up, a shadow palace. Just a simple cut of my throat, and it will

all be theirs. Every bit of my existence will be destroyed."
He sighed, sucking in another mouthful. "Find proof for me:
proof of siphoning from all the tributes and attributes to
me . . . to this throne. Then we will cleanse the evil from our
ranks, one by one. You know that I am not her son. This is
all but an illusion, a house of matchsticks that could easily be
torched and reduced to ashes."

"But Grandpa has forbidden us to do any more searching."

"Grandpa." The emperor's eyes blazed with heated emotion. "That old witch! She had the documents man hanged.
She will have you wiped off the face of this earth. If you hesi-
tate, falter for even one minor step, we are finished."

"You are acting like a lunatic! What's gotten into you?"

"This." The emperor pulled a silk scroll from under his
pillow and let it fall onto the floor. Black letters were inscribed
onto its whiteness.

It was an advisory order from the chamber of his adoptive mother, officially called the Curtain Cabinet, imposed in
reigns when the emperors were young. Such devices were described in poetic terms as having a hidden cabinet behind a
draped curtain in back of the throne whereby the emperor's
mother could, sight unseen, whisper her cares and concerns
to the leaning ears of her young son. It was under such an
administrative arrangement that this present Court was established in the wake of the untimely death of Grandpa's
late emperor husband. The dowager's whispers bore constitu-
tional heft and were entered into the Court record as having
the potency of sovereign law.

This particular directive dictated that the young emperor, due to his waning spirit and lowering temperament,

had been advised to receive a series of visitations by prominent doctors in the course of the coming moon cycle, a time
that was determined to be healing and curative due to as-
trological calculations by Court priests. The order was given
upon advisement of faithful Court counselors and ministers.
The emperor was to take no exception to it. The physicians
were to be chosen and invited only by an exclusive commit-
tee headed by his adoptive mother, in whose loving heart
lay dear concern for her son, the sole and supreme ruler
under the sun.

"A few doctors' visits? Why should you be worried about
this?" Q said, tossing the silk order back to her husband.

"You tell her." S tilted his head my way.

Clearing my throat, I gave her this grave explanation.
"Each time an advisory is given, a prelude to a coup is set in
motion. One day you are seeing a doctor, the next day you
are given the requisite herbal treatment. The day after,
you are sent to the nut house. Such was the case of a minor
reign I read about in the otherwise glorious Tang Dynasty
when a young emperor under the Curtain Cabinet administration was jailed in a bloodless coup, not as a prisoner in
name but as a patient under his mother's care."

"Why would Grandpa encourage this? Is it because of
me?" Q asked, sitting on the edge of his bed.

The ruler shook his head and sucked another potent
mouthful, which seemed to aid the flow of his words. "It is
I, always, from the very beginning. I still remember the first
time she slapped her coarse palm across my cheeks; it was
the first night after I was 'adopted.' She, as you know, had
borne a son but lost him when he was fourteen from a weak

constitution, as they say. Not even a day after her own son's death, I was taken from my mother's nursing bosom. Late at night, when I craved another feeding and called out my mother's name, she slapped me hard and cruel. My lips were swollen for days afterward. Each time I cried for my birth mother, she would threaten to never let me see her again, and I never did see her again. She was said to have caught a cursed wind, and she died at the age of twenty-three. When I threatened to kill myself upon hearing this, Grandpa had me guarded for the longest time. When she caught me painting red color on my lips, she called me a girl, accused me of possessing womanly attributes, and had me savagely beaten so I would be cured of the weakling disease. She called me unfit for the future she had fostered for me and threatened to rid me of my testicles, making me a eunuch. It would have freed me. What I crave, what I yearn for, she aimed to have me cured by having you and others marry me." He leaned forward to kiss Q on her left cheek. "And you did cure me for a while. How I adore you. But what is in me is incurable, as incurable as my love for you. And you only made worse what she feared the most: tearing this palace apart, poking and disturbing the secret order here. But it is the only way I can rule this Court, this empire, by cleansing the dirt, the graft, the embezzlement. I have received letters through my own secret envoys that taxes and levies on the provincial levels have been increasing by leaps and bounds, but here, at my end, the figures have been dwindling. I warned Grandpa of this discrepancy, but she paid no heed to my finding. On the contrary, she accused me of setting up my own shadow governing cabinet to undo hers. But what I am doing is for the health of this empire and for her. She doesn't know that, for she is misinformed by those thieving minions headed by Chief Eunuch Li. Now she issued this to me. You have to hurry or death will come our way soon."

He drew another lungful of opium before sagging back onto his bed. "Go now. I need to rest . . . ready myself for tomorrow."

26

 Samples of grease and graft were numerous, yet all would pale against the tale of a fat goat. On the meticulous ledgers, a young fat goat would leave its bucolic grazing meadow, in this case a farm at the foot of the Western Mountains. The initial price for this goat, three months or thereabouts in age as appearing in the annotated lengthy appendix attached to copious ledgers, was a mere three copper coins, which already was twice the price for an average goat of same age, but the quote was reasonably heightened, for this goat was from no ordinary stock. This particular breed of goat, short-legged and furry, boasted unique layers of fat along its belly and around its hips. Its soupy brain and marrow, when sucked raw, was said to enhance the essence of men, prolonging life. Fable or truth, the myth persisted. But the fattening of this price had only just begun.

This innocuous goat had to be fleeced pricewise by first the farmer merchant governing the land upon which this goat had grazed, adding one copper coin to the original price of three coppers. Another copper coin was collected by the market master, the man who set the daily prices in everything from rice to rubies. Then another mysterious middle man acting as an agent for the Court would add on, at this time, two more copper coins for the same goat before another three coins were to be added as the entrance fee collected by the agency specialized in scrutinizing every item coming through the gates of the palace.

Right before our goat set its gingerly hooves upon the brick ground of the royal kitchen, another fee was again exacted by the royal butcher for his special rite of dressing, attuned to the flow of blood and spirit. This fee partially was necessitated because the service of a Taoist priest was needed to bless the goat.

All fees and charges along this crooked vine were manifested with ready proof of handwritten and dated receipts, the perfection of which only managed to trigger suspicion in this auditor. It's fair to say that the dead accountant had tried a tad too hard. After a night of poring over these falsified records, it became clear what the next step must be. A necessary visit had to be paid to those imprudent merchants daring to charge the Royal Court more, and not less, for the privilege of serving the mighty emperor. Logic would demand that they charge a reduced amount for the honor and steadiness of this daily business.

Figures and numbers don't lie, but accountants do. To see beyond their spidery veil one must put in legwork. Sometimes truth is only a thin paper away, as thin as the paper whence forgery is done.

Leaving Q to accompany her spouse for the compulsory consultation with the physicians lining up in his chamber, I made several short sojourns to the markets to spot-check the accuracy in the books and ledgers.

The Western Mountain goat farm was my first stop. The hilly road was rutted and the carriage ride arduous, consuming the better part of the morning. The thin proprietor of the fat goats was perturbed and stiff at first sight of this ocean man, but he quickly turned pliant upon my introduction as a buying agent for the foreigners in the city in search of safe meat. The Boxer Rebellion had destined all food supply for foreigners to be old and tainted, if not outright poisoned. Two Shanghai-dwelling Frenchmen had perished after consuming some local escargots, and another five had been poisoned after dining on some innocuous frogs.

The proprietor was a man of practicality. He offered undisturbed delivery right to the door of the legation's kitchens without the meddling fingers of the city's middlemen, thusly ensuring the quality of his goods.

"But how could you avoid the fingers of middlemen?" I asked, feigning concern.

The farmer owner sneered, stroking his goateed beard. "I have the wherewithal to sell to anyone without any of them meddling with my business—about the only privilege that comes with selling at a discount to the royal kitchen."

"Selling at a discount?"

"The chief eunuch there demands a deep discount so that his men in the city will keep their eyes and ears half-closed and let me trade freely. It's a steady business, so I don't mind."

"What is the price of a three-month-old goat then?"

"I will quote to you the same as I do the royal kitchen, but you have to keep it a secret between you and me. Times are hard. The Boxers are still out here in the country driving away those who could afford my goats."

"How much then?"

The goat farmer pulled out a ledger from the drawer and

pointed at an entry that he had marked with red ink. "Two copper coins per goat at the tender three-month age of breeding. But I have to write him a receipt for three coins."

"Why?"

"To make it worth his while."

"The chief eunuch's while?"

He nodded. "Exactly, and I could do the same for you so it'll be worth your while if you guide all the foreigners to my goat farm."

"But what if my auditors come around to check on our dealings?"

"I always keep two books, if you know what I mean. It's done everywhere. It's the only way of dealing with the palace. So how many goats do you need, and on which days do you want them delivered?"

"I am the auditor from the palace. You will hear from the Royal Court soon," I said, showing the gaunt man the emperor's mandate. But he was neither surprised nor disturbed.

"Get out, off my farm, you blue-eyed bastard! You don't scare me with this fake mandate. It's not worth my goats' pebbly droppings. You could buy this forgery for five copper coins. Get out!" The man called on his hounds, those long-legged mountain dogs with sunken bellies and narrow hips. A pack of three leaped and pounced on me, baring their fangs. Luckily they seemed intrigued by the perfumed jacket I was wearing, tearing at it furiously. I took it off, throwing it into their midst, and they fought over it till it was all threads and rags. Jacketless I escaped holding tight to my flimsy carriage door.

A quick stop at a pawn store where a green short-collared

wool jacket of possible Austrian origin was bought and put upon my back, and I was ready to carry on the rest of this auditing, notwithstanding the chafing of my neck by the stubby collar.

Next I poked my head into a cloth store with rolls of colorful fabrics covering the counters. The entire royal household, servants and palace women included, relied on this very store to replenish and upkeep their clothing. Thousands of bales of fabric were purchased from here, seasonably and annually. When asked about a possible discount to buy the fabric by the roll, rather than by the foot or yard, for the purpose of putting on a garden party to welcome a certain American dignitary, the bespectacled store manager puffed on his pipe and chuckled. "I don't give a discount to anyone. Business is hard and getting harder by the day with these Boxers still out in the woods. Even ladies of means have stopped coming to my store, and this is supposed to be the busy autumn season, when silk and satin is switched to cotton, wool, furs, and leather. Even the most fashionable ladies have stopped coming over. I could not give a discount. The cheaper I go, the less they value me."

"How about the discount you give to there?" I tilted my head toward the formidable palace wall seen off in the distance.

"The palace?" He shook his head with disdain. "Never."

"Never?"

"If anything, I sell to them at a premium."

"But don't you have to bow down to the eunuchs? You know, give them a ready discount to make it worth their while?"

He chuckled, bemused. "You are the only ocean man who really knows how things work here, but you are still an ocean fool. This store will never have to give a discount to the palace or anyone else. No middlemen can control me; no local government tax man can tax me."

"Why is that so?"

"Because this store is owned by the honorable Chief Eunuch Li, and I am his third cousin on my mother's side."

"Does he own any other stores or businesses?"

"Why do you want to know?" He put aside his pipe, suddenly wary.

I reached into my pockets, fished out two shining silver coins, and placed them onto his palm. He smiled and bargained, "Three more silvers and you need not tell me why you want to know."

Grudgingly I parted with another three—the sum of the weekly expense for a well-to-do house of four—and he readily made me privy to all the treachery and corruption.

"From north to south and east to west, there isn't a store along this square that Cousin Li does not own, in part or in whole. The lumber-and-coffin store he bought five years ago for seventy silvers; the grain store on that far corner for ninety silvers six years ago; the tea company that imports and exports various precious varieties he gained a quarter share of by force and was stopped from owning more only by the other owner, the sheriff of Peking; the paper company that also deals in art and antiques as well as calligraphy used to be owned by a rich woman, a widow who was forced to sell so that her son might be spared a jail sentence for failing to pay a levy unreasonably imposed upon them. You see, the paper business wasn't, still isn't, taxed because in the spirit of Confucius it encourages people to read and write and be civilized. So Cousin Li made up a levy to drag them through the court. In the end it was sold to a middleman, for appearance's sake, who in turn resold it to my cousin. I can give you tale after tale; it's no secret. In one case he even coerced an old man, the owner of the jewelry store, to adopt him so he could 'inherit' legitimately from the old man."

"You seem unhappy about all this."

"Unhappy? No one is unhappy. It's all right that I am telling you, a foreigner. If I tell anyone else, though, I will not be here for long. He would take care of me in a way one wouldn't want to be taken care of, if you get my meaning. Why do you think I am here serving him, running his business?"

"Yes, why is that?"

"You want to know everything, don't you? Here, have a drink of liquor." He grabbed a jar and poured a splash into a tiny cup that he drained first before pouring again for me. His face scrunched into a painful knot, all nose and bushy brows. "This wine came from his store as well, around the corner. Now, when one is prosperous, he should take care of his own, but this cousin of mine takes care of us in his own manner and way."

Another cup was downed, this time more smoothly. "He bought our entire village—the farming land, the orchards, temples, rivers, the road, even the county administration and the sheriff. He rented the land out to others and drove all our clan to the city to serve him on his terms. Some of us are fools, pleased just to be here. They are cows," he sneered. "They don't read or write—just cows and pigs. But some of us do. I read and write. I came here as well, after my land was bought up. I came here to open the wine store, and it was good business. I bought, I sold, minding my own business. Business expanded. I was into wholesale instead of just cups and jars. People from all over the northern plain come to me for their liquor and wine. Why? Because I bought the best from the best, and I didn't put water in my liquor or color it with dye. I was a good man minding my business. Then one day a man died in my store after drinking a jar of yellow wine, warmed as he liked it. He was a poet and a painter; his art was shown in the paper store. He used to sell, but not after he started drinking. He had quite a collection over there at Zhen's. He just dropped dead, vomiting up everything he had eaten that day.

"The sheriff came to the door accusing me of mixing poison in his drink. He was poisoned, but I knew I didn't mix my wine with anything—it was the purest and best, and I am a Buddhist. I don't kill people for coin. I was to be condemned to be hung, when Cousin Li came to my rescue. What a gracious rescue that was." He pinched up his wine jar and poured himself a long draught. "He laid out one hundred petty silvers to buy my company. In return, I would be a free man and he a new owner." Slamming the jar on his table, he wiped his foamy mouth on his wide sleeve. "He didn't even offer to allow me to run his store, my old business. I was a freed but bruised man. They beat me and hung me throughout my prison stay until I signed the deed over to Cousin Li. I could have used the silver to buy some land in another town or start a store somewhere else, but my wife fell ill, and the cost of the medicine and doctors took half of it. Then I had to spend the remaining half to keep my son from being drafted. In the end, my wife jumped into a well and my son went mad and soon died as well. All these misfortunes for what? It all began with my refusal to sell the wine store to him in the first place. I should have let it go. Now look at me, aged, hopeless, with nothing to call my own, working for the man. Have you seen his mansion? Bigger and mightier than any foreign legation's mansion. It's filled with old paintings and scrolls." He paused to gaze at me with an inquisitive frown. "Do you work for the legation?"

I shook my head.

"Do you know anyone who works for the legation?"

I nodded.

"Are you or your friends in need of some genuine treasures of art, fresh from the vault from the Deep Within?" He tilted his head toward the palace.

"What kind of art?"

"Any kind you could name, for a bargain. The kind that you won't see in the front of that antique store. The rare kind from the earliest dynasties, by the grandest masters." My feigned curiosity seemed to duly ease his pains and up his pecuniary acuity. "I could be your buying agent, helping you garner the lowest prices from the sellers."

"Who are the sellers?"

"Surely not the palace itself, you know what I mean?"

"But who?"

"You don't need to know. All items will be authenticated with legal documentation for your shipment through customs. You can be assured that you are dealing with legitimate merchants."

"Who steals from the palace?"

"I wouldn't put it that way, ocean man. The palace is a mess. They are running on a deficit, and much coin needs to be raised to offset their expenditure. Things are tight in there. Each sect and division within has their needs and burdens. Taxes and levies have all risen, but they are still insufficient to meet demand, so everyone who is anyone who can lay their hands on hidden treasures is channeling things out to sell. There's a saying around here: *'Even the blind could rob the palace.'* There is another rather humorous one; you somber foreign devils will like this one. *'What are you going to find in a eunuch's trousers?'*"

The question didn't amuse me a bit.

"Say something," he urged with a smirk.

I decided to play along. "Nothing?"

"No." He shook his head. "A gold ingot and two jade balls." He burst into uproarious laughter, resulting in a lengthy spell of breathless wheezing. "Isn't that funny?"

"Not in the least." I rose up to take my leave.

"Really, I could get ahold of some of the finest pieces in our history directly from the palace. I can show you a list of what they have there. You could pick what you wish. Look." He proceeded to open his desk drawer and proudly unrolled a lengthy handwritten scroll full of minute descriptions of all the items that could be ill-gotten from within the palace. It only took two more silvers to buy this list of theft off the man's grudging hands.

"Remember," he said, wrapping the scroll inside blue cloth. "Whatever you blue-eyed devils desire, it could be had for a price. There are few devils like you who can use our tongue and know the value of our treasure. You and I could really profit from it all. I am the insider, and you the outsider. We'll split our gain half and half. What say you? Hey, don't leave yet." Before he could finish his scheming, I had rushed down the stairs and out into the bustling street.

27

Q and her spouse were somber. The day's diagnostic audience with three doctors had produced three distinct illnesses, much to Grandpa's delight and the emperor's dismay. Any of the purported sicknesses, had he had them, would render him incapacitated by the year's end, invalidating his claim to power and begetting a precarious retirement.

As the wisdom of the medicinal trade would dictate, it was always better to find something than nothing. The first one called him a head case upon viewing his pale face, nearly bloodless, and he advised a serene isolation away from the vagary of daily Court affairs. The second one could find nothing wrong with him initially with much pulse feeling and needle pricking, only to later amend his diagnostic outcome with a severe case of impotency, which he claimed could be cured by strengthening his kidneys via the daily consumption of a set of pig kidneys to be supplemented with nightly spermatic exercise by pulling and massaging his testicular sac and tickling it with certain blackened spidery legs. The third physician declared that he had contracted a rare case of leprosy from his foreign-raised spouse, Q, that had duly sucked empty his basic masculine energy. The cure for it would come only from an excessive succession of lovemaking with the purest virgins, only after each woman's first menstruation, until such libidinous leprosy was diluted and drawn away by those unfortunate virgins, who would soon die of his illness. Uncured, his potency would wither, and he would slowly lose his appendages to certain rotting that would eventually infect his entire body, causing a pain-ful end.

"Foreign leprosy," S chuckled bitterly. "A medical novelty only Grandpa could invent. What a farce! It won't be long before the order for retirement will be given to banish all of us, you included with your American leprosy." The emperor glanced at me, his eyes dull and full of darkness. "Now what did you find that couldn't wait until tomorrow?"

"The cause for the deficit in the palace finances no doubt falls on one culprit and one only: the chief eunuch, Li Liang," I pronounced.

"That's a vague and vast summation," said S, raising one brow disinterestedly.

"The prices of all goods coming in daily to this Court have all been inflated to a great extent, sometimes by as much as quadruple the price."

"Is that because the goods commanded are singularly the rarest and of choicest quality?"

"No, your highness. It can all be blamed on one fact only: they all come from one source. The businesses and stores are owned by Li Liang, in part or in whole," I declared, present-ing a list of merchants and businesses, familiar names dealing with the palace regularly.

"It's no news that Li Liang is prosperous and owns many of the businesses that supply the goods to us. It's a guarantee that all that is supplied will be good in quality and that the supply will be smooth and unhindered."

"But he knowingly inflates the prices by creating layers of phantom middlemen, making it look right and sound proper, which in itself is fraudulent."

"All this might look onerous to you, the foreign lepers." S smirked at his own humor. "But this could be argued away by the chief eunuch. He is as slippery as the mossy rocks inside a manure hole." The emperor paused for effect, raising his other eyebrow this time.

"That is a saying he gleaned from reading the popular newspapers," Q murmured. "The newspapers that I bring in for him to read."

"Another offense on Grandpa's list that won't easily be forgiven or forgotten, you unrepentant ingénue," S said lovingly to Q as she huddled next to him like a cat.

"Slippery rock he might be, but he is evil to the core." I slowly unveiled the treasure list I had bought off the shopkeeper. "Do you know what this is? Do you even want to know?"

"Surely, what other shocking news could there be?" He reached out his hand for the scroll and casually glanced at the coarsely copied items. Perusing it more intently with a deepening frown, he asked, "This is the list of famed treasures from our ancestors' trove. How—?"

"Bought it at the market . . ."

"This is only known to a few," S said, smirkless now.

". . . for two silver coins."

"But why is this list out there?" He waved the list angrily.

"This is the list of treasures for sale. You no longer own those antiques."

"But I do. They belong to the Qing Empire."

"Not anymore. Someone has helped himself to all on the list. You, my emperor, have a big hole in your pocket. All of the men working here are minions of thievery with Li Liang as their head. This is your empire only in name. It is his empire in reality. The list was sold to me by his third cousin, one of many, forming a family of companies on his behest. The whole Tartar City commerce district is his empire reaching as far as customs in Tianjin and Shanghai. How do I know? Because his cousin told me. If I wanted to buy any of the items of treasure from this list, they could also sell me the proper legal documentation to go through customs without any complications. Either they have an alliance with the customs officers or with local government officials who can dole out the documents for coin. It seems the whole empire outside is working against you, with your mightiest opponent being the eunuch in your utmost confidence and trust."

"Now you are onto something, something vital to pin down that half-man. You foreign devils never fail, do you? Your tenacity!" The elated emperor landed a kiss on the left cheek of his spouse. Addressing her, he said, "You should take my teacher to the treasure vaults tonight and record the inventory, or more pertinently, the lack of which. Create for me a list of missing items. When confirmed, this will be our scepter to fight back the wave against me. All these faux diagnoses and these medical advisers will be swept aside once Grandpa finds me useful and vital again. This will show her that I have been right all along. The entire horde of eunuchs has been against me and more important, against her and this palace. Once she sees her new foe clearly, all ill feeling toward me will be swept away. Mr. Pickens, you have no idea what this will do for me, for you, for us. You will formally be appointed to the highest rank of royal counsel. You and your heirs shall forever benefit from the enjoyment of this titular privilege for eternity, in perpetuity."

"I am honored, but I'm not doing this for my heirs. I see none coming."

"Nevertheless, the honor you shall carry. Go now, you two. At daybreak, a new sun shall rise, and we shall all breathe in fresh air. I am not unwell, as you two can see. I am just suffer⸗ ing from such anguish . . . unknowable anguish. I am about to be freed from all these accusations, all this coldness and neglect—"

"No one neglects you," Q said, embracing the emperor, holding him as a mother would her fretful child.

"The bitter coldness from Grandpa. All because she thinks I am weak like a girl, that I am useless and powerless. That's why Grandpa seeks to have me retired. I have been weak, but no longer. You two go and find proof of theft. With that one genuine thing, I can be proved right on all other matters. Grandpa will not think of me again as weak. That's all I ask for. Go, you two." He removed Q's arms from around his shoulders and pushed her away. The exertion seemed to exhaust him, sending a shiver through his frame and render⸗ ing him to seek the only solace he knew.

"Servant! Bring me the pipe."

The shadow of his servant swept in like a ghost and lit the

emperor's pipe. Such was our titular ruler. Such was the plight of this helpless soul, in which lay clarity and sweet innocence. Such was what bound me to him in ways I cannot describe, in ways that incite nostalgia, homesickness, and longing, a certain hollowness of one's heart. Fondness for another being.

Strength might be heroic, but frailty is darling, and utter fragility outright endearing, for in that weakness there is a certain strength that urged me to charge afore and lay myself down in his defense.

Helplessness is a gift in and of itself.

28

Brushing this entry, how I wish I had a second chance to relive the events that followed. Had I the opportunity to live that night one more time, I might see the blinking signs of my undoing that marred the dark night.

I had intended only to include Q in my effort to account for all the treasure piling under the roof of the Treasure Chamber, a stout building on the neglected western spur of the palace grounds. But the emperor instead sent an order to assemble a team of palace women and cursed eunuchs under the leadership of the very man about whom all these investigations were aimed. At once, this discreet act initiated by the new inspector was transformed into a full-blown affair.

"Don't worry, Li Liang will not be concerned by all this," S answered when I rushed back to question him about that decision. His naïveté was alarming. "These servants all follow my orders."

"*Wrong again, my sovereign. Haven't you seen what this palace has been reduced to?*" I wanted to shout at him. "*What a den of thieves it has become? And you are but a parody of power, a ruler of ultimate foolishness and utter idiocy.*"

How I wished to wipe that smirk off his face, as if I were the blind one seeing nothing, fumbling my way around this foreign land and alien Court. And yet how my heart ached for this helpless lamb on the chopping block.

Into the night came the firebugs and minions, the hid-den and the ugly, mutually crowding the nocturnal chamber filled to the rafters with the annual gifts from far provinces and ocean nations, offerings by empires, foreign kings and queens. Q was regal, organizing the eunuchs and palace women into queues and circles in their respective tasks. The commingling of the two—the neglected palace concubines and feminized half-men—had long been the fodder of sala-cious novels: lone and lonely men without wherewithal, and their opposite fully equipped with their wiles and whistles. The haphazard fumbling and caressing is a given, given the nature of their existence. Little though the neuters had, they became peerless experts and authorities on pleasing a woman with what organs they had remaining. I had witnessed with my own eyes a young eunuch, a kitchen hand from the north, bending over an older palace woman, his face between her thighs, his agile tongue causing her to give out delighted cries.

Night might be dark out on the palace grounds, but the chamber's interior was well lit with rows of gigantic ceremo-nial candles giving off hisses of light and fragrant scent. The palace women, the engines of this stately household, moved the wares from shelf to shelf, inspecting their provenance, voicing their gift labels to the eunuchs recording the confir-mations at hand, who in turn told other eunuchs to register them either as missing or intact. Such trigroupings repeated at length from aisle to aisle and hall to hall, seeking order amidst chaos. These halls might bear treasures, but signs of abandonment and neglect were everywhere: dust and spider-webs, and worse, the haunts of theft and embezzlement.

In its midst were vases from Versailles, clocks from Colón, little engines from the English Court, porcelain from Poland, gems from Germany—in sum and to wit, the rarities from the far corners of this earth, valuables from the high moun-tains to the deep seas.

In it all was Q, my queen bee, inspecting room to room, advising aisle to aisle. A creature of the arts, native or foreign, she possessed a sharp eye for paintings, particularly of the Baroque era, and a taste for North Soong Dynasty water-colors. It owed much to the fact that her adoptive father had been a premier collector of that period's art, from porcelain jars to poetry scrolls and silk and satin tapestry, much of which adorned the walls of Q's private study.

What ensued next I should have perceived had I posses-sion of that illusive third eye. The mystical firebugs of that long ago night must have invaded my aura without my detec-tion, flooding through unlocked doors and released window latches of those dusty rooms, creating a gale that gained pas-sage behind a scroll hanging crookedly on the western wall and causing a nearby candle flame to elongate and stretch, nipping first at the sleeves of a busy palace woman's gown. She flailed her hand frantically, aiming to douse the fire, and her arm caught the edges of the volume in a eunuch's hands. The volume, with its thin and fragile pages, was instantly aflame, sending its sparks to fly in a radius within which a silk tapestry was hung, that in turn burned quickly upward, leading the fire to squirm like some sly snake all the way to the ceiling rafter, igniting the wooden roof into a canopy of heat and dancing flames.

I was marveling at a marble sculpture of Venus when the heat wave sliced the dense air, piercing the spiderwebs as quick and palpable as lightning. The age-old rafters gave off sizzling fury as they were engulfed in flame, which soon gave way to panic. Eunuchs threw away their record books, adding fuel to the growing fire; palace women screeched, batting at the flames lighting up their dresses, their sleeves, their hair. Some ran for the door, others squatted down in confusion. A burning chunk of wood breaking off from the ceiling beam hit my shoulder. Sparks quickly nipped at my scalp, burning a few strands of my hair, dying quickly under my smothering palm.

Looking from the other side of this slippery truth, one could argue that the chamber fire had nothing to do with imagined firebugs: there had never been those flying creatures, neither in the autumn meadows of New England nor in the July air of Peking. In-In was but a liar with the sweetness of spirit to conform to his pitiful master, and their flight, nocturnal, was an astral vision by a misguided, crazed man of inborn or acquired madness. Perhaps the following was what had actually occurred.

Only a moment ago, I had a glimpse of that particular palace woman letting go of the vase she was holding, thereby toppling a giant candle toward her sleeves, which a second ago had been pushed aside by the fleeting hand of a particular eunuch with a square face and jutting chin, the kind that defies authority, the kind most liable to rebel, the kind that is ambitious beyond his means. He had not merely pushed the giant wooden candle stand but had duly kicked the stand off its support—amazing how one's memory could withhold all these truths only to be revealed later. While he concocted these sequences, his muddy eyes had darted toward me at the very second when Q ran over in excitement, a scroll half open in her hand, to tell me about a rare find, the original of a legendary poet who had hidden the answer to a riddle in another scroll, the one that she possessed.

Just a split second after, a shadow lurched behind her, one that shut closed the heavy door with a clacking noise associated with certain clinking of a heavy lock, the kind requiring two keys to open. The candle tilted, falling and alarming the palace woman, so on and so forth.

The scenario was simple. All had been well thought out, with a commanding choreographer silently mastering every single step and move within. Maybe Q's find had been planted by the same invisible master, leading her to run into the same room I was in. We had positioned ourselves in separate rooms so that two set of eyes could keep the servitude honest and diligent.

My first instinct was to fling myself toward Q, catching her in my arms as she glimpsed the fire burning the palace woman. Her move to render aid was impeded by the rush of palace women, who abandoned the wares and treasures at hand and rushed to the door. The first one to reach it yanked at the inner door knob. It didn't budge. The second one leaped over her, pulling at the latch, but the door seemed stuck. The look on their faces was telling—frightened and anguished. Together, they aimed their shoulders at the door, giving it a mighty slam. The door stood firmly as it was so meant.

The fire had by now flooded the room like a raging tide spitting up sparks and sparkles, turning the area into an instant pond of flames. The heat rose, stifling our noses and throats. I did my best to shield Q within my arms, holding her thin frame close to my chest into which her shouts and screams could be felt vibrating, muffled against my rib cage.

Some palace women collapsed; others dashed from one corner to another, their clothes and hair aflame. A handful of eunuchs, all young and vital, were taking turns trying to break down the door with precious jars and statues. Nothing gave. The air turned denser, the heat rising, clawing at our skin, eyelashes, and hair.

"Window? Is there a window in here?" I shouted, only to be muted by falling debris from above. The only one who heard me was my Q. She pushed herself away from my chest to leap on a stool partially aflame and quickly rip away a watercolor hanging on the eastern wall. There an ingenious window was revealed, barred by three iron rods.

It would take three men, six eunuchs that is, to break out the iron rods. Q was the first to be pushed out the window. Following her, I crawled through the narrow passage, my boots nipped by ferocious flames. Only two other eunuchs made it out. The rest were all entombed within, burned to embers and ashes.

29

Let's now borrow a passage or two from the palace record, which is so regularly wrong and fictive that at times it could not help itself being right. The Court historian hereby wrote:

> *The perpetrator of this flame of sin is none other than the royal ocean tutor, the one and only outsider, employed to inspect the management of the age-old Royal Court. His doing, or rather undoing, has thus far caused havoc among us. Another case of suicide by rope is also said to be blamed on this intruder.*
>
> *As such, the august emperor himself has temporarily taken leave from the throne to tend to his ailments of holy body and sacred spirit. The ocean tutor is relieved from all his duties and chores, his digression and dereliction making null and void the employment contract formed at the outset of his arrival. This announcement takes effect immediately. Empress Qiu Rong, the fourth consort, is under house arrest for her greed and misconduct. Several priceless missing treasures have been found in her possession. She hence awaits demotion or other punishment.*

Fear shrinks a dwarf but only stirs a gallant. Only a fool would linger in the aftermath of the fire to read in this jaun, diced publication his own fate and the condemnation of those involved. In the evening twilight, what little I had I packed up within a small trunk, and I headed out through a backyard grove of secretive bamboo. From there I was to make my way to a curtained rickshaw awaiting me outside the western gate, which In In had summoned with two silver ingots to ensure his way. By then my house was already being watched by the eyes of a platoon that had to be fooled by the stage props of a lit lantern in my bedroom shining opaquely on a bulbous bed wherein lay, as my substitute, a stool covered snugly by a silk quilt.

A hidden door allowed me to exit my damp vault into a garden of peonies now felled aground by their own heavy, dewy blooms. I crawled through the peony patch next to leaning bamboo trees following a mental topography mapped for this very circumstance. This route of evasion was to be best trampled in summer's lush leaves and thick shrubbery while winter urgency would have dictated an alternate course. Next the rising hedges of stout pine bushes led me to a dock over an eel pond whereby I poled to shore a discreet boat from its moor under a bridge among swaying lotus stems, in a morass of turtles and rotting leaves near the garden of Q's mansionette.

All along, my guilt, my sorrow, was heavy with a certain pending premonition. My imagining eye could see a singular profile of Q, not supine or prone, but encircled by a casket of stillness, with summer heat chilled around her.

Quickly I threw open her lacquered door. Her living chamber was empty, gray in twilight, no maids or servants in sight. I stormed next into the bedroom. I didn't see her right away. On the wall was projected an elongated silhouette hung by a thin rope from a ceiling beam, her head bent in equanimity, her arms dangling in surrender.

Sadness weakened my knees and my arms yet I leaped at her, lifting her feet up. The noose atop slackened around her neck, and she slumped over my fetching shoulder.

Next I reached for the handle of a boot-plunged knife and stepping on a chair gave the hanging rope quick slashes. It gave finally, and gently I laid her on a rumpled bed. Save for a garish cut beneath her petite larynx and some spittle smearing her lower lip and the corners of her mouth, she looked utterly unhurt, at peace in slumber. I sheathed the Arab knife and fished from my trouser pocket a tiny leather holder containing a pin-sharp silver toothpick, with which I would now perform that ancient art of the Needle Cure. One prick, needlewise, at a certain hot-blooded nerve point beneath a woman's tender ankle and she would coil with rampant desire and contort for condign punishments. No province of carnal knowledge or precincts of fancy were beyond my reach.

With the makeshift needle, I aimed at the vertical furrow above the upper lip. The philtrum, as it is otherwise known, had linear filaments running to the brain. To stir the tender groove was to awaken the life within.

The sharp point pricked into her pale skin. A living man would leap in an unbearable pain, but in her it cajoled not a twitch or a wince, leaving me with one last resort: the tip of her *digitus medius,* or middle finger, a secret burrow to the ventricles of her heart. If this failed, I did not know what would become of me.

I forced my slender tool inside the tenderness between her nail and flesh, at once inducing a bead of blood. My fingers went into frenzy, spinning its stem, stirring its tip deeper down in, trying to call forth that residual flame remnant in her. After only exerting the full length of my bloody toothpick did I finally make Q quiver.

Maddeningly I kept on the task with my scepter of life whilst pasting my ear over the diamond of her chest, listening for her heartbeat. She jerked again, this time heaving up with a long-lodged sigh. Soon I sensed Q's weak arteries pulsing and her fey bosom heaving, but she was still blue. Wiping the copious mucous from her face, I sealed my lips around her mouth, pinched shut her nose, and inflated her lungs. In four breaths she was pink. She then gurgled, as if some blockage had just given way, and opened her big eyes, looking puzzled.

"What are you doing here, Big Man?" she inquired weakly, easing herself up with a haunted look on her face as if seeing ghosts. "Quick, Big Man, get me out of here. They tried to kill me!"

"Who tried to kill you?"

"The servants! Eunuchs. A band of them forced their way in. Did they try to kill you, too?" she asked, cupping my face with her cold hands.

"Not yet."

"How did you know to come rescue me?"

Carefully I caressed the bruise around her neck as tears

rolled down her cheeks. "I only knew I had to come take you far away from this place."

"Where are we going?"

"Wherever you wish to go."

"To my parents' residence then." She climbed off her bed, still weak but able.

My Q, my innocent. Her purity jabbed my tender heart.

I carried her out of the house across her garden into the bobbing boat. It was dead quiet. Such would be the case, with her unwatched and unguarded, giving her ample time to hang, limp and dead, while resident ghosts preyed on her, until the shocking discovery in the morn. A case of suicide would be made with evidence strewn all over her abode. A note of demise would be forwarded to her princely adoptive father, who would only be allowed to view her body at her burial, a hush-hush affair in the royal cemetery.

What fallacy! But before we could pole away into safety, I had to do one more deed. Leaving Q alone on the stern of the boat, I trudged back into her home, picked up the short-ened candle, and fed its waning flame to the hem of a curtain where some rude boot had stomped on its fringe. Slowly it caught with a sizzling crawl upward.

By the time we reached the opposite bank of this palace pond, the tongues of fire were visible, squirming up other curtains and drapery. When I carried her, my delicate liv-ing ghost, into the carriage at the foot of that deserted west-ern gate, the sound of gongs and the fury of shouts were faintly audible, just enough to distract the vigilance of the gate guard.

To avoid easy pursuit, I told the rickshaw man to take a shortcut along a quiet moat away from the boulevards and streets to the American legation, a stopover to let Q heal her wounds and calm her fragile soul. But the asylum of ambas-sadorial protection was not to be had easily.

Colonel Winthrop, the tic and tac man, only grudgingly acquiesced to a two-day stay if I rendered a diary of events leading to the unexpected departure. When I let it be known the circumstances wherein, he nearly fainted. The stout man of courtly manners had to lean on a frail railing to let the spell pass. His facial tics resumed frantically, contorting the right side of his face. But it was when Q's identity was whispered to him by an aide of his, a well-heeled nobody who'd had a chance encounter with Q a summer before at her chrysanthemum tea party in the Jing Garden, that Win-throp stomped into our room threatening to turn us into the palace if I didn't take to the road at once. It was after midnight, mind you. He could not wait till daybreak when carriages could be summoned. Only after lengthy pleading on the point of my delicate company would he let us stay until sunrise. By then, when the main gate of the walled Tartar City had opened, not only was a notice of apprehen-sion of two treasonous fugitives, Q and I, posted but so was an announcement of the honorable Prince Qiu's death by self-hanging.

When I informed her of the tragedy, Q was pale and strengthless, leaning on her bedpost. Neither the gentle voice with which I delivered the news nor the ensuing words of comfort could soothe her. She shook her head violently, ask-ing, "Why him? My poor papa. Why is my path filled with death? Why are you still here with me? Why aren't you gone like the rest? I am cursed. I must be." She wasn't speaking to me in particular. She seemed to be repenting to someone, her God perhaps.

How I wished I could answer her. All I could do was rock her in my arms till she fell into a jerking, sobbing sleep.

30

The world outside could be windy and stormy in June heat, but in here, within our haven, all was calm. Q and I found refuge for the next two nights in a petite alley inn, deftly named Ye Ying Tang, the Nightingale's Nest. After‑ward I often thought of it as some winsome device off pages of myth and folklore.

The inn hid behind a willow garden, barely visible from an archway crawled by long‑neck peonies. It came into my view only when, our carriage freshly discharged from the le‑gation's rear gate, the Mongol stallion suddenly veered left without the urging of the reins, taking us into a narrow alley as if sensing danger ahead. At the alley's end, the Nightin‑gale's Nest came into view.

It could have been the sound of men in arms two blocks down that frightened the intuitive beast or its innate beastly spirit sensing danger afar. Whatever the cause, the horse brought us even farther down the alley, trotting forcefully, notwithstanding the whipping and cussing by its master, till it stopped at an archway upon which a bell hung. Homer would have spirited it so that the white‑furred beast used its snout to ring the bell to announce our arrival to the innkeeper, who might in turn be a three‑breasted horned beast, but the feat was already angelic enough without the aid of literal fanfare as the Greeks were prone to do or overdo. I paid an extra silver tael to the driver for additional hay to be fed the beatific beast. The man patted his animal proudly and bowed rapidly in thanks.

The innkeeper was a dwarf paired with a fully grown wife. They greeted us like a vaudeville comic show. All they had for the night was one single room in a quiet corner of their establishment, said the impish innkeeper with a child-like voice.

Q had draped her head and shoulders with a scarf, a gift from the congenial Mrs. Winthrop upon leaving the besieged legation, which concealed all but her downcast eyes. I murmured some gibberish to the effect that she was my daughter, adding with my mangled Mandarin that we were awaiting arrival of her sick mother who was recovering at Union Hospital and that the single should suffice with a mat and satin quilt for my daughter. The innkeeper was agreeable, and he led us to our enchanted nest with a window overlooking a willow grove.

"A single room?" Q said as soon as I shut the door. "Are you mad? I am not your daughter, and you will not come near my bed. You'll stay on the floor for as long as we have to stay here." Her eyes darted about our chamber with disdain as she cast away the scarf and dove into the fluffy bed, curling herself up under the blanket.

I ordered our supper to be brought to our chamber, on account that my darling daughter was infirm and a whiff of outside wind would only worsen her fragility. The host was quick to oblige. Q quietly ate two servings of soft corn crepes and crusty fried pork skin, a culinary affliction with which all Manchurians were cursed. Before tea could be served, she yawned and dozed off, lying on a bamboo pillow.

You all might assume that with all the stumbling blocks removed and my pet safely caged, dozing with a smile on her impish face, that I would be free to make my final claim of my prey—all that had transpired before had not involved the ultimate act of burying myself inside her yet—but all I could think of was to dash out into the hallway and down to the parlor to find a jar of spirits to calm my nerves. Lust was all guts and nerves, a shaky rope bridge over a roaring river—sin without redemption, nightmare without end save for the promise of some fleeting bliss.

I strolled the parlor, lit by a Baroque chandelier, surrounded by a mural of horses and their forlorn shepherds, who gazed singularly and silently at the lone interloper among the crowd. A low murmur of piano music crawled the air. A German duke and his dull duchess were chattering over a candled table with some English gentry, a surgeon and his skinny and much younger mistress. An Indian guard's white teeth, eyeball sclera, and turban could be seen, but not the contours of his lunar face. In the corner was a lone woman, French possibly, sitting with her pubescent daughter—ten, twelve tops—a fresh breeze among the opaque curly locks, earthy blond, the kind one found in the French countryside among vineyards or on the beaches of Nice with sand on bare ankles, tan lines veining her virgin thighs, eyes blue like the inquisitive ocean, smelling of summer's angst and languorous unripe lust. Youth always calls on me.

I picked my way around an Italian man, moustached and idling with a jade pipe, framed in his own quaint smoke, no doubt looking to squeeze in on any rich widows and lonely women.

"What a beauty your daughter is," he offered to me with a gleaming shine in his eyes. "I saw you two pulling up in front of the inn. I'd love to meet her. She reminds me of—"

I cut him off bluntly with, "She is sick, under the weather," and chose a chair next to the bored child and her spinsterly mother.

Haven't I just hoarded one as juvenile and ready for the ravaging of my loving lust? Why was I eyeing the knees of another child while a sleeping siren lay upstairs, weak and supine on my bed? Am I to prefer those far-flung butterflies other than the ones in my net? Is it the dream or reality I craved?

Before long the French girl turned and smiled at me. "*Bon-soir*, monsieur," she said sweetly.

"Good evening," I said uneasily. Lust is never at ease.

"Are you English?" She managed another smile, arch-ing her left brow while crossing and recrossing her skirted legs. Oh, those bare knees! There were even scars rounding one cap.

"American."

"American. From New York?" She picked herself up and sat at my table. "Me and my mama are from Paris. Would you like to buy my mama a drink?" She cast a glance at her stoic mom who smiled shyly at me.

"I'm merely here to—"

"She could join you, if you desire?"

Quite a twin of hustlers, weren't they? I shook my head,

but the child was persistent. She came over to sit on my lap. "We can drink together. Don't go yet."

"My daughter is waiting."

"Just one cocktail. Mama and I were left behind by my père, a ship engineer who drowned. We have to find our way home. Our ship abandoned us." She ground her bony but‑ tocks hard on my taut lap and slung her thin arms around my shoulders, her armpits emitting the stench of some coarse perfume.

In my crooked search for the young and frail, I had been approached and handled by old hacks, swarthy men, and hairy‑chested brutes. But never ever had I been solicited by a child in service of her own mother. But was she her real mother, or was it another convenient pairing in the com‑ merce of flesh, demure they might all pretend to be?

Quietly I declined, causing the girl to roll her eyes. She got up from my lap after giving it another grind.

"Ask for Claudia's chamber at monsieur's convenience, *oui*? If not tonight, tomorrow maybe, or tomorrow after to‑ morrow perhaps." She left, dusting the hem of her short skirt.

I had to be further insulted by the Italian count, who gallantly ordered one cocktail each for the juvenile young madam and her geisha mama before casting me a dark look. It would surprise me not at all if the count was a cog of the threesome.

"Leave him alone, Claudia," said the petite innkeeper coming to my rescue. His hair was well combed, and he was dressed in evening wear, a snug child‑size tuxedo, all four feet of him. "Monsieur is not to be disturbed." He waved his short arm with authority at Claudia, nodding in my direction before moving on to others.

The sound of gongs could be heard dismally through the window, drowning the murmuring trickle of a moaning piano manned by a player barely visible.

Urgency suddenly laid bare my lust. In haste, I paid for a bottle of sugarcane rum and downed half the contents half-way to my cold nest. The Caribbean spirit ransacked through my heaving innards, sanctifying the urge, purifying its end goal. How could I have slowed my hooves this near the final trough that would sate the deepest of my yearning and seek-ing? That faraway ethereal pledge made by my heavenly An-nabelle was now earthbound, a thin wall away awaiting my claiming.

I fumbled out the key with shaking hand and opened the door. In a quiet light, lying in repose was no longer Q but the earthen solid object of my longing, a flesh and bone rein-carnation of my tragic Annabelle. The candle shed soft light on her horizontal form, her childish hipbone barely rising with an arm under her neck, her head resting on the bam-boo pillow the same way Annabelle had posed under that long ago summer moon. Infantile rouge had climbed up her cheeks and parted her lips red like summer berries. Tipping sideways were her pear-size breasts with darkened nipples slipping out of her loosened nightgown. Her other arm was draped softly over her thin thighs, bony fingers partially bent. The gown had ridden up her thighs baring her thin knees and pubescent calves, her feet arched and toes curled.

The rum throbbed my temples and tickled my nether-dom, numbing the outer world to a wavy periphery. Draining

the bottle, I unbuttoned the bulky jacket, shed the cumber-
some trousers, and kicked off my socks and boots in the slow
deliberation of a lion readying for his bloody feast. My head
was swarming now with firebugs of yesteryear, each stinging me with bitefuls of delight; my senses were doused with
the fragrance of rampant weeds tinctured by cow manure,
sodden mud, and dirty feet, transporting me back to that
hazy night among haystacks. The evocation was vital to this
enterprise, without which it would be just a meal and not at
all a feast. This was what spanned the bridge that arcs from
the living to the dead, hell to fierier hell. This was to be my
coronation.

I lay unrobed alongside my darling; the prelude would be
brief. Lust's eyes had long envisioned this moment as finality.
As gentle as a monster could bear, I lifted the white satin off
her soft, dewy skin, untying the sash over her waist, opening its seam and letting it fall behind the small of her back.
She unleashed a sigh, eyes still closed, lashes casting lengthy
shadows down over her cheeks. She moved her bare shoulder
blades causing a slight jiggle of young breast, taut and unripe. Slowly I fondled her bud with trembling fingers. A light
pinch caused a moan to escape her lips. Softly I cupped her
juvenile mounds, too small to feed even the tiniest of babies,
and suckled her with my abject lips and mournful tongue.

She eased her chest and bare belly toward me and with
the faintest moan whispered the following fateful words, "I've
been waiting for so long."

31

"You brute!" She turned her head, staring at my stark nakedness. "Who were you making love to?"

"You, my darling, you," I said drowsily, drained by her exuberance.

"Why were you calling my birth mother's name?"

"Mmm?"

"And you bruised me so," she said in a hurt voice.

"My darling little soul." I swept her into my arms, my heart swollen with madness, and violently ravaged her all over again, causing her to moan with little cries.

"You know I was just a virgin. Please . . ."

At her announcement, I trembled and shattered with gushes only to be met by her blood-stained juice dripping down my shaft and her bare, parted thighs. Tightly I held her, covering her nose, lips, neck, and breasts with the tenderest kisses as tears of gratitude wet my sallow cheeks.

All cultures worship the sanctity of the cherry, which in Chinese was labeled delicately as the peach blossom. Certain Mongolian tribes would spread white silk beneath the bride's buttocks to catch the wedding night stains. If no redness was discerned, the bride would be returned to her father with a penalty of three horses, though the same culture also adhered to polyandry whereby a wife is shared tacitly and tactfully among brothers living in the same yurt.

The blood of this cherry from Q offered hidden clues to the viability of her mother, Annabelle, much like the blood-line visible in the white of a hen's egg when shone against the bright sun. Like the imprint of a lovesick soul, lost and regained through her daughter, her living vessel. Radiant proof that that which was lost is now living. It was Annabelle's virginity I had ravaged, her cherry I had suckled and broken, her lips I had kissed, her heart I had throbbed.

Oh, my darling and dear Annabelle. How I have missed you. Now in my arms, on my lap, you are whole again, unburned and uncharcoaled.

What lay ahead mattered not at all. What lay within could never ever be lost again.

32

Gray marred our window when I heard a knock on our door.

"Mister, open the door, please," someone said urgently.

I leaped off the bed and opened our door to the sight of the dwarf and his white-toothed Bengal servant.

"Royal guards are downstairs," the innkeeper whispered.

"What for?" I asked, shielding my sleeping beauty from their view.

"They are here with a palace warrant to search for the runaway empress and her cohort, a tall and white ocean man." Knowledge was in his voice.

"Why are you telling me this?" I calmly asked, though my heart was in my throat.

"You know why. I might not know who you are, but I knew her." He stretched his neck to peep around my waist. "I was a guest at her father's princely tea party once. I am here to help you. Let's waste no more time."

"Who brought them here?"

"Who, indeed? Someone has led them here, someone who knows your whereabouts."

I darted a glance up and down the corridor. "What do you suppose you can do?"

"He will help you gather your things," the dwarf said,

pushing his servant forward. "Then I will show you the way out."

Q, without urging, was already off the bed and dressing. "What's the matter?" she asked.

"They are here, after us. We must go."

"You've bitten more than you can chew, Big Man," she said, wrapping herself up in the scarf. "Maybe it's better that we surrender. We can plea for mercy."

"There will not be mercy or pity."

"This is all to fulfill some sort of fantasy for you, isn't it?"

"No, I am trying to save you from certain death."

"And how do you propose we do that—running from one nest to another?"

"We have a final destination."

"Where?"

"The home of Wang Dan, seventy miles south of Peking."

"The home of the bloodthirsty rebel?"

"The father that you have never met."

"What good would this meeting bring?"

"We can stay at his home temporarily, and he has an army to defend us."

"This is all a nightmare. I can't leave behind my husband."

"You can and you must, if you are to save him."

Without words, things were gathered and the trunk shut. The servant grabbed it up in his mighty hand, and Q and I were out of our chamber following the innkeeper along the corridor, down the stairs, into a willow garden via a back door. There in the back alley was a tall horse and a roofed carriage. The innkeeper opened the door for us, bowing. "Your high-ness," he murmured, his eyes on the ground.

"Who are these people?" Q asked.

That was when I noticed that we weren't alone. Claudia, the youthful pimp, and her stiff mother were already seated inside the carriage. They bowed as I helped Q inward, and I bowed back in thanks.

The innkeeper pulled me aside and whispered, "I asked them to ride with you and pretend to be your family, four people instead of the two they are searching for. They can travel as far as you need them."

Gratitude flooded my heart. Rarely do I deserve such grace.

I pressed five silvers into the tiny palm of the innkeeper. He refused, pushing it back. "I was once a guest of her fragrant house. I can never repay the honor bestowed upon me, but please do compensate the pair who will accompany you farther. You know, they aren't even family. Claudia is French, her 'mother' a Russian widow. They have a roof above them, paying when they can, and they help me when I am in need, as is the case now."

"Why are you helping her?" I asked.

"We are distant cousins on her princely father's side. I render aid, if not for blood then the clan name." He slapped the horse's belly with his hand. "Off you go."

"Where are we going?" I asked him.

"Don't worry, I am not sending you through the gates. They have been crowded with royal inspectors since yesterday. A boat man will meet you at a loading dock."

With the facade of a benign family of four, we negotiated through the streets of Peking lined and guarded by the minions of the palace, every street corner a hooded guard, every block an alert inspector.

The metropolis was a convenient amphitheater and the foursome a well-chosen cast in which I played the doting father touring the northern plains in pursuit of possible tea trading, if inquired, with the Russian widow as my indifferent wife, eyes downcast, mouth sagging, lips dried, whom I had cajoled with extra coin to lean woodenly on my left shoulder while the French girl sprawled across my thighs as my lap pet. Q, my grumpy older daughter, was wrapped up in her scarf and ensconced in the back row obscured by the dark carriage roof.

Our rider chose to traverse the quiet back alleys and narrow lanes to avoid the eyes and grid of the dragnet. The beast, a beauty he was, trotted with measured gait, hurried but not harried. Above our moving theater an agile storm gathered, ominously lurching among the surrounding tree-tops. Thunder soon rumbled like a string of cow moos following us from street to street, from lane to narrower lane in slow chase of our squeaky wheels as if it could detect us among this movable maze, pinpointing the exactitude of our whereabouts amidst the massive landscape, then the all-seeing eye in heaven began pelting us with bullet-size raindrops beating mercilessly upon our roof and on our horse's back. The earth was hushed by this sudden downpour, the world silenced. I could see that only two streets away the ground was dry and the earth was unstirred and sun drenched. The space flanking us, a narrow lane with a Buddhist temple two corners away, was all clear, without a cloud above, but wherever our carriage rode, a valley of dark rain preceded us, not by much, only a detrimental ten yards—enough that our beast could never outrun it. In our trail, a river of wetness gleamed in the reappearing sun.

It was beneath this mystical rumble of rain and thun⸱ der over us, and over us only, that we journeyed smoothly through the western part of the city after passing two inevi⸱ table checkpoints—shabby kiosks filled with drenched pal⸱ ace police, who might have been outside waving their swords, stopping this very chariot had they not sought shelter from the rain. By midmorning we reached the city's edge with its stone wall looming, arriving at a loading dock of a small trib⸱ utary of the Grand Canal. A boatman was introduced to us by the rider, who drove back the tragic Russian and French duet after boarding us on a flat⸱bottomed boat filled to its brim with cookery and humble belongings—chinaware and sacks of wheat and rice under the leaky roof among which we were to hide. An infant's cry, the boatman's son, perfected this drizzling portrait of familial bliss: chimney and pets (two nuzzling Pekingese afoot), dangling chimes, and two older sons. With his wife making a fire in an earthen stove to warm up the noon meal, the boatman, a pigtailed Chinaman of no discernible age, poled his vessel along the mossy root of the city wall whose mightiness could not stop the rain or echoing thunder claps. Gliding serenely among the dimpled surface of the mucky canal, with the rain still umbrellaing us, the boat snuck through an underpass beneath an arched base of the city wall, an egress granted only to certain merchants or mercenaries carrying a green flag at their stern.

As we disappeared from one side of the wall, the rain was

thinning and clouds clearing. By the time we emerged on the other side, the sky was as blue as a blue jay with no peep of prior thunder or a morsel of previous moisture. Beyond that wall summer noon smiled at us with clarity and radiance. Even that certain Bard of Avon could not have envisioned such theatrics.

33

For three days and nights, we sheltered in the negligible houseboat, inching southeast at a snail's pace from the canal's northernmost terminus toward Tianjin. Among slumbering grain barges, flower rafts, and wobbling sampans filled with cabbages and melons, the boatman's two brooding sons took turns walking the rocky shore, a rope over their shoulders, hauling the boat forward while the father sat on the deck smoking his pipe, minding its course. When not cooking, the man's wife could be seen rocking their youngest seed, an unclad infant in a round-bottomed bamboo cradle on deck.

The sun rose and set, left to right; the moon trailed us, to and fro. Q suffered some feverish chills by night that could not be soothed by either fish soup or green tea brewed from the wife's stove. My sickened empress kept murmuring "Father . . . Father" in her delirium. I dared not leave her alone even for a short repose. Her feverish lips were burning hot, and her nether Venus an unadulterated thermal inferno threatening to inflame not just my part but my whole. Lovemaking, absent proper medicine, was the only amalgam I could tender aboard this floating vessel. It's the air and the sun, God and his invisible goddess. It's the Taoist way, the Buddhist nirvana, and the Christians' paradise. The truth dwelled right here between man and his woman. It was in the entwining of bodies that the ideal of God was conceived—it was that essential.

Talking of vessel, Q during those three drenched, vulgar days of copulation wasn't just serving as her own tool but as a bifurcated subvessel of her ancestor. Yes, ladies and gentle-men, the arbiters of my dying soul, in all our couplings I stretched my vision beyond what lay before me to that far-away end goal. When loving her, I also loved her twin, that spirited mother, Annabelle.

For three cycles of the sun, I never left her. Three dark nights, water gurgling beside us, she lay coiled in my arms. There was the water police we had to evade, a tariff collec-tor's barge we had to negotiate; there might have even been some thunder or storms, but the only climatic wonders oc-curred under our soggy roof upon the flat bottom of the shaking boat.

34

The Grand Canal skirted the vast rice fields nearly ripened for harvest. Ears of rice, abundant and bending, eavesdropped on our affairs on this shameless boat. The country widened and the land flattened; more willows whispered and more birds twittered. Schools of young fish trailed our wake with leggy storks and throaty pelicans shimmering in the fringed shallows.

The fourth morning greeted us with a fishermen's song sung along the shore, which woke my empress, my darling. Q was like the face of a mountain washed fresh by the thunderous storm: her cheeks were dimpled roses, her eyes ponds of liquid shimmering with light; her hair, a bird's nest of chaos, only enhanced her unblemished beauty. The fishermen's singing didn't wake her; my swan song did when I slyly mounted her for the first and last time from her forbidden back garden. All the three days and nights of passion could only end in this fiery way: heaven and hell together.

From that morning after, intimate privilege was deprived me for more reason than I could account for. I thought it was Annabelle who gave the order to cut me off, though it could have been God, that we all fear, or his blushing bride, the Goddess—she was shamed by what underwent and what was undertaken. I must say in hindsight that if I were to give up something so precious that the final coition should suffice me, not just for the rest of my earthly life but for all the end-time I had to endure.

On that day, Q emerged from under the roof a tad more womanly. There was an accusatory expression on her face each time she looked my way as we journeyed from our load-ing dock and took a carriage to the township of Wang, her presumed father. But there was no blame in her eyes, only a new light, a light of wisdom and insight, a newly gained confidence and higher strength, all earned by having been so deeply and maddeningly loved.

"Are you ready to face your father?" I asked. "I've heard bloody things about the man."

"Anyone who could have loved my mother would not be a killer," she said.

"Yes, but what right do we really have to come to his for-tress uninvited?" I asked.

"My birthright," she answered, her eyes looking afield.

Amidst the greenery of willows, summer corn, the gur-gling rivulets, and quietly swimming geese suddenly emerged a mirage of humanity. A leafy townlet loomed against the range of a gentle hill, overgrown with blossoms of lavender. A faint and quaint aroma preceded, permeating the fresh air, framing the town as a garden, a sea of petals, an ocean of colors, vibrant and seasonal.

Q inhaled deeply, her eyes closed. "So fragrant."

"They call it the 'rebel's fortress.' "

"Mother must have fallen in love on her way here, her Bible in hand. I can see her in her white frock and white hat, a pale butterfly amidst the green, feel her urgent heart beating, measure her rhythm with mine. There is something in the air. . . . Then the lord of the manor opens his gate, and her heart softens, and forever she is his slave."

"Mine, too."

"You never got to love her."

"But I did through you."

"You are a rude man. Ugh, you ruined my vision, my pleasure." She struck my shoulder with her bony fist. "What if his soldiers chase us away? What if he doesn't want to see me? Is he even really my father?"

"There is no doubt."

"What if I told him what you made me do?" she asked wickedly.

"You wouldn't, would you?"

"They should probably lock you up to keep the young girls safe," she said.

My paws would have choked her skinny neck had not the pull-bridge come into view marking the end of our ride. Three white uniformed soldiers kicked dirt toward us, stopping our carriage with their pointy spears.

The bridge guard took our arrival notice, a note that I had scribed with the most elegant characters I could summon during the three taxing days of passion, about the only exterior task I accomplished, which coaxed not admiration but only a cold chuckle from Q. Curtly it said that the guest was of importance, and that the consequence of seeing such would be beneficial to him and us mutually. The note ended succinctly, denoting Reverend Pickens, indicating my rank in the business of God, hoping to gain a tad closer entry to this crazed specimen who, in this bleakest of time, was our only ray of hope in a dark sea.

Half an hour ensued without seeing the messenger's return. Then another hour lapsed before a grim official of Wang's clan rode to us on a blinking mule.

"His lordship has taken ill; therefore no visitor of any rank or officialdom will be granted audience."

No sooner had the man swallowed the last syllable of his announcement than Q jumped off our carriage and slung herself onto the mule's back, clutching the skinny man's veiny neck.

"Listen, you worthless man of self-importance. Do you even know who I am?"

"No, please!" gasped the male on the mule.

"I am a reigning empress of the Qing Empire on my royal inspection tour to weed out remnants of our kingdom such as you. Get down this very moment and offer me twelve kowtows or my royal ocean tutor will sever your head and sell your scalp to the Indians of America. Do you even know what they will do with your soul? They will boil your scalp and eat it with their coarse wine and make you into the lowest animal form ever so that you will never rise again."

The man humbly bowed twelve times and docilely took us to the very hall where his Lord on Earth presided, as Wang Dan declared himself since the day of his own awakening.

The township of Wang was an enclave in itself, cut off from the northern plain by a manmade river serving as its outer moat. A town wall stood erect barring any intruders;

only a main ironclad gate allowed passage inward. Atop the gate were his flags, a red one with a roaring lion, a white one with a blue fish sign, and a black flag with a white moon. Sentries were posted, much as at the Forbidden City. One would imagine this to be an empty town with only soldiers, barracks, cannons, and gunpowder, but one would be proven wrong.

The gate led one to a conjuncture with three streets sprouting onward north. The main road was called Paradise Boulevard. It led one not to a palatial establishment but a domed sanctuary with a fronting piazza. There was even a balcony to overlook an absent throng. The streets were of northern variety paved with gray stone, the stores and shops all flying the red flag. Children, all donned in white tunics and accompanied by their mamas and papas, were running about as carefree as the birds above them and the deer and peacocks around them. There was a serenity to the place untouched by what lay outside no more than a short mile away. Soldiers sang and marched in columns along the streets, patrolling the township; women were covered under black scarves, moving about like shadows on the street, carrying baskets of vegetables and grain. The kites flown by the children were white bearing the blue fish symbols.

Upon Paradise Boulevard, with the ingratiating official accompanying us, the citizenry of Wang Township paused to acknowledge us with a bow and a one-knee bending, for sure an act borrowed from some faraway ocean practice. The children followed us as children anywhere would follow visitors and outsiders.

"Are you here to pay witness to our Messiah's return?" a boy asked, sweetly tugging Q's sleeve. "Are you?"

"Whose return?"

"His father, our Lord in Heaven, has sent for him. That is why Messiah Wang has been preparing his body and mind for the inevitable."

"And what if we are here to see him return?"

"Then you are still days too early. God isn't ready for him. But you can always give your heavenly tithing early so heaven's gate will be open to you when you are ready."

Q frowned and whispered to me, "What is this place?"

"The only safe harbor for you."

By the time we arrived at the piazza in front of Wang's sanctuary, it was already crowded with a throng of noon chanters singing in pious voice, looking up to the balcony where an elder was seen hitting a bronze bell, marking the passage of the meridian. An orchestra of Mandarin instruments played a majestic passage, no doubt some imitation of palace music, punctuated by the striking of gongs and rambling beat of mighty cowhide drums standing on their sides as in a Japanese drum ceremony. All these indeed conspired to give off if not a heavenly ambience, then a deeply somber one, unimaginable only a short while ago beyond that pull-bridge. But what plucked an onlooker's heartstring was not the faux grandeur of this wacky vaudeville invention but the piety borne by the noontime mass who had apparently dropped whatever at hand to hurry here to the heart of the township to observe this daily ceremony. There was a look of hunger, of yearning, on their faces.

Entering the stone archway crafted with images of dragons

and *chi lin*, mighty mythical creatures, I followed Q, letting her lead. Her gait was blithe and her pose regal.

She walked proudly in a carefree gait of a loved and adored wife with her tamed spouse following behind her. She had a knowing stride, sure of herself and even better, of the lame pup at her heels.

On the dais of the empty sanctuary, a man leaned fee﹍ bly on the arm of his throne, plopped upright by cushions and pillows. He was racking up quite a mouthful of phlegm, spitting it into a spittoon held up by a girl in a red tunic. The effort left him breathless. Another young nurse soothed the man by gently patting his back while urging him along with words of endearment. Sensing our approach, he curtly pushed away the spittoon, signaling with a turn of his head for the young nurse to stop. He frowned, deep furrows lin﹍ ing his forehead, as the official leaned over to whisper into his ear. The words stiffened him. He lifted his chin up and widened his eyes as Q and I offered our bow.

"On your knees in the presence of his sacredness," a guard commanded.

"You don't know who she is, do you?" I asked with cool command.

"All must bow, especially women." Before the guard could strike me, Lord Wang Dan pushed him away with a long﹍ stemmed pipe that bore the traces of darkened burn over its silver head.

"You look familiar. Come closer," Wang said. Q stood quietly, letting the stranger examine her.

In my prior zealous jealousy, I had tried to mold, in my mind, the closest likeness of this man who had robbed me of Annabelle's virginity, the man who had stood tall in the way of her pristine past. But nothing would or could have come close to this. Before me was no man of Herculean proportion, full of rigor and martial bearing and religious zest, but instead a decrepit man on his dying path, inches away from the heaven of his own making. There were endless reasons making this, and every man, such. Leading its way, no doubt, would be some prevailing venereal infirmity evidenced by the gauntness of his body, his sunken cheeks, and protruding forehead with open sores dotting his trembling hands and thin neck. One shouldn't be surprised, considering the number of wives and concubines he possessed and the horde of whores and courtesans he kept. I had even met some of his discarded favorites during the sordid days of my ennui.

"Is that you, Annie?" Wang Dan asked in a thin voice. The exertion kicked him into a fit of spasmodic coughing, shaking him like a windblasted sea reed.

"No, I'm her daughter, Qiu Rong," said Q, leaning forward, unperturbed by his gory appearance. "Annabelle is my mother."

"Ah, my poor eyesight and old age." More phlegm gurgled in his throat, prompting his young nurse to drum his back for relief.

"Are you really Annie's daughter?" he asked when the fit had passed, reaching out a trembling hand.

Undaunted, Q took his hand and cupped it between her soft palms. "I am."

"God have mercy," he exclaimed, shaking his head incredulously. "I could never have imagined this day coming."

"Why not?" asked Q.

"If you only knew the circumstance of your birth." He examined her face closely with his jaundiced eyes, gauging her as if she were an objet d'art.

"What did you come to me for, my pearl?" he asked, already giving her a term of endearment. What a fraud. I began to state our cause, only to be slapped silent on my knee by Q's grudging hand.

Vividly and modestly, my nymphet empress regaled her plight, dating from the fire in the Treasure Chamber to her near death by hanging, to this very moment of relief. The word *kindness* surfaced often but never in conjunction with my name; indeed, it was as if I were a singular sadistic culprit drowning her already precarious destiny. I vied to correct her in her telling of the tale leading us this far but was pushed away by Q in disgust.

"So what good are you, ocean tutor?" Wang asked, after much nodding at the conclusion of Q's tale. "You foreigners are outstanding in getting what you want and forsaking what you desire not."

"I am merely here to plead for her safety," I said stiffly.

"And not your own?"

"Never. How dare you question my motive!"

"The motive of an ocean man." He chuckled. "It's always beyond reproach, isn't it? You took her as surety to keep your own life in flight."

Had he not been so sickly a sight, I would have shown him the potency of my pugilist fist, but calm I kept, if not for propriety's sake, then for my suddenly curt Q.

"Where is my Annie? Where is she?" the old man inquired,

craning his thin neck to look beyond us. "Is she hiding in the back trying to fool this old man's weak heart? Where is she?" There was such playfulness. Utterly unbecoming!

"She is dead," I said.

Wang was incredulous. "Dead? How?"

Q nudged my back with her sharp fist but I had to take this shot at the smug man, so I related the aromatic circum/ stances under which her and my life converged, our hearts colliding like stars, and colluded stealthily to the finality of the hay fire that ultimately claimed her, taking her away from me.

"She cannot be dead!"

"But dead she is," I said pissily. I could not explain my agitation. The very thought that this man had preceded me in seniority and possibly in depth of intimacy with the one and only Annabelle leadened the day and moment beyond my reckoning.

"One shining so bright shouldn't have died so soon," he murmured, frowning as if saddened. After a long pause, he added, "I have missed her every day since she left me."

That just about did it. The sordid, fraudulent philistine! I started to sputter but Wang waved me to silence and parted his robe, revealing a sunken chest covered with reddened sores and open wounds oozing with yellow exudate. In one, several maggots squirmed, feeding on his rotten flesh. I had heard of such archaic manner of healing by worm debridement but never imagined seeing such in practice. Wang gently picked the fattened ones up and placed them in his mouth, chewing them, replacing them with some thin, hungry ones from a nearby jar to continue the cleansing.

Q's jaw dropped and she hid behind me after seeing the spectacle.

"Ailments and sickness: nothing new in this life or next," Wang muttered. "Trials and tribulations—I have seen them all and yet more still come my way. Buddhists call this earthly life the 'sea of bitter sorrows.' I see it no differently. This is the old way of curing these cursed wounds. The larvae all come down to me from above to soak up my drippings." He sighed and looked up to the sunlit dome of his chapel, wonderment in his eyes, a seeming gesture of thanksgiving to his god before returning his piercing gaze back to me. "Annie belongs up there, beholden to none, least of all you. But hardly can I blame you. We are all love's fools."

"Lord Wang," said Q. "Tell me if I am your daughter as the hospital record shows."

"I could not be your father," Wang Dan said, his face stern and frowning.

"What?"

"Annie was seeded by another, not I."

"And you call yourself the Messiah." I jabbed at the man bitterly.

"But I am. It all started with my mother and the way I came to this earth. She was seeded not by my father but in a dream granted by God himself as the Virgin Mary was in that heavenly way. Mother was a maid working in the kitchen of a priest named Father Lafarge, the present cardinal of Quebec. Mother must have been touched by the holy spirit of that grand man."

She had surely been touched, and by more than holiness. God, these frauds! When would they cease such treachery?

"My earthly father was just like Joseph, the husband of the Virgin Mary. My earthly father, a well-to-do scion of prosperity, was persuaded by Father Lafarge to wed my mother so that I, the begotten son, would have a home of warmth and wealth to be reared in. He brought me up without any complaints or bitterness, going on to bear no other sons or daughters of his own, devoting himself utterly to my well-being."

"This is a Catholic cathedral then?" I asked, looking about me.

"No, not Catholic but one of my own faith. I am the only living truth, as Jesus, my brother, was to all Christendom."

"Have you thought of the possibility that you might have been tricked by that Canadian cardinal?"

Wang chuckled, looking only to Q, ignoring my eyes altogether. "Petty minds think pithy thoughts. I would not expect anything less from this ocean tutor. I have been called bastard by foreigners, but never by my own people."

"Because your Canadian father taught you his tricks of the trade?" I could not help jabbing, which readily begot Q's assault, this time a nail-digging pinch of my leg.

"My followers have the faith and conviction that you all lack. They see my white skin as a rarity, my blue eyes as windows to heaven, and my tall, straight nose as uncommon authority and esteem among them."

In Chinese belief, fair skin is regarded as a sign of wealth and exalted social station since commoners toiled under the unclenching sun, imbuing them with dark, leathery skin, and in a nation of flat-nosed citizenry, any unbroken nose of Caucasian extraction would be looked upon as indicative of leadership. It was, at best, a national bias rather than truth, from which this man was wringing every drop of superstitious credence to fool his gullible parishioners.

So here we had the forsaken and bastardly seed of some salacious Quebecian fraud who had obviously fornicated upon Wang's poor mother, the lurching kitchen maid—a shy virgin or a vile tease, no one would know—in some apron-over-her-head variety of coition that duly produced this child of ill fate, whose bastardry was concealed by the easy fallacy of a holy birth. I had seen and heard many improbable things in life, but never had I been more inflamed than by this brazen lie told by the one lied to. Was I to pity this man or despise him? I knew not which. The conviction in Wang Dan of his own life story was so complete that I could not help bending his way in the hope of gaining some truth from this contorted man.

"I am heirless as my brother Jesus was, made so by our mutual Father in heaven," continued the self-proclaimed messiah. "All potency remains with our Father, as you know, even though wives I have many."

"How many wives did you have when Annie came to you?" I asked.

He shook his head, avoiding my eyes. "It makes no difference how many. I am without any heir. You, my empress, will never be my child, though given the chance I would give my heart to claim you as mine.

"The battle I had with the Hawthorn Congregational Church started not with me but with them. Many of their parishioners came over to me, for their high tithing rendered the poor even poorer, and their strict canons and laws suffocated them to breathlessness. First they came to me by the dozens, then the hundreds. I was in no need of any more; I had thousands and thousands in this region, with thirteen sanctuaries to tend to. I had no need to fight to gain more followers, but they came to me like flocks to their shepherd.

"Reverend Hawthorn armed his parishioners, and they stormed into my township demanding that his people be returned, but they did not want to go back, so Hawthorn's soldiers beat them. That was when I came to their defense.

"Once I became a foe of Hawthorn, then a foe I was to all colonists, for he was the leader of all foreign Christians—if he feared me, all feared me. Allied forces came to be organized among the French, Americans, English, and Portuguese; even the Japanese and Germans united in their goal to annihilate me. To survive, I had to arm my parishioners.

"My victories soon gained the notice of the Royal Court, those imbecilic fools who have been beaten in every battle and nearly every war. Here I was defeating them all. The dowager approached with an offer to make us their army and fight in their name. My supplies by then were drained, with thirty thousand hungry and desperate men on the verge of rebelling when the Court came knocking. So I bent, thinking that our aim and theirs were one. Of course the palace readily betrayed me." He paused here and asked his maid to fill his pipe with opium, which she expertly did. After a few puffs, the man glowed with a faint rosiness that colored his wrinkled forehead and sagging cheeks. "My medicine, if you will."

I merely nodded.

"Annie came to me to plead for peace. The day she came, she seemed to have brought a flock of butterflies with her. They flitted around her like a water lily framed by a beauteous pond. She stormed into my sanctuary, her skirt the purity of white, her face tender like silk; her cheeks were rosy, her breath fragrant, and smile charming; her strides were blithe and her voice sweet. My heart thumped at the sight of her. I almost mistook her as a heavenly vision."

Another puff.

"How I adored hearing her read the Bible and sing her hymns to me. After she left, how I craved to see again her bare limbs, blue eyes, golden hair, and sweet lips. She answered my yearning by returning once more. We made love. She even shed her virgin's blood. Petite she was, just like you." His dead oyster eyes lingered on Q, the tip of his tongue licking his dry lips.

"How can you say I am not your child?" exclaimed Q. "My mother's virgin blood you spilled!"

"Youth is so impatient. Your mother was just as rosy as you," Lord Wang observed, reaching a shaky hand out to pinch Q's left cheek. "Like summer days, love invites thunder and storms. Her surreptitious visits were soon discovered by Hawthorn's spies. One night when she returned to her father's house, the devil ambushed her. Despicable evil awaited her."

"What happened?" asked Q, attentive like a schoolgirl.

"She did not come back. After the first month passed, I sent an envoy to inquire the cause. He was robbed of his horse and returned to me bloody and beaten with no word of what had befallen my Annie. What loneliness I felt."

"Didn't your other wives keep you warm and your pillow soft during these lonely days?" I snidely asked.

Lord Wang ignored my question. "Annie was a jewel. Hundreds of others would not be her equal. I breached the truce negotiated by Annie and led my army toward Reverend Hawthorn's camp in good faith to ask for Annie's hand in marriage, but they met me with nothing but cannon shells and bullets, no matter that we made our peaceful intentions known. Fortunately she escaped the confinement her father had placed her in and came to me, fearless in the midst of battle. I carried her away to safety. That night she told me that new life grew inside her but that it was not my child planted within her."

"Who else's could it be then?" asked Q.

Wang only shook his head and resumed his tale. "Much pain and sickness she suffered. She could not return to her home, for her father had threatened to cut the infant out of her womb, but your mother never once swayed on her conviction to keep you. Then one day in April she fell ill and began to bleed. I had to seek audience with the dowager to gain Annie admission into Union Hospital, the one and only way to save you and her both. The palace saw this as an opportunity for peace and me as a sacrificial lamb. No sooner had I surrendered your mother to the hospital than I was taken to serve a three-year sentence imposed not by my own emperor but by the American legation by will of Reverend Hawthorn." He paused, shaking his head. "But I did not suffer in vain. I pleaded that you, the child, be kept alive on the promise that I would not mobilize my far-flung army to riot against them, which I could have done even from behind iron bars. So a bargain was forged and your life kept."

Q seemed stunned, tears glistening her slanting eyes.

"A wonderful tale," I said, "but you still refuse to acknowledge fatherhood and to provide protection for the empress's safety."

He pondered the weight of my words for a second before saying firmly, "I will show you the truth, and then you must be on your way."

"What truth?" I asked belligerently.

"Scientific truth." Wang gestured toward the foyer. "Come to my wash chamber. Just you."

I followed the hunched, limping man to the near chamber, which contained a wooden bucket and a face basin. Without much ado, he lifted up the front of his gown showing me what seemed a suitable case of pseudo-hermaphroditism—a fully formed vagina, lipped and layered, upon which protruded an atypical genital organ that was larger than a clitoris but smaller than a normal penis, less than a pinkie in size and length.

"See for yourself," Wang Dan said, his chin up and tone full of pride. "This is what God has given me."

I was utterly unprepared for his revelation. The sight overwhelmed me, rushing instant hot tears into my cold eyes of judgment. It was a long lull before I could speak again. "But how . . . ?"

"How, indeed? I can pleasure and be pleasured, but no child can ever be obtained from my matings."

This was the first time I glimpsed this abnormality with my own eyes. The pictorial depictions of such were hardly as

shocking, what I had perused in the journals and encyclope-
dias I had scouted. Some African tribes were known to hack
away the dwarfish penises on young female children after
stroking the abnormal organ to its fullest hardness, which
was then burned to ashes and mixed in with wine so the child
could drink the cocktail to rid herself of any residual mascu-
linity. The child would then be sold off as a prized bride to
a tribal chief. It was said, when excited, that the stem, that
residual node, would still harden, giving the male lover added
pleasure.

"Who then could have impregnated our Annie?" I
demanded.

"Not your Annie—mine."

Such stubbornness.

"I will tell you if you promise to confide this to no other,
especially the empress," he said grimly.

"Fine," I agreed.

"It was her father, the Reverend Hawthorn himself. Annie
told me so."

I was struck mute as if by clapping thunder right overhead.

"But why?" I asked.

"To rid her of my supposed seed in a moment of madness."

This left me quiet and somber for a long while.

Poor Annabelle! My poor darling nymphet love! What
a foul fate God had struck you with. What tragedy! Never
in my maddest moments would I have ever conjectured this
truth. My poor lamb, to have hoarded such ugly and slander-
ous shame.

Had she, in all my encounters, ever uttered or proffered
the echoes of her pain? Had all her joyousness been but a

disguise to conceal her sorrow, a way to cleanse the tarnished stain of her past?

Why hadn't God struck her father down with his thunderous wrath? Why hadn't providence been more plentiful in blessing her, the wronged one, instead of cutting short her young life in punishment for the despicable deeds of another?

How had she penetrated through all the lies, coming to the truth that her child had survived her? How could she have known to guide me this far, searching for her living child?

Whatever the answer, the road ahead was straightened for me, and the path clear of all clouds and mist, disguises and camouflage.

Silent I must remain. Promise I must keep.

When inquired and probed by a frustrated Q, all I could offer her was a foul and disquieted mood. All I uttered to her regarding her birth and this trickery of a man was the comment, "He cannot have fathered you. He cannot father any child."

For the next two hours, when supper was served and banal pleasantry exchanged between our host and Q, I stayed silent and moody. Our coughing lord gazed at me with certain smugness, content with having defeated my glibness.

At the conclusion of the meal, he rasped, "Now it is time for you to be gone from my township, royal tutor, but she can stay." His lewd eyes darted to Q.

I was about to agree to this manly pact when Q stood up. "If my companion cannot stay, then I shall leave as well."

I would have fought her, but something in her eyes warned

otherwise. She was, after all, more like her mother than not, unwilling to discard me in service of herself. What grace, what providence!

One could feel Wang Dan's anger rise in his heaving chest, then in his reddening neck. But that was that. The road might be crooked ahead and tomorrow utterly uncertain, but sure was my heart, rhyming the same beat with Q, my beauteous queen.

Farewell we bid our host, and off we walked away from the sanctuary of Wang Dan with the moon over our shoulder, a light breeze fluttering the hem of summer night. A carriage was dispatched for our use until we reached Tianjin, a token of kindness that I readily accepted. Crossing the pull-bridge, I looked back at the golden sanctuary to see a flock of butterflies suddenly emerge chasing after us in sweeping plumes of colorful clouds.

"Why didn't you stay and take that man's offering?" I asked as the carriage jolted into motion.

"You said he was not my father," she replied. Leaning against me, eyes half-closed, she asked, "What are we to do after we arrive in Tianjin?"

"We will go to America."

"But this is my land, my father's land."

"Your adoptive father's land from which we are being driven away."

"Who will look after me?"

"I shall, and if not I, then your very own grandparents."

"My grandparents? But I am an empress. I cannot leave my husband. We are bound forever in life and death."

"He is probably already onto his next life if Grandpa has her way. The slaughtering has already begun, with your adoptive father being the first to go."

She covered her mouth and sobbed. "I am fatherless, now and forever."

I could not answer her. Some truths were best left untold.

She cried all the way through the frigid night as we journeyed along the pitted road.

35

When they came upon me, after I left Q at the modest lodging near Tianjin Wharf, it was not hard to conjecture the culprit behind the betrayal. I had, the previous day, paid a visit to the American consulate there to inquire about certain rights given not just to current citizens as I was but also to one born of an American mother.

The clerk was some haughty youth wearing a glaring orange tie. At once, he had excused himself, departing his post for a good minute, returning with his superior, a chargé d'affaires, to be sure, who in turn seemed confounded by the simple query. What useless minions! All that pomposity and no one seemed certain of anything. A third person was consulted, a minor legal officer, a typical Columbia man who knew everything and nothing. A fool he was, citing all sorts of irrelevant legalities and farfetched treaties that had little to do with my pointed inquiry.

Between the three philistines a precious half hour was squandered, during which time a telephone call could have been made to the legation in Peking into the ear of my nemesis, Colonel Winthrop, whose duty it was to keep an acute eye on me, or a messenger could have been dispatched to the nearest Manchurian sheriff from which an envoy could have been deputized for my seizure. Or even more tantalizingly so, Wang Dan himself could have personally ridden out to the gate of the Forbidden City to whisper his intelligence into the waiting ears of his former cohort, the dowager, reporting to her the whereabouts of the prized fugitives for an unimaginable award befitting the task.

Why would I suspect that Wang would betray us? Why not, indeed? The lordship had, after all, given Q away once. Why wouldn't he do it again to regain his former glory? All was within the realm of possibility.

When they came upon me in that glaring noon sun, I felt a sigh of relief unleash from my chest, as if this was destined and certain to occur sooner than later. My obsession and possession had steered me into the dark in search of that everlasting light. It had been tiring, and such fatigue only came upon me now, rightly and punctually.

Only two hours before, I had awakened in our love nest, my love slave still warm in my snug arms, my scepter ready and upright for mellow morning lust. We might be in flight—who in this world wasn't in flight from one thing or another?—but this was, after all, our honeymoon with sweetened days numbered. She called me many things: brute, ape, thug, and animal. And yet she had delighted in every groan and every moan. Her playfulness had all but hidden a rather shy self, and only lust could lay bare her real self, a rosy, bigeyed novice in the game of coition. The days and nights on the flat-bottomed boat had provided a prelude to this full blossoming, how timely and opportune. Flight and lust were intertwined, one urging the other. How monstrously I adored and craved her. The more I loved, the more wretched the craving.

I could never have envisioned an end to all this, and yet end it would and must. I had long been living on borrowed time, an allowance proffered by Annabelle, surely not for this base devouring but for a far loftier aim—that I well knew—and when the time came, I would redeem myself.

As she lay in the morning light, I had placed a pair of tickets marked for Kyoto en route to Hawaii, garnered with money earned by giving a dizzying pint of blood in direct transfusion to a dying Frenchman at the Tianjin Hospital—white man's blood being the fluid of gold. On the same desk I had laid a bagful of gold, the last of my inheritance from my departed parents, sufficient for Q to live not a queenly life but a comfortable one anywhere she would call home. Little did I know that it would be the last time we would kiss, and never would I have thought it to be the finality of it all. I glimpsed her one last time, my heart full of contentment, my eyes smiling, wet with pearls of my improbable tears, though it wasn't a moment for crying or parting, yet it all came to be that way. Any clearer glimpse of my destiny, I would have had to have been pried away by the likes of Hercules; another moment longer and I would not have left her side at all. Now as they came upon me, I felt ready. My heart was set for the inevitable and the unavoidable. Redemption was coming. So was the final judgment.

In life one makes choices, which in turn became sign-posts of your path serving as beacons that shine upon you when weakening and dwindling. In the end, life is accounted for only by the measure of these tangible marvels: all other things fade like water, like light.

So I gave myself in to them, all the alleys swamped with

the shadows of royal guards. There might have been sailors from the English navy among them, German and Portuguese soldiers in the midst guarding their domiciliary docks and sanguine ships, but they all seemed indifferent, letting the Manchurians undo me, watching me dragged to a waiting carriage, and if there were Americans there among them, I did not see them. They were the invisible bunch, good for nothing.

36

There was a lengthy interrogation during the travel back, with me bound and blindfolded. Judging by the voice, my interrogator could only be the viperine Chief Eunuch Li, that emasculated pseudo-husband of the dowager. The old tree could have just as easily been identified by his ignoble stench resultant from a mélange of fragrance Grandpa insisted he wear to ward off his own fetid body odor, unique among the half-men with their overly quick trait to sweat; consequently he smelled like a street harlot of Canton.

Among the trotting, and later galloping, sounds of eight rigorous horses, the chief eunuch began by asking me, "Where is the empress?"

I told him that no price would pry me open to give that secret away even though had they searched door by door within a block of the dripping wharf, they could have easily snatched and snarled her. She was only two stores away from the site of my capture.

"You'll suffer dearly for your crime." He didn't raise his voice, had no need to do so. The pitch of his voice was already high and venomous enough. "The kind unimaginable to an ocean man like you."

In reply I said something to the effect that nothing would be unimaginable in the hands of thugs like him.

He chuckled, though in a most sinister manner.

I taunted him about the so-called crimes he mentioned.

"It was the paramount crime, the unmentionable," he returned.

This time I chuckled and he slapped me.

"You know, you have a woman's hand, and you strike like one."

He slapped me once again, this time backhanding me with sufficient force to throw me to the corner of the carriage. A lull ensued, and all I heard was his wheezing: a leaky valve, the warbling of his steaming wrath. We came to a rolling stop at an apparent rail crossing, allowing a train to rumble by. The Tianjin-Peking Express it must have been, heading inland as we were.

"You have no right to treat me as such. I outrank you by two degrees," I said the moment the carriage swayed into motion once more, referring to the honorary rank given me as a royal tutor. "An august position you will never come near."

A sinister chuckle. "Your crime strips you of your honors— a decree issued by Grandpa."

"Is it really from Grandpa, or did you falsify it as you did many other decrees and favors?"

He did not answer.

"I know all about your graft, your thefts, your cunning."

"Good that you know who you are facing."

"I will report all this to the emperor, and you will lose more than just your manhood."

"Too late. Your master was retired to the Isle of Solitude two days ago."

"I am an American, you know. My legation will come to claim me."

"Your legation was the one who gave me your whereabouts," Li told me.

"That's a lie!"

He chuckled. "No, it is the sweet truth. They had a duty to turn you in, since you have violated the laws of this sovereignty. You committed the crime of consorting with a royal spouse, and infracted a few more, the least of which was the murder of the hanged royal accountant and the arson that burned our priceless treasure hall to ruin. Where is Qiu Rong?" he demanded, his spittle flying over me.

"You will never find her."

By nightfall the next day we arrived in Peking and passed through a gate, entering the palace. The carriage jostled over the cobbled yards, making the wheels squeak and carriage sway.

My blindfold was removed, and my eyes opened to view the interior of a hollow chamber, a lone table of butchery at its center. One ominous rope hung from a pulley secured to the ceiling beam. On the wall were devices of torture and torment: saws, cleavers, whips, and such like. Four unsmiling hyenas and jackals of the bloody trade stood nearby, bald and swarthy, somber and mirthless, aiders and abettors in the willing game of my death, a thing that I dreaded not at all. I smiled at them, causing puzzlement to frame their faces.

"I do not fear death," I proclaimed to the chief eunuch.

"Death you don't deserve, Mr. Pickens." His thin voice echoed in the chamber from the corner armchair he sat in.

"You have much to suffer, and you shall suffer like no white man has ever suffered before. Disrobe him."

The four men held me down on the table, still soggy with fluids from the last man there, and ripped off my clothes. The last shred was nipped off my loins by a sharp dagger. Nude, I was tied onto the rough surface with leather straps over my neck, chest, and pelvis. Both ankles were secured to the legs of the table so that I was splayed open. As for the purpose of that dangling rope, I would not know of its vile use until later.

"What is this all about?" I shouted at the eunuch, whose face was perfectly framed in the vee of my crotch.

"You have given me little choice but to order the ultimate punishment of castration for breaking our jade vase," Li said, employing the euphemism describing the act of defiling a royal empress. "Our thousand years of righteousness and dignity were ruined by your act of transgression. Without your penile wantonness, you will not be able to insult us anymore."

Deafening thunder struck my thin scalp and the world around me revolved in circularity and bare muteness. The bottom of my heart gave way. Barely audible were the rest of Li's wrathful soliloquy. "You have broken one of our cardinal rules. You will now live your residual time of life as we do, to pay for your grave sin."

Adamantly I pleaded for him to behead me instead, to take my heart out, cut off my limbs. Not this.

He went on, ignoring my plea. "Did you know that it was I who brought her home to her adoptive father the day she came to this earth? Did you know it was I who convinced the dowager to keep her for adoption rather than drowning her as

a peace offering? Qiu Rong ascended to the august station as
the fourth consort, reaching a sacred rank beyond reproach,
and then you came along to bring her to ruination and utmost shame. You have one last chance to spare yourself. Tell
us where she is and you will go free, a whole man."

His glib words flowed and echoed, vibrating the walls of
the chamber. "Qiu Rong or castration?" he asked again.

When the choice is that simple, then choosing is no labor
whatsoever. I spat at him.

At the chief eunuch's nod, one of the foursome snatched
the ax from the wall, gliding his thumb down the blade to
test its sharpness. I steeled myself, taking in a deep breath.
Another executioner lit a bundle of incense sticks from which
arose a pungent aroma. He circled it over my face and above
my loins. In the dense smoke, a spectral fortress was miraged,
encircling me. Within me, imagination took flight. In view was
that inescapable summer fire above which winged Annabelle,
hovering with searing firebugs and incendiary butterflies, the
hem of her skirt rising and falling as the ventricles of my
heart clenched and spasmed. That which eluded me became
my last cocoon, my holy hearth around which I would lay in
repose with no lament or sorrow. All the halfmen before me
had chosen ignoble emasculation for glory. I would do so for
want of such: for my twin archangels, A and her kindred Q.

What ensued was coarse and crude. I watched the sequence as if witnessing the morning birds fly above me or
the summer river flowing past me.

Someone pried my bare thighs farther apart. A shaving
blade scraped over me before a cold hand seized my scrotum,
tying my mast and testicular lump near the base tight and

taut with that hanging rope. Then came one clean swing of the ax, hacking it all off in a single blow.

Oh, what deathly numbing shock and pain! Shrieks burst from my throat as the bloody chunk was yanked up by the rigorous rope, the messy lump twirling in the air. Then the curtains of my eyes descended, closing out the tragic play. Darkness soothed, overcoming me.

37

I was moved out of the palace to a nameless infirmary somewhere on the fringe of Tartar City, barely clinging to consciousness. Passage of time was punctured by bouts of seething pain as if hot lava was searing the core of the open wound, three inches in diameter and rough-edged all around. Blood trickled, wetting my buttocks and my inner thighs, and droplets crawled down my calves.

The wound had swollen to a mound looking like a crimson crater from within. Flies buzzed over the gaping hole, some landing precariously on the edges, others picking away at the core irking the raw nerve endings, their mouths cutting like dagger tips. I could hardly raise my hand to swipe them away. It was In-In who dispersed them, fanning a palm leaf. Yet even his gentlest breeze incurred tenderness to the unshielded gash, scraping it like a knife's blade.

✦ ✦ ✦

The urge to urinate woke me from a painful dream. In it I was legless, stranded alone on an island with no land or ship in sight, only the silence of despair and helplessness. Worms squirmed toward me in full assault. Only when a thunderous storm doused the island with belts of rain, clapping with deafening thunders, did the worms scurry away, but the rain kept falling, pouring, compelling my guts to tighten and groins to ache. Urgent pain flooded my lower belly, threatening to burst through, to rip me apart. Every cry was in vain, every surfeit of agony cause enough to immolate myself on my own pyre of sin and transgressions.

Reality dawned on me soon as the pain persisted. What one took in must come out. The painful urge to urinate was blocked by a severed course now muddy with blood and pustule.

In-In presented me with an opium pipe, an expediency I knew not how he had acquired.

"What do I do now?" I asked, whimpering pitifully.

In-In lit the pipe for me and fed it into my mouth. An abject drag filled the chambers of my lungs, immediately calming the scathing pain. Producing a dried reed stalk with a hollow center, In-In squatted between my thighs. Bend-ing over my injured area, he carefully inserted one end of the stem inside the wound, finding the burrow of my urinal track. Slowly he sipped out my liquid excretion through the straw, spitting out what he had sucked up, drawing up some of the glutinous discharge as well so that now the face of castration revealed itself. Gone were the tree and its root, the sac and its marbles. Gone also was that which I had abided by, my manhood, leaving behind just the inchoate terrain of nothingness. Here, before your naked eyes, my ladies and sorrowful gentlemen, lies in all its inglorious rusticity, to wit, the very mournful specimen of my own nomadic no-man's-land.

My first inclination was an irresistible itch at self-ridicule. Had I not still been in such pain and a full-length mirror granted, I would have stood up to gaze at my new self, twirling around in display, laughing at my flatness. What simplicity!

Should I eulogize the bygones as a blind man his missing sight, or trees their fallen fruits and wilted blossoms? Should I lament with bleeding heart and torrential tears that would never run dry?

Retreating from my reverie, I asked, "How did you learn to clean me like this?"

"I was served this way by another boy, one who shared the ward with me, but he died not long after from infection." Standing up, In-In rinsed himself over a spittoon, leaving the stem still inserted in me.

"You forgot to remove the reed," I said.

"No, it has to stay there so when you heal the opening will be intact and not close up."

So young yet so wise.

"Where did you find the money to buy me this?" I asked, waving my pipe.

His head bent low, his pointy chin resting on his bony chest. "I'd rather not say."

"Tell me, please."

"My severance wage."

"They drove you out?"

He nodded. "When one's master goes, so does the ser-vant. There will not be riches waiting for me anymore, just a slow death. I asked to serve you, which earned me this sever-ance wage."

Oh, tender was the boy. Tenderer yet his love.

"It is the only medicine that could heal you. I wished a puff or two when I was chopped." He pulled out a silk bag from a drawer and showed it to me. "Here is my treasure, all dried and useless."

"What are you to do with it?"

"I am to be buried with it so in the next life I will be made whole again. Here is your sack." He held up a wet bag still damp with blood and carefully laid it beside me. "Keep it with you always."

How I wished I could offer him riches and gold, but I had nothing, only gratitude.

38

One November day when the sky was dreary with pending snow, Qiu Rong appeared at our ward. She was radiant, her cheeks rouged, her eyes smiling. I made little drama at seeing her by my side, by which time it had been three months. The wound had healed by then.

"Why are you here? Shouldn't you be hiding somewhere?" I asked.

"I heard, and I wanted to see you. Besides, I missed the ship. It left port before I could get there."

I wanted to hold her and cry out all my anguish, but I could not even open my arms to her. Such rigidity I felt, standing there like a frozen tree.

She came to me, hugging my gaunt frame—I had grown thin. Even then I could not embrace her. Something had gone out of me, and something was different about her.

Only an interval of a hundred days and some, and yet in my eyes she seemed to have aged, not by moons but by years and years. Her face had filled up, becoming round, and though her dimples were still deep, her eyes had lost that gleaming luster so typical of youth and were now on the verge of turning dull. The blond hair had darkened a shade, and the lush and meaty succulence of her lips now looked dry and chapped. Her bosom had grown rounder and fuller, and her slender waist seemed to have widened by inches.

"I am pregnant," she announced with an unsure smile.

"Who is the father?" I asked.

"You."

Doubt stirred in me. "Have you had other lovers?"

She slapped me hard with her cold palm.

I could find no words of adequacy to convey what was and wasn't within me, and I was confused and confounded by my own lack of enthusiasm, of former zest, of even curiosity. I seemed to have aged reversely back to my childish years of uncertainty, shyness, and witlessness.

"Aren't you going to say something?" she snapped. "I said it's yours. Aren't you happy now that you've lost your . . ." Q bit her lip.

I sighed. Something was aground, forcefully barring me from reaching her, from loving her as I had always dreamed of loving. Something dull and leaden was holding me back. Something new was asserting a fence of forbearance where formerly there had been none. All I could utter was, "Look at what you've done to yourself."

She looked at me, hurt.

I broke down like a defenseless child right before her, my earthly love-mate, my incarnated wife, the quintessence of what I had once held dear and deemed perfect—the only tangible trace of my entangled and contorted love.

That was all I could say.

What shame! What sorrow!

She turned on her heel and walked away.

39

After Q's brief visit, In·In and I settled into the fabled three·room shanty built by the Reverend Hawthorn. It was in this locale that I learned about the fate of Q and the lordly Wang Dan.

Once Q missed her ship, heading for Kyoto, that good man, Wang Dan, came to her rescue, taking her away from the Tianjin Wharf after my capture, keeping her safe from the murderous hands of the dowager.

The palace pursued Wang Dan for aiding the fugitive em·press. The royal army besieged his township, and not long after Wang surrendered himself. By then Q was long gone, some say to far south Canton where the flames of revolution were spreading. Others said she had gone to Kyoto where she had spent her formative years. Still others said she had fled to Boston. All, however, said she had left with a child growing in her—her child, my child, our child.

I had heard by then that it was really the young emperor himself who had ordered Q to be hanged that night of our flight. The poor fellow was given a choice of no choice by the dowager: get rid of Qiu Rong or he would be dethroned. He chose to hang her, knowing well it would neither save his crown nor his life. He was said to have died lamenting the loss of his last empress. Was he a villain or a victim? Both, I would say.

The dowager had Wang Dan buried alive, nailing him down in his coffin like Christ to his cross, weighing his tomb with layers of rock in an unmarked crypt. When his followers unearthed his tomb and exhumed his body several days later, they found not only the anomaly of his pseudohermaphrodite state but also a surprising syndactyly of his toes, specifically webbing between his second and third toes, the very same state afflicting Q.

I will leave it to you all to judge. After all, you are my sitting jury. I will just say what needs to be said and no more. Wang's webbed toes tell an utterly enchanting tale: that he is the father of Qiu Rong, and considering the ambiguity of his manhood and sexuality, it could only be by means of a godly way.

As for my Annabelle, the truth that I have come to see is that passion blinds a man, but love keeps him alive. I would have died a long time ago, finding the world empty and life hollow without much aim, dying if not by natural means then by hanging myself, many a time and chance, but Annabelle's phantom possession gave my living a florid content and my journey a worthy destination. Now every day that I live in this childhood house of hers, looking with my wane eyes at the hawthorn trees she had planted and deciphering drawings her fingers made along the walls, I am one with her, flying with her tribe of butterflies in that evergreen summer garden. Summers and childhood are synonyms equating themselves in turn with our initial love; they are the foremost hieroglyphs of our waking souls, thus making us long for them as such.

Quiet nights, I hear Annabelle's footfalls, and mornings her giggles, echoes of her youth. Seasons come and go. Our hawthorn trees blossom and bloom. In this grace, I await nothing but my end to go to her.

The desire and lust are gone, leaving behind a clear-eyed lucidity in which sweet love for her infuses my every breath. Each day I ponder, gaining new insight. Each sunset and sunrise marks my slow and sure steps toward her.

ACKNOWLEDGMENTS

No book is ever done alone in utter isolation. I wish to give thanks and credit to the following people for creating a forest around me, and allowing this book to blossom:

My beautiful wife, Sunny. My first and foremost editor, she labored over every single word in this book, making sure diction and phrases were properly applied. My gratitude for her is deep and vast. Her literary gift is abundant in the marvelous fictions she publishes with Berkeley/Penguin Group.

My mother for her rice noodles with shrimp, oysters, and cilantro. Her calm smiles are always filled with enough love for me to soak myself in.

My children, Victoria and Michael. You make us proud and bring a smile to our faces every day.

Mrs. and Mr. Liu, my in-laws, the most loving and generous people. We are much blessed by your love.

Uncle (Dr.) Nate, Auntie Mil, and their children, Austin, Sam, Erica, and Hudson. You are our inspiration in more ways than you know.

ACKNOWLEDGMENTS

My sister, Ke, her husband, and my niece Si: for your generous and loyal support.

Our dear friends Marcia Gay Harden and Thaddaeus Scheel. New Year's Day skating at your lake house is a beloved tradition and warm celebration of friendship and goodwill.

Elliot Figman, much celebrated poet and founder of *Poets & Writers,* who has watched over me from the very onset of my publishing career. There is no worthier cause than Elliot's P&W Foundation. Donate!

My dear colleagues Elizabeth Hastings and Dr. Michael White, celebrated novelist and director of Fairfield University's MFA program in creative writing, which I am proudly a part of. You are my heroes on Enders Island. Thanks to all my FUMFAers for their love and general awesomeness.

Glen Loveland. Thanks for making sure that all my southerner's pin-yin spellings are correct.

My literary agent, Alex Glass, of Trident Media Group, who cares deeply about fine books, and even more deeply about his authors. I am most fortunate to have your friendship, dedication, and wise counsel.

My deep appreciation to Jenny Frost and Shaye Areheart.

Kate Kennedy, whom I cannot thank enough for shaping this book to its essence.

My most heartfelt thanks to Alexis Washam, my brilliant editor, for launching this book. Another shout of thanks to her amazing assistant, Christine Kopprasch. To the esteemed Maya Mavjee, Molly Stern, and Tina Constable, thank you for your brilliant leadership at Crown.

Finally, I have to acknowledge that the idea first sparked

for this story when I was invited to speak at Yale University and saw the portrait of Mr. Horace Tracy Pitkin (class of 1892) hanging in the Woolsey rotunda. His heroism inspired me to write this book, but all the characters and scenes are purely of my own imagining and creation.

ABOUT THE AUTHOR

DA CHEN is the author of the *New York Times* bestselling memoir *Colors of the Mountain,* and the award-winning novel *Brothers.* He teaches creative writing at Fairfield University's MFA program. For more information, please visit www.dachen.org.